As I step into the room, a silver flash blurs my vision.
Before I can take a breath, the world falls away.

Brianna has always felt invisible. People stare right past her, including the one boy she can't resist, Blake Williams. But everything changes at a house party when Brianna's charm bracelet slips off and time stands still. In that one frozen, silver moment, Blake not only sees her, he recognizes something deep inside her that she's been hiding even from herself.

Discovering she is descended from Danu, the legendary bandia of Celtic myth, Brianna finds herself questioning the truth of who she is. And when she accidentally binds her soul to Blake's, their mutual attraction becomes undeniable.

But Blake has his own secret, one that could prove deadly for them both.

Bound together by forbidden magic, Brianna and Blake find themselves at the heart of an ancient feud that threatens to destroy their lives and their love.

SILVER

For Sammy and Hunter: Never stop dreaming.

TALIA VANCE

SILVER

flux™
Woodbury, Minnesota

First Edition
First Printing, 2012

Book design by Bob Gaul
Cover design by Ellen Lawson
Cover artist © 2012: Brenda Meelker/Embrision Arts
Cover images © Night sky: Shutterstock Images/Presniakov Oleksandr
Woman: iStockphoto.com/RelaxFoto.de
Title art © Llewellyn art department

Flux, an imprint of Llewellyn Worldwide Ltd.

This is a work of fiction. Names, characters, places, and incidents are either the product of the author's imagination or are used fictitiously, and any resemblance to actual persons living or dead, business establishments, events, or locales is entirely coincidental. Cover model used for illustrative purposes only and may not endorse or represent the book's subject.

Library of Congress Cataloging-in-Publication Data
Vance, Talia.
Silver/Talia Vance.—1st ed.
p. cm.
Summary: In a frozen, silver moment, Brianna, used to being invisible to boys, is seen by handsome Blake Williams who recognizes her as a descendant of Danu—legendary beings his family is sworn to hunt—but before Brianna understands the truth she accidentally binds her soul to Blake.
ISBN 978-0-7387-3303-6
[1. Supernatural—Fiction. 2. Mythology, Celtic—Fiction. 3. Goddesses—Fiction. 4. Dating (Social customs)—Fiction. 5. High schools—Fiction. 6. Schools—Fiction.] I. Title.
PZ7.V39853Sil 2012
[Fic]—dc23

2012009866

Flux
Llewellyn Worldwide Ltd.
2143 Wooddale Drive
Woodbury, MN 55125-2989
www.fluxnow.com

Printed in the United States of America

Acknowledgments

So many wonderful people helped bring this book into the world, and I couldn't have done it without any of them. Sarah Davies, you are a goddess—smart, beautiful, and fierce. Thank you for the master class in plotting, and for your amazing business savvy and guidance.

To the team at Flux: you have been a joy from start to finish. Thank you, Brian Farrey-Latz, for your sharp insight and unwavering support. Thanks to the brilliant Sandy Sullivan, continuity queen, and public relations champions Marissa Pederson and Steven Pomije. Thanks to Ellen Lawson and Brenda Meelker for the gorgeous cover design and illustration.

To the aptly named YA Muses, Veronica Rossi, Katherine Longshore, Donna Cooner, and Bret Ballou: you inspire me on a daily basis. Your support and encouragement made everything feel more real, more bearable, and completely doable. Thank you for sharing this journey with me.

Thanks, Mom and Dad, for encouraging my creative side for as long as I can remember. Thanks to Crystina Smith for letting me steal your best quips. And to my real-life love interest, Jeff Vance, thank you for believing in me even when I didn't, for supporting me unconditionally, and for giving me the freedom to live my dreams.

ONE

Beauty is pointless when no one's looking. And no one ever looks. People weave around me without making eye contact. I'm the tree that falls in the forest with no one around to see or hear it. I can't remember the last time someone besides Haley or Christy talked to me at a party.

Not that there aren't advantages to fading into the background. No one cares that I didn't have time to straighten my hair, and no one notices that I can barely walk in the four-inch heels Haley talked me into buying. And everyone is so much safer.

The party is what Haley calls a rager, the perfect combination of no parents, cute guys, and alcohol-fueled hookups. I can almost smell the pheromones. Then again, it could be the guy in the Padres jersey sweating tequila from his pores.

Haley scans the crowded living room one more time.

"He's not here." She checks her cell for a message from Oscar, or Otto, some senior from McMillan Prep she met at Magic Beans. Another rich kid who's too good to slum it out at Rancho Domingo High with the rest of us, even though it's the top-rated school in San Diego County. It's Otto's party, so presumably he's here somewhere.

I mean to help her look, but I'm distracted by the blond waves of Blake Williams' hair. It's too long, brushing his neck in the back and his ears on the side, the kind of layered mess that is too flattering to be unintentional.

I know the second Blake spots Haley. He turns his head just a fraction and his green eyes brighten so they're almost silver. He moves with the stealthy grace of a panther as he weaves through the crowd. I'm already standing near the wall, but I inch back the rest of the way. It's not like he's coming to talk to me or anything, but I prefer to watch Blake from a distance.

He stops in front of Haley. Dimples frame a smile that's probably charmed more than a few girls out of their underwear.

One of said girls strides up behind him, not missing a step despite the spiky heels on her vinyl boots. She leans into him, flashing a strategically placed tear in her fishnet stockings.

Haley hammers out a text, ignoring Blake and his territorial indie girl. I'd say something to them myself, but they give no sign that they even know I'm here. A small twinge of disappointment flares in my chest before I can stamp it out. Then I do. Ruthlessly.

Haley finally looks up from her phone. "Blake, right?" She flips a long strand of blond hair over her shoulder. "Austin's friend?"

Blake's dimples grow impossibly deeper. "And here I thought I was *your* friend."

Fishnet squeezes closer to Blake.

Game on. Haley gazes from beneath her eyelashes in a way that seems entirely unaffected. I know firsthand how many hours in front of a mirror have gone into perfecting this particular look, which simultaneously broadcasts complete innocence and the promise of seduction. "What's up?" she asks.

"I heard there was this pretty crazy party going on." Blake's voice is laced with sarcasm. "I was thinking of checking it out. What about you?" Blake's eyes ask another question. The same question every guy, and even the occasional girl, wants to ask Haley.

She lets her lids fall. "I could be up for a party." Haley's a master. I probably should be taking notes.

"Blake's bartending." Fishnet's voice is a purr, in contrast to the death rays that beam from her eyes. She loops an arm around Blake's elbow. "He makes the best screwdrivers." I almost feel sorry for her. Haley's shadow can be a cold dark place.

Blake breaks free from Fishnet's hold. His fingers brush my wrist as he steps to the side, creating a spark of static electricity. I flinch, scratching my arm so it looks like I have an itch or something. At least I hope that's how it looks. Not that anyone notices.

"Do you know Brianna?" Haley asks.

Here it comes.

Blake finally looks at me.

I start to smile, but his gaze is already back on Haley. My lips fall and I stare down at the shiny blue straps that crisscross my feet. I'm like an abused puppy, so desperate for attention that it's almost a surprise when I get belted in the gut.

Again.

Fishnet pulls on Blake's sleeve. "Let's go. I'm thirsty."

Blake graces Haley with one more gorgeous smile before he follows Fishnet to the other side of the living room. He holds open a swinging door as she walks through. This minor act of chivalry is marred by the fact that his gaze never leaves her butt.

Haley sniffs at my hair. "Eww, Brie."

"That bad?" I grab a dark curl and hold it to my nose. My riding lesson ran late. Even after a quick shower, I still reek of horse.

Haley rifles through her bag until she finds a small spray bottle. She spritzes my hair with something that smells like vanilla. "Better. And I love the shoes."

"Thanks, but tell that to my toes." Not only do my feet hurt, I suspect my hair now smells like a cross between eau de equine and a milkshake.

"Love the shoes!" Haley yells at my feet.

"You talking to me?" The guy in the Padres jersey sloshes his beer as he leans toward us, spraying my toes with Budweiser. Perfect. Now I smell like a sticky patch of pave-

ment at the state fair. A magnet for future farmers and car-
nies alike.

Haley leads me away, but Padre staggers after us. "Hey!
I'm not done talking to you!"

Haley stops, pulling me to a halt beside her. Padre's
reaction time is predictably feeble. He lurches forward,
bumping into me and spilling more beer on my jeans. He
tries to prop himself up on my shoulder, grabbing at my
sweater. I push him away. His arms flail, catching my wrist
before gravity takes over and he's sprawled on the floor. I
nearly topple over with him, but Haley grabs my arm just
in time.

"Jerk." I rub at the wet spot on the front of my jeans
with the sleeve of my sweater.

"Your bracelet!" Haley kneels to pick up the silver
chain, giving it a quick once-over. "The clasp is broken."
The silver charms still hang from the thick chain.

"It's fine. I'll get it fixed tomorrow."

"Are you sure? We can find Christy and go home if
you want." Haley puts the bracelet in her bag, watching
me closely. No way she wants to leave before we find Otto.

"No. Let's just get something to drink." This is already
shaping up to be a night I want to forget.

Haley lifts a strand of my hair and sniffs it again. "I
think it's working. Your hair looks amazing." I doubt that
a scented spray could have any effect on my wild curls, but
there's no point arguing with Haley.

We're nearly to the kitchen when I remember that

Blake is in there. Here I come again, tail wagging, tongue out. Stupid little puppy.

Blake is mixing a pitcher of screwdrivers at an island counter, Fishnet velcroed to his side. They both laugh at the shared secret Blake whispers in her ear.

As I step into the room, a silver flash blurs my vision. It's like seeing spots when you're dizzy, only I don't feel the least bit faint. Before I can take a breath, my foot lands on the tile floor and the world falls away. The sounds of the party disappear, cloaking me in a shadow of absolute silence. The quiet has a distinct sound of its own, as if the sudden absence of sensation has created a void that echoes in deep, passing waves.

I'm surrounded in blackness, unable to make out even the outline of shapes or movement in the dark. I feel, rather than see, the stillness that envelops the room. A shiver pulses down my spine, the only sign that I'm still alive and breathing.

The room comes into focus gradually, the tones appearing brighter now. Everyone is exactly where they were a second ago. *Exactly.* Frozen in place as if someone pressed pause on a DVD. Haley is stuck in mid-stride, her foot hanging in the air.

Blake and Fishnet stand at the island. She stares at him with pure adoration. Blake focuses on the pitcher in front of him, his expression light from whatever they laughed about a second before. His right hand is raised, pouring a bottle of vodka. A trail of clear liquid from the bottle is frozen in mid-stream, stopping just before it makes contact with the orange juice in the pitcher below.

Out of the stillness, Blake raises his chin and turns his head toward me. The movement is slow and deliberate. My breath catches in my throat. His eyes lock with mine. There is nothing effortless or light about the way they burn through me now, dark and relentless. I shudder as the shiver in my spine twists into an icy wave.

Blake's lips curve into a smile.

"Mine," he whispers, shattering the silence.

Before I can react, there's another flash of silver light and the room is filled with laughter and music and movement as the party rages on.

TWO

I take a deep breath and close my eyes. When I open them again, everything is as it should be. People move, talk, laugh. The music blares. Blake sets down the bottle, laughing. The only indication that anything just happened is my racing heart.

Blake's attention goes right to Haley as she approaches, his grin out in full force. Definitely normal.

Until his eyes slide to mine. And stay there.

His smile vanishes.

I have to quell the urge to turn and run. Running screaming from the room won't exactly help my social standing. I just need to go back to being invisible girl. I straighten my spine and walk to the island, taking a position next to Haley where I'm sure to disappear.

It will only be a second before he looks back at Haley.

One.

Two.

Any second now.

Blake doesn't look away, so I do. I concentrate on one blue shoe. Stupid, uncomfortable, way-too-high shoe. Like running was ever an option.

He sees me.

It's what I thought I wanted, but I'm even more pathetic than I realized. Turns out I go into all-out panic mode, complete with hallucinations, at the first sign that a guy notices me. I can't be *that* much of a loser. I force myself to look at him again.

"Where have you been hiding?" His smile is lethal.

I cling to the counter, glad for the four-foot island between us. It's a few seconds before I realize everyone is watching me, waiting for an answer. "Sorry?"

Blake snorts back a laugh. He grabs a beer from a bucket on the floor and points the neck at me. I hold my ground. So it's been more than ten seconds and he hasn't written me off completely. Maybe he's slow. I reach for the beer.

"Do I know you?" he asks.

Yes to slow. "We've kind of met." Like six times, but who's counting? "At Magic Beans?" In the living room, five minutes ago? I pick up a bottle opener from the counter and try to maneuver it over the cap on my beer, hoping he won't notice my burning cheeks. Still no response as I struggle with the opener. "Brianna Paxton? Haley's friend?"

Blake tries my name out on his tongue. "Very pretty."

The opener flies out of my hand, barely missing the

pitcher of screwdrivers before it lands with a clang in front of Fishnet. She makes no effort to hold back an unkind laugh, correctly determining that I pose no threat whatsoever.

Blake's laugh is nicer as he holds his hand out, palm up. I set the bottle in his hand with surgical precision, careful not to make any physical contact. He removes the cap easily with his bare hands. "Twist off," he says as he holds the beer out to me again.

"You could've said something sooner."

"I could have." He holds onto the base as I grab the neck, trapping me for a few seconds while he leans over the counter until his head is even with mine. His breath is warm against my ear. Hot. "But I was enjoying watching you."

I can't breathe. Can't. Breathe.

As he lets go of the bottle and backs away, our eyes meet again. There's a tingling in my fingers, almost like they're not getting enough oxygen. I'm having some kind of anxiety attack. The tingling grows stronger, little shocks of electricity sparking and arcing through my hands. It's not unpleasant. Far from it. I lift my hand from the counter, my palm facing Blake.

No, no, no. This can't be happening. Not again.

Blake's eyes narrow, almost like he knows that someone's just turned on the crazy switch at the back of my brain. He reaches across the counter and jerks my hand back down to the counter. "Easy, bandia."

My wrist burns where he holds it, but his words bring

the cold chill in my spine front and center. "What did you say?"

"You heard me." There's a spark of silver behind his eyes. It's just a hallucination, but it looks so real. I pull my hand away, breaking his hold.

I try to push down the panic before it turns into something I can't control. *4. 16. 64. 256.* By the time I get to the sixth exponent in the sequence, I feel almost normal.

Haley leans forward on the counter, letting her shirt fall open to reveal the kind of natural cleavage that plastic surgeons can never fully emulate. "Can I get one of those?" She points toward the cooler.

Blake must not hear. He flips the cap of my beer through his fingers absently and his eyes don't leave mine.

Get away.

The thought comes from nowhere, strong and insistent. I force myself to keep it together. Rationally, I know there's no such thing as death by dimples. So Blake is talking to me; there's nothing to freak over.

Haley steps around the counter to grab a beer. She twists it open herself and takes a long, slow swig. When Blake still doesn't look in her direction, she wanders back toward the living room, abandoning me.

Blake still stares.

"Didn't you get the memo? Haley's the hot one." I want to take the words back as soon as they're out. I need serious help. Blurters Anonymous.

Blake looks at me like I'm crazy. It hits a little too close to home. "Is that what you think?"

"Me and the entire human population."

He laughs. Whatever show he has playing in his head is far more entertaining than our actual conversation. "You're not kidding?"

It's my turn to look at him like he's nuts. Which he obviously is.

He runs his fingers through his hair. "You don't know what you are?"

A rush of adrenaline sends my pulse skittering. "And what, exactly, would that be?" For a second it's like he sees right through me, like he knows that everything I do, from analyzing anti-matter to solving equations, is one giant lie. A distraction to keep the crazy at bay.

"Only the hottest thing to grace this planet in several generations."

I release a breath. What did I expect him to say anyway? I might be inexperienced when it comes to these things, but even I can spot a line when it's served up with that much cheese. "Wow," I murmur. "You didn't strike me as stupid, but I guess first impressions are deceiving."

He leans closer, his voice a warm whisper. "I might know what I'm talking about."

This time I don't fight the instinct to run. I get out of the room as fast as I can. I sail blindly around a corner, stopping only when I reach a group of people sitting around a dark wood table. Safety in numbers and all that. I hold the back of an empty chair and try to remember how to breathe.

Bandia. It's a word I haven't heard since my grandma

died—her nickname for me. Blake couldn't know that. There's no way. Just like time did not stop. And there was no silver light. So Blake said hi to me. It's an outlier, sure, but statistically, it was bound to happen sooner or later.

A preppy girl at the end of the table rolls a quarter off her nose and bounces it toward a glass in front of her. The coin hits the glass and falls back on the table. "Off the rim has to drink," the guy next to her says too loudly, even with the music. The girl flashes him a defiant stare as she picks up a large cup to her left and chugs the liquid inside. She never breaks eye contact even as she slams the empty cup back down. Modern mating rituals at their finest.

"You gonna sit down or are you busy holding up that chair?" A thin guy lifts his head slightly. I've seen him with Blake before. They were seniors last year at McMillan Prep, but now I think they both go to U.R.D.

I take the seat next to him, willing my pulse to slow down but not quite succeeding.

The thin guy slides the glass and quarter to me. He has hair like a fifties greaser, combed back and teased high. An unlit Marlboro hangs from the corner of his mouth. He's a dark-haired James Dean wannabe, except for the Green-peace tattoo on his left forearm. He might actually have a cause.

I take the quarter between my shaking fingers. I should be good at this game; it's just basic physics. Force, energy, trajectory. But understanding how something works and being able to execute it are two different things. Entirely. I line up the coin, concentrating on staving off the adrenaline that still courses through my blood. When I let the quarter go, it makes a loud plink before it skews dead right, landing in front of a guy in a red T-shirt.

"Oh, we're in trouble now, aren't we?" Red Shirt Guy says in a soft accent that sounds like a cross between my grandmother and a character from *Harry Potter*. His brown eyes crinkle at the corners as he smiles, a lopsided smile that doesn't send me into a panic. To the contrary, I relax a little.

"I'm just warming up." I try another shot, closing my eyes as I let the quarter go. No one is more surprised than me to hear it settle at the bottom of the glass.

"Well done." The soft lilt in Red Shirt's voice is soothing, like a lullaby.

I pour a healthy shot from a pitcher of screwdrivers in the center of the table with little difficulty, the shaking in my hands gone. I push the cup in the direction of Red Shirt. "Drink." Before I can stop myself, I add, in a bad imitation of his accent, "Unless you would prefer a spot of tea?"

"I'll have you know I take my tea very seriously." He raises the cup in a toast. "But I prefer vodka." He presses the cup to his lips and downs the drink in one swallow.

I smile. At least for now, my psyche does not fall apart just because a cute guy is talking to me. I even feel a little normal.

"Much better." He laughs, almost to himself. "A shame that this will end badly."

"What? You don't think I can make another one?" I

take the quarter between my fingers and line it up with the glass again.

"I have no idea. I was speaking of our relationship."

It's my turn to laugh. The idea of me and him, me and any guy, is a joke in itself. "We don't even know each other."

His dark brown bangs fall forward, covering one eye. "Yet."

I toss the quarter at the table. It bounces left and lands on the ground. Back in form.

Red Shirt Guy fills the glass with a screwdriver. "Off the table has to drink."

I gulp it down before I can think about it. The liquid leaves a trail of fire from the back of my throat to my stomach. His eyes meet mine, and for a second it's like he knows that the heat that fills me isn't entirely caused by the alcohol.

To my left, Greenpeace removes the unlit cigarette from his lips, sipping from a can of Pepsi before he picks up the quarter from the floor.

"C'mon Joe!" The girl at the end of the table is ready for the game to get back underway.

Joe takes aim and makes it easily. He points at my chest. The guy might be worse at the whole small-talk thing than me.

Red Shirt refills the glass. "The fair Juliet drinks again."

"This is cheating, right?" I say. "Joe's not even drinking."

"All's fair in love and quarters."

"I'm pretty sure Romeo didn't need to get Juliet drunk."

Red Shirt laughs. "That might be the best news I've heard all night." He downs the screwdriver himself, then stands up, holding out his hand. Waiting.

I hesitate for only a second, placing my hand in his and letting him pull me from my chair. There's no burning heat where our hands touch. I shouldn't be disappointed. It has to be a good sign. I'm not going to lose control with him.

We weave through the partygoers until we reach a darkened room at the end of a hallway. I don't stop to think about why we're here or what it might mean. I already know. And the answer is yes. Please. His hand is a solid branch on a slippery hillside, and I cling to it for all I'm worth.

The door shuts behind us, cloaking us in darkness. For a second it's almost too much, reminding me of the scene in the kitchen. But there's no silver light and the sounds of the party are still audible in the distance. When his free hand circles my waist, the only shiver I feel is one of anticipation. The good kind.

Definitely the good kind.

THREE

He pulls me against his red shirt. "Is this okay?"

"Yes," I manage to say. The place where his hand touches my waist tingles, the nerves jumping despite the barrier of my sweater.

He lowers his head until his lips brush mine, so softly I barely feel it. Then they're gone. Just as I'm wondering if that was it, his lips are back, the pressure stronger. It's weird at first, to taste someone's breath, but it's nice, too, like sharing a secret. His tongue licks at my lower lip and I pull back.

He loosens his hold on my waist but doesn't move away from me. "It's okay," he whispers. "I won't hurt you. Not ever."

It's an odd thing to say to someone you've just met. "You can't know that."

He laughs. "You'd be surprised." I feel his breath against

my cheek and then his lips are on mine again. The weight of his chest pushes me back against the door as his tongue invades my mouth. His hand moves underneath my sweater, his fingers brushing bare skin.

I don't stop him. I wait to see if I feel anything strange. But there's nothing. No electric shock, no flash of light. No risk that I'm going to go pyro on him. His touch is soft and warm and soothing. Not hot like Blake's.

Red Shirt's hands travel further north, bringing me back into the moment. Damn. I should not be thinking about Blake right now.

I put my hands on his shoulders and kiss him back. I press closer until there's nothing but the feel of his lips, his mouth, his hands.

He breaks the kiss, his fingers still moving across my skin. His thumbs rub circles on my lower back. I can just make out his face in the dark. He looks different here in the shadows, better-looking than I thought at first, with impossibly high cheekbones and a strong jaw. There's a question in his eyes as he watches me, an invitation.

I'm exposed and defenseless, like a white blood cell pressed on a glass slide. I have to look away. I focus on the ceiling, where hundreds of glowing stars float in intricate patterns, a perfect starry night. An illusion. The stars are the kind you can buy in a fancy toy store, simple phosphors that can be energized with light.

His hand moves along my waist to my belly button, flirting with the button of my jeans. "I'm Austin," he says.

A nervous laugh escapes before I can stop it. "Just when I was getting used to thinking of you as Red Shirt Guy."

His lips curve into a crooked smile, an imperfection that makes his face seem more human and less Greek god. "Not Romeo?"

Not Romeo. And before I can stop myself from thinking it—*not Blake.*

A pounding on the door startles us both.

"Brianna?" The door pushes against my back as it opens and I have to jump out of its path, away from Austin. Blake's shoulders fill the frame. "Is everything okay?"

I try to process this. It was one thing for Blake to talk to me when I approached him in the kitchen, but there is no reason whatsoever for him to be here now. None. A tickle of nervous energy makes my stomach tighten. Is he jealous? I try not to let myself hope for things that can't possibly be true.

"We're fine," Austin says. He slides his arm around me and pulls me back to him.

For the second time, Blake looks directly at me. "Your friends are looking for you." The words are neutral, but everything about his posture is tense. The slightest pressure and he'll snap. "They're ready to go."

"She can stay here if she likes." Austin doesn't even try to make the sentence sound innocent.

Blake emits a low guttural sound that's almost a growl. I shrink back. "I should find out what they want."

Austin whispers in my ear. "Back here in five minutes." It's not a question.

I step forward, but Blake still stands in the doorway, blocking my way. We're too close, inches apart. I almost feel the current of electricity that hangs in the air between us. Only the fact that Austin is right behind me keeps me from running to the farthest corner of the room.

"Excuse me?" I say.

Blake blinks and takes a small step back. "They're in the kitchen."

I slide past Blake, twisting my shoulders so my body doesn't touch any part of his. Then I nearly run, snaking through the people milling in the hallway.

Christy heads me off in the living room. "Omigod, Brie." She rakes her hands through her black hair, creating body that will only last as long as she continues the motion. "What's going on?"

I almost launch into the whole story. About the weird hallucination with Blake and my kiss with Austin, but the worry in her tone stops me. "What do you mean?"

"What are you doing with Austin?"

"Nothing." The answer is pure reflex. It's far easier than trying to sort out the truth.

Christy looks around to make sure no one's listening. "Haley saw you go off with him. She's freaking."

Join the club, I want to say. Instead, I just wait, knowing Christy won't be able to resist filling me in on whatever Haley's latest drama involves.

"Hello? You hooked up with Austin! What were you thinking?"

Not much beyond "yes," if she wants the truth. It's not

like Christy can judge, given her own track record. She picks up guys the way an adrenaline junkie picks up hobbies. The more dangerous, the better.

Christy pouts. "Austin's the guy Haley came here to see in the first place. She really likes him, right?"

I almost laugh. Austin is Otto? It figures that the one guy to show any interest in me since I moved here nearly three years ago is Haley's latest boytoy. My life is a series of cruel ironies. The pretty girl no one sees. The horse I have to sell. The kiss I can't keep.

It's not that I'm unattractive, exactly, but people always seem surprised when they see a picture of me—as if they never noticed I was pretty before. It's not as obvious a thing with girls, but it still happens. It's like I'm missing some key ingredient when I'm around people in person.

Christy grabs my elbow and leads me out to a patio that's serving as an impromptu smoking section. "I can't believe you're doing this to Haley," she says, like I planned it or something.

I'm grateful for the cloak the cloud of smoke provides. It's a relief to disappear. "I swear, I didn't know."

Christy bums a cigarette from a group of skaters in the corner even though she doesn't really smoke. "I knew you wouldn't do this on purpose."

"I didn't know," I say again, hoping if I repeat it enough I can absolve myself of my sins.

She lights the cigarette and takes short puffs without inhaling. "Did you do something different with your makeup?"

I shake my head. "Haley put something in my hair."

"That must be it." Christy looks back toward the house. "We might be able to fix this. It's not like you're in love with Austin or anything, right?"

In love? The fact that he even noticed me is an anomaly in itself. Even I'm not foolish enough to pretend that love is part of the equation. "I just met him."

"And nothing happened?"

"I swear."

More than anything, I want to get out of here. To run back to my coach before it turns back into a pumpkin. Too soon, the clock will strike midnight and I'll have to fade back into my reality. Once Prince Charming sobers up and realizes he can have Haley, he won't be making the rounds with any glass slippers.

"So? How do we fix this?" I ask.

Christy's plan is simple. The old bait and switch. Haley will go into Austin's bedroom in my place. Once Austin sees her, he'll forget all about me. It's practically a *fait accompli*. Guys don't say no to Haley Marvell.

I wait outside while Christy goes in to save my friendship and kill any hope of a budding romance. I find an empty spot along the wall where I can be alone, more comfortable than I've been all night.

I know the second Blake walks outside. The skin on the back of my neck burns under his fiery gaze. I turn to face him, every instinct telling me to meet him from a position of strength.

He stops about fifteen feet away, his face indecisive.

I want him closer. Much, much closer.

Christy brushes past Blake as she rushes up to me. "It's done."

Blake turns away and walks back into the house. I feel sick.

"I think it worked. Haley's in with Austin now." Christy claps her hands together. "I'm sure we'll hear all about it tomorrow."

So I have that to look forward to.

Christy reaches into her pocket. "Oh, Haley said to give you this." She sets the broken charm bracelet into my palm. It's hardly a fair trade.

It's not until we reach the car that I realize I never asked Blake how he knew my grandma's nickname for me. My stomach lurches.

I'm definitely going to be sick.

FOUR

I pour myself a glass of orange juice before I can think better of it. The smell is at once sweet and repulsive. It sits on the kitchen table, untouched.

Dad looks like a bad quilt, in a plaid bathrobe wrapped around a set of flannel pajamas. He brings me a cup of coffee, the newspaper tucked under his arm. The mug says *Paxton Insurance Services—Because your life is your most valuable asset.* If Mom was up, I'd get the one with her picture on it and the tagline *Cyndi Paxton sells dreams!* The Paxtons are big on branding.

He catches me frowning at the mug. "Someday you'll have your own: *Brianna Paxton saves the world.*" Dad has been teasing me about being some kind of environmental extremist ever since I announced my plans to study biology in the eighth grade. He doesn't realize that science is my escape, not my calling.

When I don't answer, Dad pulls the sports section out and skims the front page. "Heading out to see Piece of Meat?"

"His name's Dart."

"Well, don't go getting attached." This is shorthand for Dad's Lecture Number 376, *That Horse is Just an Investment*. The full lecture includes reminders that the money we used to buy Dart off the racetrack came from my college fund, and that I'll have to sell him before I can apply for college in the fall. It goes on from there, but thankfully today Dad is more interested in the Padres' opening week than my progress with training and selling Dart.

Or not. Dad pushes the corner of the paper down. "When do you think you'll be ready to sell him?"

"Another month or so. After the Del Mar National."

Dad goes back to his paper. With the wall of newsprint between us, I rub my temples.

"You feeling okay?" Dad misses nothing, even at six a.m.

"Just tired." I take my still-full glass of orange juice to the sink and pour it down the drain.

"Hot date last night?"

"You know it." My standard response to our running joke feels heavy on my tongue. I'm not ready to think about last night. But it's unavoidable. "Hey Dad?" He sets down the newspaper and looks over to where I still stand, holding the empty glass. "Remember how Nana used to call me 'bandia'?"

He nods. "You could take your grandmother out of

Ireland, but you could never take Ireland out of your grandmother."

"It meant something, right? The name?"

Dad pushes his glasses back against the bridge of his nose. "Why the sudden interest in your grandmother's superstitions?"

Not an answer. He's watching me like I'm about to sprout horns or something, but I'm not backing down. "I was just thinking that Beltane is coming up and it made me think of her, that's all." Our family has celebrated Beltane for as long as I can remember. Nana made sure we celebrated both half-year eves. It went right along with keeping away from black cats and wearing sprigs of mint around our wrists when we got a cold.

Dad smiles. "Your mother isn't going to make us eat that nettle soup again, is she?"

"She always does." In the two years since Nana's death, my mom has continued the tradition.

"You sure you can't talk her into a nice chicken tortilla or tomato bisque?"

"Sounds very Irish. Good luck with that."

Dad picks up his coffee. "She'll listen to you. You're the one she does this for."

I have to grab the sink for support. "Me?"

Dad's eyes widen and I can tell he wants to take back what he just said. Then he sets down his coffee, resigned. "Honey, I know how hard it was for you when Nana died. And then we had to move here when I took over the branch office." He doesn't mention the other reason we moved. I don't blame him. No one mentions it. "Your mom is trying."

"Mom's trying to do what? She doesn't have to pretend for my benefit, okay?" For the last few years, Mom's been a ghost, a beautiful specter who floats in and out of our house on a breeze, her brilliant smile reserved for bus stops and coffee mugs. She avoids me. The only exception was when she sat me down to ask if I'd started the wildfire that burned nearly two hundred homes in Rancho Domingo last fall. We're close like that. I'm halfway to the front door before Dad can respond.

"Brianna." The tone of his voice stops me. "Try not to be so hard on her. It's been rough for her too. She lost her mother."

I can only nod and sigh. I don't say what I'm thinking: *So did I.*

"Say hi to Piece of Meat for me," Dad says, our discussion over.

I drive to Bridle Oaks as fast as the Blue Box can manage—which means I almost make it to fifty-five miles an hour. My old hatchback has seen better days. When I enter the stable, Dart is nestled in a corner of his stall polishing off a flake of alfalfa. I pull a carrot from my pocket, drawing a welcoming nicker. He walks over and devours the carrot in two bites, sniffing for more. Once he determines I'm out, he goes back to his hay. He always eats like he doesn't know when he'll see his next meal. When I first saw him, he was all ribs and withers, nearly starved after an unsuccessful year on the racetrack. Now he looks like a different horse.

Parker Winslow leads her bay hunter, Tristan, down the barn aisle. I can't tell if she notices me in the stall with Dart or not, but it hardly matters, since she's never spoken to me in the three years I've worked here. Parker and I are the same age. That's pretty much the full extent of what we have in common. Parker goes to McMillan Prep, drives a convertible Lexus, and has three horses in training with Sam Sabatini, the grand prix rider. I'm just the hired help, teaching beginning riding lessons to spoiled ten-year-olds in exchange for Dart's board and my own lessons with Sam's assistant Marcy.

I lean back against the stall. Everything feels so normal in the light of day. Normal is good.

"Hello? Excuse me!" Parker Winslow stands in front of the stall door. Tristan's reins are now looped under her arm as she pulls on a pair of black leather gloves. She doesn't look quite so perfect up close. Her face is a bit too narrow and her chin sharpens to a point. I can't fault her body, though. Her cashmere sweater molds to her chest in all the right places. Effective, if not exactly practical. The seafoam color sets off a touch of green in her hazel eyes. Parker knows how to accentuate the positive.

"Hey," I say.

She gestures toward Dart without looking at him. "Sam wants me to try this horse. Bring him to the main ring at nine." She walks away, leading the big bay behind her, not waiting for a response.

I know that Marcy told Sam I would be selling Dart soon. Still, I can't imagine that Parker Winslow is interested in my rescue horse. Even if he's bloomed into a handsome prince, to Parker it would be like buying designer clothes at an outlet mall. There's no point.

That doesn't stop me from spending the next half hour brushing Dart until he gleams. Even I have to admit that Dart will fit right in next to the expensive warmbloods that Sam's students normally ride. In some ways Dart, a thoroughbred, is even more beautiful. He has the graceful athleticism that comes from a hundred years of selective breeding.

I bring Dart to the center of the arena, where Sam and Marcy stand. Parker rides toward us, bringing Tristan to a halt. She dismounts and pulls the reins over his head, handing them to me so I'm holding one horse in each hand. She unbuckles the girth and slides her saddle from Tristan's back. She marches around to Dart, cinching the saddle in place without once looking at him. She takes the reins from me in silence.

"He's afraid of crops." It's Dart's one quirk from his days on the track. I learned it the hard way.

"I think I know how to ride a horse." Parker mounts with one smooth motion and guides Dart to the rail, easing into a trot. It's been a long time since I've seen anyone else ride Dart, and I'm amazed at how he seems to float across the ground. Sam occasionally comments to Marcy and smiles.

After just a few laps around the arena, Parker pulls Dart

up and walks him back to Sam. "I don't like him." She says it loud enough so I can hear. Me and half the county. "His trot is jarring, and he doesn't understand lateral aids."

Sam laughs and then I hear his elegant voice. "Parker, dear, you're just not used to so much extension. He's a ten."

"Well, he needs some *professional* training." Parker has already dismounted and is running her stirrup iron up the leather. Within seconds, her saddle is off and on the bench next to Marcy and Sam. She hands Dart back to me without another word, holding out the reins and simultaneously grabbing Tristan's. Her long platinum braid sways in time with her steps as she marches out of the arena without a backward glance.

Marcy walks over to where I stand fuming. Her face breaks into a huge grin.

"What are you so happy about?" I stroke Dart's neck, insulted for both of us.

"Sam *loves* him."

"Really?" My spirits lift. Sam's buyers shop in an entirely different stratosphere than the riders on the local show circuit where Marcy and I toil. If I have to sell Dart, I could do a lot worse than one of Sam's clients.

When I'm done teaching my lessons, I hack Dart around the smaller arena designated for Marcy's students. I try not to notice that his trot might be a little bit bouncy, or that he doesn't exactly respond when I squeeze my inside leg to push him toward the rail.

FIVE

The next afternoon, Christy and I make a quick trip to the mall. Christy buys a life-sized cutout of the celebrity du jour and I get my bracelet fixed. We're back in the car before I broach the subject I've been avoiding all weekend. "So? Did you talk to Haley?"

"No. You?"

I shake my head. I can't bring myself to ask Haley about Austin. I'm not jealous, exactly, but I can't help feeling sad that my first kiss has to stay buried in the dark room where it happened. I'm dying to tell someone. It occurs to me that I could tell Blake, that I want him to know. It's a stupid idea. For one thing, Blake already has a good idea what happened. For another, he couldn't possibly care. And it's not like I should even consider talking to Blake again.

Haley's already waiting in front of her house when we

pull into the cul-de-sac. At least we won't have to risk facing her mom. As Christy moves to the back seat, I brace myself for the play-by-play.

It hasn't always been this way with Haley. She was boyfriend-free until September of sophomore year, when she fell head over heels for Tyler Laredo, a senior and wannabe musician. All his songs were about OD'ing on Vicodin, but he was cute in an artsy way, and he worshiped the ground Haley walked on. Tyler lasted a whole six weeks before she broke it off. Since then, Haley's been in perpetual motion—falling madly in love, losing interest, and then starting all over with someone else. By my count, Austin will be lucky number thirteen. If he plays his cards right, he's probably in for the best three weeks of his life.

And my first kiss never happened.

———————

Haley spends the drive talking about a biography on Ayn Rand she's reading. There's no mention of Austin. And I can't bring myself to ask.

Magic Beans is empty for now, but the Sunday night special will start in about fifteen minutes. Nothing brings out the college crowd like two-for-one espresso drinks.

Max Carroll snaps his fingers as soon as we walk in. "Girls. Lovely. Fresh. The first sign of Spring." He has the annoying habit of turning every sentence into spoken word poetry.

Haley puts on a blue apron and ducks behind the

counter to make our drinks. "You know spring started like three weeks ago, right?"

Max rolls his eyes and pumps vanilla into an oversized mug. "Killjoy. Heartless. Weak. Murderer of all that is good."

Christy giggles. Max is almost weird enough for her. Too bad he isn't a little less harmless.

I wander toward the back, navigating the silk vines that hang from the shop's signature beanstalk, a floor-to-ceiling monstrosity that takes up most of the square footage. The door to the back office is open. If the coffee shop is an exercise in overindulgence, the tiny office in the back is its complete opposite. Only a handwritten shift schedule adorns the white walls.

Kimmy sits in a metal folding chair, hunched over a ledger. She's spending more time here since her husband left, which, depending on what kind of mood Haley's in, is a good or bad thing. She doesn't look up from her list of numbers.

"Brie!" Christy calls from a table under the beanstalk. "Come on." She sets three white candles in a circle in front of her.

I make my way over to Christy. "Are we drinking our lattes by candlelight now?" It wouldn't be the first time Christy insisted we do something like this for better feng shui or chi or something equally arcane. I wander back toward the table, arriving just as Haley sits down with our drinks.

Christy shakes her head and reaches into her bag,

pulling out a thick hardcover. "Delia sent me this amazing book."

I eye the book with some skepticism. Christy is not by nature an avid reader. Aside from a book on sexual techniques she stole from her sister Delia's college dorm room, she hasn't read anything more substantial than *People* magazine in the last two years.

"It's a book of spells," Christy says. "We're going to cast a love spell."

Even Haley looks pensive. "Are you sure this is a good idea?"

"Of course! We can all use more love in our lives, right?" Christy thumbs through the large book. "Delia says we should try the simple spell on page sixty-seven to start."

Delia never met a psychic she wouldn't shell out fifty bucks for. Like Christy, she's drawn to all things corrupt. It must be genetic.

"Here it is!" Christy reads the page in earnest, her lips moving as her fingers follow the path of the words on the page. "We sit in a circle, then we each take a turn lighting a candle and saying the spell."

"So is this witchcraft or something?" Haley grabs the book.

"White magic. It's totally fine."

"My mom will flip out," Haley says. She is so in.

I shake my head. "Don't look at me."

It's not that I believe in witchcraft, exactly. But you don't grow up in a house with my grandmother without having a few old-world superstitions conditioned into your subconscious. And this superstition is a big one: Nana always claimed the women in our family were "touched." So, to practice witchcraft was to actually invite trouble from spirits and faeries. Or worse, to attract the attention of the Milesians, men of God who would burn us at the stake.

Yeah, Nana was a few centuries behind the times. Still, she would've freaked if she thought I was even contemplating messing with witchcraft. Especially so close to Beltane.

Haley is laughing at me. "Don't tell me Ms. Uber-Science is afraid of a little magic?"

"It's a waste of time." It sounds like a lame excuse even as I say it, but I'm not going to admit to some crazy superstition I don't even believe in.

Christy shrugs. "It's your love life. Or lack thereof. You can just watch if you want."

Haley's attention is back on the book. "No, she can't. We need a circle of three."

"Get Kimmy," I say, making one more attempt at an out.

"Kimmy's not ready to date yet." Haley's emphasis on the word "Kimmy" is a not-so-subtle reminder that I am ready. And in need of all the help I can get.

I take the book from Haley. Peer pressure: one. Brianna: zero.

Christy goes first. She reads the verse, her face filled with excitement. When she lights the candle, no fire and brimstone rain into the coffee shop. Nothing happens at all. Not that I expected anything to happen. Not really. I'm just a little on edge after last night.

Haley goes next, striking a match and saying the verse. Her candle also lights without fanfare. I let out a breath, relaxing a little.

My turn. "Hear my wish, loud as the raven's cry." My voice cracks a little. "Send out my magic. Send it high." That part comes out smoother. No problem. "Let the magic hear my plea. Let me meet the guy for me."

My fingers barely shake as I light the match. "So it will be."

I lower the flame to the wick. The candle flares to life in a perfectly normal orange flame, completing the circle.

Christy grins from across the table.

I smile back, about to laugh at my own unfounded fear, but I'm stopped by a gust of wind that has no place in the shop. It swirls around me, lifting the hair off my back and whipping it around my face. Bright silver light floods my vision. Then the coffee shop is gone and I'm lost in a vortex of mist and blinding light, the wind whipping faster and faster. I spin around, unable to get my bearings, surrounded as I am in light and fog. I reach out, searching for something to ground me, but find only empty air.

The outline of a man materializes in the distance, moving toward me. I can't make out his features, just the dark shape of his body, sinewy and strong. I wrap my arms around myself, bracing against the cold, wet air. The man's hand extends in my direction, a beacon of strength and safety in this strange world. I reach out, desperate to touch something solid, but my fingers don't quite reach. I strain to stretch another millimeter, frantic. At last, our fingers brush. At the touch, a searing white heat pools in my abdomen, primal and strong. The contact breaks, but the warmth remains, filling me with strength and power. He drifts away, farther and farther, until the mist swallows him.

I push forward, grabbing at the wind, begging for another glimpse of the dark figure, for one more touch. But there is nothing. I am completely alone. The wind turns to ice, cutting to the bone, removing any last trace of warmth from my body. From somewhere in the distance, a desolate shriek slices through the air. I shiver and spin away from the sound. But there is nowhere to run.

The mist fades and there's ground beneath my feet. Damp, moist ground. Bright rays of sunlight dot the landscape, illuminating the greenest grass I've ever seen, each blade more vivid than the last. To the right is a wall of stacked gray stone, intricately arranged and packed with mud. To the left is a field of endless emerald, dotted with yellow and purple wildflowers and large boulders that seem to grow right out of the ground. Even with the sun, the air is cold and everything feels wet.

A young woman walks beside the stone wall, her hand trailing along the stacks of rock. She wears a flowing blue dress, just a shade lighter than her indigo eyes. Dark curls spiral down to her waist. A crown of violet flowers makes her look like she stepped right out of a fairy tale. She graces me with a benevolent smile, like she knows how lost I am.

"Can you help me?" I ask. "I need to get home."

She laughs. When she speaks, her voice is a soft brogue. "Do you not know me then?" She reaches out to brush a strand of hair away from my face. "Do you not know yourself?"

I blink at her. "Should I know you?"

She shrugs. "In time you will know me well enough. I'll not be the one to tell you. I remember well the peace that comes with ignorance."

I tremble, though whether it's from the cold or the ominous tone of her voice, I can't say.

Her hands come to my face, palms warm against my cheeks. "Welcome home, child!" Her smile is so bright that even the white light fades in comparison. And then there is nothing but darkness.

"Get some water!" Haley's voice is far and distant. A hand presses against my shoulder. "Brie!" Haley screams in my ear.

I'm on my back on the cold tile floor, staring up at the silk and wire beanstalk. Not again. Two bizarre hallucinations in as many days. I did it to myself this time, freaking myself out over Christy's stupid spell. Still, this can't be good.

"She's okay!" Haley searches my face. "You're okay, right?"

I nod, even though I'm not okay. I'm nowhere close to it. I start counting in exponential sequences again, this time with the number seven. It takes more concentration, the calculations getting more difficult with each number. It's almost enough to make me forget that it's happening again, that I'm losing my fragile grip on reality. That no one is safe.

Christy runs over with a bottle of water. "Omigod, Brianna, you completely passed out. Do you think it was the spell?"

"No." I sit up on my elbows. "I just fainted, I guess." It doesn't sound convincing, but I'm trying.

Christy nods. "It happened to me once. Remember when I was on that fasting diet?"

I stand up slowly, grabbing the back of a chair for support. "I'm fine." *16,807. 117,649.*

A bell rings, and the door at the front of the shop opens.

"Omigod!" Christy stares at the front door. "It worked!"

I follow Christy's gaze.

A group of preps walks into the shop. Blake is leading the way, his shining smile drawing all of my attention. Our eyes meet and my heart leaps to my throat, nearly choking me. But it's the briefest of seconds before he looks away. To stare at Haley.

His blond hair catches on a silk vine that hangs down in front of him, but he pushes the vine to the side and walks right toward her. I grip the back of the chair harder. It's nothing more than the same scene I've watched play out dozens of times before. The ache in my chest is there anyway. I fight against it, but today there's no denying the disappointment. I don't know what I expected. So he talked to me last night. It was inevitable that whatever buzz he had going would wear off and things would go back to normal. But hope is addictive, and I've been chasing this particular dragon for over a year.

"Good party last night," Blake says. His eyes brighten as he takes in Haley's perfect features, and I can't help the tide of envy that rises inside. I try to go back to counting. Jealousy and crazy are the psychological equivalent of mixing an acid and a base. Explosive.

"It was okay." Haley sounds bored.

Blake smiles. "I was thinking you might give me Brianna's number?"

Only my grip on the chair keeps me from falling over.

"Why don't you just ask her yourself?"

"Hey," I say, before I can stop myself.

Blake barely glances at me. Then he does a double take, his eyes narrowed. "Brianna?"

"Last time I checked."

Blake stares, the question on his face now blatant. He shakes his head and looks at the ground. "Can I get your number?"

My little adrenaline rush is stamped on and squished into a wet puddle of reality. I almost don't give my number to him at all, but then I do. It's safe enough, now that he's seen me in person minus the beer goggles. It's not like he's going to call me.

Sure enough, he programs the number into his phone without saying another word. It's not even a surprise when he walks away.

SIX

There are four or five people in line for coffee, so Haley heads behind the counter to help Matt.

Christy nods toward the line. "Who's that?"

I only see her from the back, but I recognize the cherry red stripes slashing through Fishnet's onyx hair. "The girl who was with Blake last night?"

"Eww, no. The hottie on her right." The guy next to Fishnet catches us looking at him. He flashes Christy a ravenous grin that holds none of the charm of Blake's smile. A shiver of warning creeps along my spine.

Christy bounces on her heels. "The spell is so working!"

The guy strolls across the shop. Slowly, so Christy has plenty of time to take in the perfect dark waves in his hair and his chiseled arms. He stops directly in front of her, closer than is strictly polite. "Hello gorgeous," he says, his gaze glued to the point of the V on Christy's top.

Christy waggles her fingers and giggles.

"I'm Jonah," he says to Christy's chest. "I haven't seen you before. You don't go to McMillan." He doesn't bother hiding the air of superiority in his tone.

She giggles again, and the reservations I have about the guy are instantly confirmed. It's like Christy has a built-in jerk detector. A good thing, if you know how to use it.

She doesn't.

"Well, good seeing you," I say to no one in particular. At least no one who's listening. I'm not in the mood to watch Christy throw herself in front of a bus. But I've seen this particular drama enough times to know there's no stopping her.

I take my latte over to Mariah, a life-sized stuffed cow with built-in containers offering a variety of creamers and sweeteners. My vanilla latte doesn't need more milk or sugar; I just want to look like I'm doing something besides standing in the corner by myself. Which is exactly what I'm doing. I examine a packet of Splenda.

Austin's soft lilt comes from behind me. "Would you mind handing me one of those?"

I freeze, one hand hovering over a little yellow packet. I finally turn my head. He's looking right at me. My fingers shake a little. His eyes are friendly enough, but it's still awkward.

"Hi, Juliet."

I hand him the packet, watching as he rips the little envelope and lets the white powder fall into a cup of dark tea before swirling it with a stirrer. He blows on the brown liquid before bringing the cup to his lips and taking a tentative sip.

"I'm surprised you remember me," I blurt.

"Why would you think that?" The front of his hair drifts down onto his forehead. "Perhaps I've been counting the hours until the exact moment when I would see you again." His lips curve into a crooked smile. "Just so I could get some sweetener for my tea."

I laugh. "Glad I didn't let you down."

"A good start. But it remains to be seen, doesn't it?"

"I'm not following."

"Whether you let me down."

"You're the one who said this would end badly." Of course, it already has. It ended the minute I sent Haley into his room.

"Yes, but we've a long way to go before we get to the sad part, don't you think?" Austin takes another sip of tea.

I look around the shop for Blake, almost hoping he'll see the way Austin is smiling at me. But Blake is standing at the counter, watching Haley make his drink. Joe stands next to him, sipping a black coffee while he fingers an unlit cigarette in his other hand. Blake doesn't look over. Good. I can't afford to let myself lose control again.

Christy walks over with Jonah trailing close behind. He's watching her like he wants to eat her for breakfast. And lunch. And dinner. Before I can even say anything, Jonah extends a hand to Christy. "Walk with me?"

Christy places her hand in Jonah's. She leans in and

whispers, too loud, "I told you it worked!" They disappear outside, toward the park across the lot.

Whatever. I'd rather be by myself anyway. It's funny. All this time I thought I wanted to be seen, but at the moment, I just want to be left alone. Haley keeps peeking at Austin from behind the counter, but he doesn't look in her direction. Not once.

Blake grabs his iced coffee and glides across the shop with Joe. Out of sheer habit, my eyes follow Blake as he moves through the front door, his every step more graceful and effortless than the last. It's almost a crime to waste so much beauty on a boy, especially one who tosses it around so carelessly.

Fishnet leans against Blake's SUV in a too-short skirt and too-low top. A second girl with round, fake boobs whispers in her ear as they watch Blake approach. The ache inside me mixes with something darker, converging into a stew of emotion that borders on violence.

I'm halfway out the door when Austin grabs my arm, stopping me.

I take a deep breath. *16,807. 117…*

"Leaving so soon?" Austin lets go of my arm as I turn to face him.

"No." It takes every ounce of concentration I have to keep from running out of the shop, but I hold my ground.

Austin is watching me with a hint of curiosity. "I *do* remember you."

"We've established that."

"I just imagined things would be different when we saw each other again."

I feel myself start to blush. "Different how?"

"I'm not sure. I think I expected you to be more ... affectionate."

Wow. Does he think since we kissed once, I'd just throw myself at him? After Haley? "Sorry to disappoint." I look out to the parking lot, to where Blake leans against his car, angled toward Fishnet.

Austin follows my gaze and nods toward Blake. "Am I late to the party?"

"What?"

"I saw you watching him."

"It's not what you think."

And it's not. Not exactly.

I have this theory. My hypothesis is that I lack the pheromone that attracts people to one another. Or if I do have it, there's some major imbalance. There's been more than enough evidence to support it.

Sure, Sherri Milliken invited me to be on the freshman math team on the fourteenth day of ninth grade, but that was based entirely on the fact that I solved a quadratic equation in my head during trig and the Mathletes were in dire need of a fourth member. It wasn't like she was much of a friend. We stopped hanging out once I quit the team.

It was more of a shock when Haley stopped me in the hall a few weeks later to ask me about my concert T-shirt. Turned out that the Matches were Haley's favorite band, and she couldn't believe I'd actually been to their one reunion shows at Slim's in San Francisco. She introduced me to Christy, and the three of us have been together ever since. Again, explainable—it was the Matches, not me, that got Haley's attention. Pathetic as my social life might be, I wouldn't even have one if it weren't for Haley.

Last spring, Haley dated a senior from McMillan Prep who hung in Blake's crowd, so there were plenty of opportunities to see him. And Blake kept coming to Magic Beans long after Haley broke up with his friend, even after he started college at U.R.D. Now he usually has a backpack and a medical textbook with him.

Blake is the perfect test subject for me. He enthralls girl after girl, one perfect smile at a time. And there have been lots of them. He flirts with virtually every woman he meets, young or old, small or large, pretty or plain. All except one.

Blake is my litmus test. My control group. My proof. I am the girl no one sees.

Until last night, my theory was unassailable.

SEVEN

I catch Haley watching Austin again, from behind the counter. She flashes me a nervous smile. As if I need to be reminded that Austin is spoken for.

I blink at Austin. "I should go."

For a second, his eyes seem almost black. It's there and gone so quickly, I can't be sure. I take a step forward and it happens again. His eyes darken so much that the irises almost disappear. "Stay," he says. The word is an anchor, pulling me along with a force so strong that there's no hope of my ever making my way back to the surface.

My heart drums out a staccato rhythm, pleading with me to stay with him. Hell, go with him. *Be* with him. It takes all the strength I have to pull my eyes away. I glance at Haley. She still watches, twisting her hair into a tight spiral.

"I can't." I stumble over the words, not chancing a look back at Austin.

"You can't or you won't?"

Of course I *could*. It would be easy to be with Austin. It's not just that he's adorable and has an accent that's romantic as hell, though those things don't hurt. It's that he might be the one boy in the whole world who looks at me and likes what he sees. Something must be seriously wrong with him.

I don't trust myself to resist him a second time, so I just turn away and walk outside. I need to escape. I send a text to Christy. After a couple of minutes staring at my phone, I send another one, in all caps.

I glance back into the shop and catch Austin staring. His smile pulls at me. My hand is on the front door before I catch myself and spin back around. I nearly run through the parking lot.

I move past the group by Blake's SUV like a wraith. Blake never looks up even though I deliberately move close enough to invade his personal space. So my theory's not totally dead. There's a small measure of comfort in that, even if my heart breaks just a little.

I end up at the park on the other side of the parking lot, where Christy and Jonah were headed. I turn down a path that heads to the man-made lake in the center. There are a few lights along the way, but it's darker than the parking lot.

There's no sign of Christy, just some chirping crickets and my own footsteps. A cold breeze licks at the back of my neck, sending goose bumps along my arms. The sensation is eerily like the cold I felt when I fainted. Silver light flashes. No, no, no. I rub my arms, concentrating on chasing away the rising tide of fear of what's coming.

"Brianna," Blake says from behind me.

I stifle a scream as I turn to face him. He's standing right next to me, even though I never heard him approach. "God! You scared me. Where'd you come from?" I shake my head. Everything seems normal. Blake stands there on the path with his hands in his pockets.

He cocks his head, like he can't believe how different I look without the alcohol buzz. This supports my theory: the vanilla spritzer Haley applied to my hair masked my lack of pheromones. That, combined with the fact that Blake and Austin were both drinking, is the only explanation for what happened. Maybe Austin drank something before he came to Magic Beans tonight.

Blake looks down at the ground. "I was hoping we could talk."

"Now you want to talk? What's wrong? Did your date with the Boobsie Twins fall through?"

He laughs. "You mean Sierra and Kendra? You think I wouldn't mind a break from their inane chatter?"

"Is that what we're calling it these days? Chatting?"

"If chatting still means an informal conversation with one's peers." When it's clear I'm not going to respond to his comment, he adds, "I didn't come here to see them. I wanted to see you."

I want to believe him. I shouldn't, but I do. "Right. That's why you ignored me completely and hung out with the stripper sisters. Got it." I walk away.

Blake follows, his long strides easily matching my hurried ones. We come to a grassy bank at the edge of the lake.

When I turn to face him again, he's staring. It's hard to breathe when I know he's watching me.

"Are you going to tell me how you're doing that?" He asks.

He's caught me completely off guard. "Doing what?"

"Hiding."

"I'm right here."

He shakes his head. "It's like you're here, but you're not. I can't explain it. It's brilliant. I would never have even known you were doing it if you hadn't stopped."

"Stopped?"

"Last night, when you walked into the kitchen. Not this shadow of you, but *you*. Thank God I've learned to master my impulses. If I'd met you a year ago, I don't know what I would've done." His expression is dead serious.

"I hate to break this to you, but you did meet me a year ago. And I'm not *doing* anything. The only person who showed up last night was me." *Which means that you are a psycho schizoid*, I almost add. "Don't blame your drinking binge on me."

He curves his lips so softly that my heart nearly stops in its tracks. I can't prevent the out-of-control feeling that follows, the high that comes from the perfect chemical cocktail of endorphins and adrenaline. I can't let myself imagine his smile is for me. This is exactly the kind of thing I should be avoiding now that my crazy is back.

"You really don't know?" He asks. "It's hard to believe. Next thing you'll tell me is that the fire was an accident."

Oh my God. I want to run. Yet the smile on his lips

keeps me here. "The fire?" How does he know about the fire? It's not like I told anyone. And the records were supposed to be sealed. Anyway, it was an accident. Sort of.

He looks away. "We lost our house and everything in it."

The wildfire. He's talking about the wildfire that burned through R.D. last fall. Not my fire. He doesn't know.

He steps closer. "You're not even going to deny it, are you?"

My legs shake, poised to run, but I hold my ground. "Deny what?"

"The fire." His eyes find mine again, searching. "It doesn't matter. We know it was you."

I had nothing to do with the wildfire. I was at a horse show with Marcy in L.A. But it can't be a coincidence that two people suspect me of starting it. Mom, I get, because she knows about the fire I did start. But Blake doesn't.

"You don't even know me," I say.

He laughs, mocking me. "I know enough."

"What was the point of your coming out here? To call me a criminal, or to figure out why you can't even look at me?"

"The latter. Just watching you for more than a few seconds is hard. It takes conscious effort, and a lot of it. Even when I try, it's hard to see you."

Ouch. If his accusation about the wildfire wasn't enough, this proof of my undesirability hits like a bucket of ice water against my skull. Bucket first. I step away from him.

His hand catches my wrist, sending an electric shock

of heat up my arm. "Let me explain." He looks at me then, his eyes vulnerable.

I feel myself melting. *Please, no.* I may have fantasized about him from afar, but if there was ever any doubt about why I shouldn't be around him, it's been confirmed to the hundredth power. He suspects too much. He makes me feel things I shouldn't. Even as I think this, the heat from his touch is spreading to parts of my body that should not have a direct line to my wrist.

"Two minutes," I tell him.

"The first thing you need to understand is that I do want you." He closes his eyes. "The real you. Just the memory makes me crazy. But right now, it's like you're not even here. I mean, I can see a girl in front of me. I can even tell you're pretty, but it doesn't mean anything. Everything about you pushes me away instead of drawing me in."

I pull my hand away. "So I repel you."

"Not like you think. You're a ghost of yourself. If I hadn't seen you last night, *really* seen you, I never would have suspected a thing."

I swallow, instantly back in that frozen silver moment. I was so exposed in the stillness of the room, and then he turned and spoke to me. It's impossible. The whole thing was in my head, a manifestation of a latent psychosis I thought I'd buried three years ago.

He steps closer still. "Even now, it makes me question everything. But I know I'm not crazy."

"That makes one of us." I laugh at the irony of this statement.

"Help me figure this out, Brianna. Before last night, we'd met at the coffee shop, right?"

"Several times." Six, to be exact, not even counting the fifty-one times he came in without seeing me at all. "And we were introduced again in the living room at the party."

"So something must have changed before you walked into the kitchen. What?"

"Nothing." Everything changed after.

"Did you say something unusual? Did anyone else?"

I wrack my brain for any details. "No. Haley and I were just talking, and some drunk guy hit on her. He spilled beer on me. Are you into Budweiser?" My hand instinctively finds my wrist, fingering the chain that circles it.

His eyes follow my hand. "Do you always wear that?"

"Yes." I close my fingers around the bracelet, shielding it from his gaze.

"And in the living room?"

I nod.

"In the kitchen?"

I hesitate.

"Were you wearing that bracelet when you came into the kitchen?" His voice is more insistent.

My voice shakes. "Not in the kitchen."

"Can I see it?" His eyes glow with a silver sparkle that shouldn't be visible in the dark.

Here it comes. I wait for the darkness, the silence that I know will follow the silver light. I've always heard that people who are really insane aren't aware of it, yet here I am, not only aware of the hallucinations but anticipating them.

The hallucination doesn't come. Blake still stands in front of me, waiting for an answer. I step back, easing toward the trail. "Why?"

"I just want to look." His voice is soft, seductive.

I don't move. He lowers his chin and looks out from underneath thick lashes. I know it's just a bracelet, an accessory. There's no logical reason for me to keep it from him. But nothing about Blake or the feelings he stirs in me has anything to do with logic. Everything is driven by some primitive instinct, animalistic urges that I should damn well ignore. I unfurl my fingers, one at a time, still covering the bracelet with my palm.

Blake eases forward, placing his hand over mine. I pull my hand away from the heat of his touch. "Shhh," he says, like he knows I'm a hair's breadth away from bolting. He reaches for my hand again, taking the bracelet between his fingers and rubbing it lightly. He examines the charms one at a time, stopping to touch the flower for a few seconds before his cocky smile is back. "Someone in your family has a wicked sense of humor."

"What do you mean?" How does he know that the charms came from my family?

"This one. Do you know what kind of flower it is?"

"Yes." At last, something tangible I can discuss intelligently. "Monkshood. It grows in the northern hemisphere. My grandma even managed to grow some in her yard in San Francisco."

"Wolfsbane." Blake laughs again. "Just like you. Hiding in plain sight."

I push his hand away. His eyes shine again in the dark, reflecting the stars. I've been waiting so long for him to see me that it's every bit as terrifying as it is amazing.

"Can you take it off for a minute?"

I cover the bracelet with my hand again.

"Just to see if I'm right. You can put it right back on."

There have to be at least a dozen better explanations for my condition than a simple silver charm. Maybe my pheromones are finally kicking in, albeit erratically. Or maybe Blake is just jealous of Austin. Or he's drunk again. I twist the chain and slowly unhook the shiny new clasp. I let the bracelet drop into the palm of my hand, closing my fingers around it.

Blake stares at me harder.

"Still me?"

"I think you have to let go."

I close my fingers tighter, not wanting to part with the chain in my hand. I know the flower is just a charm. An odd little flower cast in silver. I still don't let go.

The bracelet has been in our family forever, so old that the story of its origin was lost generations ago. Nana gave it to me shortly after the fire, my fire. She said it would protect me. I love the little horse and horseshoe charms that hang on either side of the strange flower, but I haven't really thought much about the bracelet since she gave it to me. I've just always worn it.

Until last night.

Blake stretches out his hand. "Humor me." He flashes his "you can't resist me" grin.

All this time I've been waiting for him to grace me with that smile, and tonight it has no effect on me. I've seen him use it too many times to think it means anything beyond a calculated effort to get what he wants. I clutch the bracelet tighter.

"Why don't you humor me?" I ask. "Maybe I don't want to give this to you. Maybe there's a reason I can't." I link the chain back around my wrist.

"Listen to yourself." Blake's voice is quiet. "There is a reason."

"What?"

"So you can hide."

I try to keep the panic from my voice. "And what exactly am I hiding from?"

His dimples are out in full force. "Bastards like me."

EIGHT

There's a rustling behind us. Christy comes down the trail, staring at the ground. She looks up only when she nearly runs into me. "Brie! What are you doing here?"

I look around for Blake, but there's no sign of him. He's gone. "Looking for you," I say, though at the moment I'm scanning the bushes for any sign of Blake. It's like he was never here. Where the hell did he go?

Christy sniffs loudly, barely stifling a sob. Even in the dark, her eyes appear puffy and swollen.

"What happened?"

Christy just shakes her head.

She'll talk when she's ready. I put my arm around her and lead her back up the path. "Let's go."

Christy doesn't say a word the entire drive back to her house. She just stares out the passenger-side window. I shut the engine off in her driveway. Neither of us makes a move to get out of the car.

"Are you going to tell me what that creepshow did to you?" I ask.

Christy wipes her nose with the sleeve of her sweater.

"You're getting snot on your Ralph Lauren. He's so not worth it."

"True." She grabs her bag and rummages through it, at last emerging with a crumpled tissue.

"So, spill."

"It's embarrassing." Christy balls the tissue in her hands.

"Did he hurt you?"

"No!" Christy's voice is two octaves higher than normal.

"He made you cry. I want to kill the guy." Whoa. I might not just be saying this. I can feel the seeds of violence growing in my heart. Not good.

"It's just embarrassing," Christy repeats. Her cheeks redden.

"What?" *8. 64.* Breathe.

Christy lets out a long exhale. "It wasn't his fault exactly. It was more me. I kind of, well, I guess I didn't ... " She pauses before she adds, "Swallow."

"Oh." The shock of Christy's words is enough to draw me back into the moment.

Now that she's started talking, there's no stopping her. She doesn't even take a breath as she recounts the entire story. "One minute everything's fine, and then, well, it just kind of happened without any warning. I mean it barely started, so I totally wasn't expecting it, and it was really gross, and I just gagged and spit and I was like, retching, you know?"

"Who wouldn't? That guy is majorly gross."

"It was kind of gross."

"Don't tell me you're crying because of that? His premature ejaculation is not your problem."

"He started yelling and freaking out. Then he just left."

"I can't believe he yelled at you."

"It wasn't that bad, really. I'm just embarrassed is all. Next time, I'll be ready for it."

"Tell me you are not even considering a next time!" She's completely off the cliff if she thinks she is going to see that loser again.

"Maybe. I don't know."

"Christy, you've only met the guy once, and already you know he's a complete bastard. Add in the fact that he expects sex right away and even suffers from some kind of sexual dysfunction, and the guy has *nothing* going for him."

"You don't think he's cute?"

"Since when does yelling at a girl qualify as cute?"

Christy's expression turns from uncertain to defiant. "I knew I shouldn't have said anything."

"I'm sorry. But maybe you shouldn't be so quick to go off with a guy you just met. What if he hurt you?"

Christy glares at me. "I don't need your holier-than-thou attitude right now."

Holier than thou? Is that what she thinks? Just because I

don't support her crazy infatuation with a guy who's already shown he's a creep of the highest order.

"And how is my going off with Jonah any different than your going off with Austin last night?" Christy raises her eyebrow. She knows she has me. "It's not like Jonah is Haley's boyfriend."

I twist uncomfortably in my seat. I want to defend myself, but I don't. "Look, if you don't want to talk about the Jonah situation, fine."

"Fine." There's a tense silence before she speaks again. "I saw you flirting with Austin."

So much for our tentative truce. "We were just talking."

"You know Haley still likes him, right?"

"She never once mentioned him today."

"That's because he's different. He's not one of her flings, you know? She's really into him." Christy dares me to disagree.

"Fine." I'm not going to have this discussion now. It doesn't matter anyway—I'm not trying to steal Austin from Haley. "It's not like there's anything going on."

"I thought so."

Right. Because on what planet could I ever consider being with a guy like Austin? Any guy? At least Christy is no longer crying over Jonah, and we manage to part on okay terms.

When I get home, Mom and Dad are camped on the couch watching old episodes of *Veronica Mars*. "Home early?" Dad asks.

I throw myself on the empty loveseat. "Looks that way."

Mom looks up and gives me a closed-mouth smile.

Dad grins. "Couldn't resist an evening with your mom and dad, is that it? I can make popcorn and put in the *Lion King*." *The Lion King* is my parents' cure-all, whether I'm sick or just having a bad day.

"Do I look like I need a *Lion King* intervention?" I wonder if the cracks in my façade are starting to show. If they can tell that it's starting again.

Dad shakes his head. "No. But it's been a while since we've watched it. What with your busy social schedule and all."

Mom gets up and heads to the kitchen. I pull a purple afghan Nana crocheted around my shoulders. I'm tempted to take Dad up on the offer, but I'm tired and need to work on my pheromone project. *The Lion King* will only help for ninety minutes or so. A new theory could carry me for a couple of months at least.

"Thanks, Dad, but I'm kind of tired. Maybe we can watch it for my birthday?" My birthday is just a couple weeks away, and watching the movie then might spare me the torture of sitting through an entire meal at a restaurant listening to my mom talk about the local real estate market.

"It's a date. For a second there I was worried you'd outgrown it."

I laugh. "Funny, I was thinking the same thing about you."

Dad grins and restarts the show they were watching. My

mom wanders back in from the kitchen with a Diet Coke and sits down next to him. It's my cue to leave.

I crawl into bed, pulling out the notebook stuffed underneath the mattress. Fifty-seven entries, all neatly organized in chronological order: a scientific survey of my every encounter with Blake up to last night. I skim a few pages, like I need the reminder of who I am. Like tonight's strange discussion with Blake wasn't all the proof I need.

I've barely started making some notes when my cell phone starts barking. Literally barking, like actual dogs howling and yelping. Haley's idea of joke. She always downloads weird ringtones when I'm not paying attention. I grab the flashing rectangle, but it stops before I can answer it. The message light blinks on and off. I don't recognize the number on the screen; it's probably Haley using Kimmy's cell, since hers was confiscated by her mom. I debate whether to read the message now or wait until morning. But if I don't answer now, Haley will keep calling. I flip it open.

Where are you? the message blinks.

Haley has no way of knowing that Christy and I went straight home. *In bed*, I type, hoping she'll get the hint.

After I send the message, I start writing again. I'm tempted to omit the details about the silver flash and frozen time. "Stress-induced hallucination" should cover it.

The barking and yelping are back. I groan and roll over. I'm going to have to turn off the ringer.

Yum, can I come?

I sit up straight, instantly alert. Definitely not Haley.

Who is this? I tap back.

I stare at the phone, waiting for a reply. I can hear my own breathing. After what seems an eternity, the phone finally lights up.

Who do you think? The message teases me in the dark.

It occurs to me that there are two possibilities, and that fact alone is something I wouldn't even have comprehended two nights ago. I twist the bracelet around my wrist self-consciously.

Blake was talking nonsense; this bracelet is just a good luck charm, nothing more. Nana gave it to me my first day home from my three-night hospital stay. They said I was kept there for observation, to make sure I didn't go into shock, yet they kept asking me questions about whether I was suicidal or hearing voices. I wasn't. I wished I could blame what I'd done on voices in my head or suicidal depression, but when it came down to it, there was no one to blame but the monster that is me.

My old middle school always held a pajama party lock-in, an overnight event with games and movies and pizza that marked the beginning of eighth grade. It was a rite of passage that set the stage for where you'd fit in the school hierarchy, an event with a secret underground of spin the bottle and thermoses full of cheap sparkling wine. At thirteen, before my pheromone problem kicked in, I was a minor deity in a clique of girls poised to take control of the school. That night, Derek Kingston, the cutest boy in our class, asked me to meet him in the chemistry lab at one in the morning. I was convinced that not only was I going to get my first kiss, I was going to land an amazing boyfriend, securing my place at the top of the pecking order.

It all seems so stupid now, but at the time I was foolish enough to think that being pretty meant something.

At one o'clock, I put on the fuzzy yellow slippers I'd bought to match my sun-and-stars pajamas and told a yawning chaperone that I was going to use the restroom by the gym. The chemistry lab was dark when I got there, and at first I couldn't make out anything but shadows. There was a shuffling noise in the back. Gradually my eyes adjusted, and I made my way along the rows of tables. I could just see the silhouette of the spikes in Derek's hair. I started to walk faster, but stopped when I heard a giggle from behind him.

"Shhh," he said. "She'll hear you."

"Hear who?" My voice came out higher than it should have, a nervous squeak.

"No one. Brie, is that you?" Derek hurried to meet me, glancing back over his shoulder. "Hey," he said as he grabbed my hand and guided me to the front of the room. "You're early."

Another giggle came from the back, and everything fell into place. I was not the only girl Derek Kingston had invited to the chemistry lab. I was just his one o'clock appointment.

That's when I snapped.

The phone starts to vibrate and "The Final Countdown" starts playing. I can't blame Haley for this ringtone. I downloaded it myself.

"Hello?"

"I'm hurt," a teasing male voice says.

I release a breath I haven't realized I'm holding. "Blake." Of course Blake sent the messages—I gave him my number, after all. "What are you doing?"

"Looking for you. You left without saying goodbye."

I almost laugh at the absurdity of this statement. "Last time I checked, you were the one who took off." Vanished is more like it.

"It looked like your friend needed you. But we aren't finished."

The thumping in my chest is so loud I'm afraid he can hear it through the phone. Defenses down, I go on the offense. "And behind door number two we have Blake Williams' psychotic stalker personality, not to be confused with his aloof, 'everything about you pushes me away' personality."

He laughs. "I thought we were past that. Besides, I think I know how to fix it."

I sigh into the phone. Maybe I don't want to fix it. Maybe I want someone to see me whether they've been drinking or not. I hang up the phone before I admit as much to Blake.

The phone rings again before I can turn it off. I answer it for no other reason than to stop the music from blaring. "What?"

"I'm sorry, okay?"

"Don't be." I don't want him to be sorry. I don't want him to be anything.

"This whole thing is crazy. I can't stop thinking about you, and then I see you and it's all messed up."

"There's only one explanation for it." Not that I'm about to share my pheromone theory with the control subject.

"I know." Blake sounds thoughtful.

"Multiple Personality Disorder."

He laughs. "Is it okay if I call you?" He sounds like he might even care what the answer will be.

"I think you just did." I am so caving. This is not good. I can't afford to play around with someone who makes me feel like Blake Williams does. I'm better off being invisible. He's a million times better off. I should just let this go.

His voice is a low purr. "I was kind of hoping I might get to use this number more than once."

"I think you just did." I should hang up now. I don't.

"Right. You never did answer my other question."

"What question is that?"

"Can I come over?"

I almost say yes, but catch myself. "Some other time."

"How's tomorrow? We could go out."

"It's a school night." God, I sound like I'm ten.

"Saturday, then."

I want to say no. I have to say no. Things have already gone too far with Blake. How many more warning flashes of silver am I going to get before something really happens?

"Okay," I say before I can stop myself. "Meet me at Magic Beans at eight."

And so I have the first real date of my pathetic teenage life. My traitorous heart rejoices, not caring at all that it's about to be sent on what can only be a suicide mission.

NINE

By the end of the week, things almost settle back to normal. Parker Winslow disappears back into her rich little world, ignoring me and Dart every day after school like always. There are no more stress-induced hallucinations just because a guy talked to me. No more silver flashes of light. I almost begin to think I've dodged a bullet, that everything is back under control.

School goes by in a blur of boredom, saved only by a Friday guest speaker in AP biology, a scientist from a biotech company that's working on isolating genes from DNA. Dr. McKay is probably my parents' age, but so good-looking that the girls in my class all start whispering as soon as he walks in.

"Who can tell us about phantom genes?" he asks, which is kind of a cop-out since he's here to share his expertise with us, not the other way around.

When no one raises their hand, I reluctantly do. He nods at me.

"Strings of genes that were once believed to have a function, but which don't really do anything," I say.

"Very good. So, the question is, why do we have full strands of genetic material with no purpose?" He looks at me expectantly.

I try to formulate an answer. "Maybe there was a function at one time, but for something we don't need anymore. Something from the early stages of human evolution."

He's still smiling, so hopefully I'm on the right track. "Like an appendix or tonsil? Possibly. An interesting theory. But I have a different idea."

Everyone in the room is quiet, waiting to hear what he will say.

"Perhaps phantom genes are not genes from our past. Perhaps these genes are the building blocks of our future. Recessive traits that will someday be triggered by cataclysmic change or the pairing with a perfect genetic partner. The proverbial lightning strike."

Whoa. His theory is way out there, but something about it is appealing.

He turns to the class as a whole. "That's the beauty of genetics. It's the direct link to our ancestors, but also the map to the future of the human race." He flips on a Power Point slide.

I have to hand it to the guy; he knows how to put on a show. He spends the next hour explaining how his company has been working on isolating genes that not only determine physical characteristics, but also genes that spur certain personality traits, intelligence, and athletic ability.

It's pretty cool stuff. In fact, I might love the concept. As fixed as our genetic code may be, there's still hope for change. Hope that some secret element of my DNA could rise up in response to a disaster, fight off a disease, or make me normal.

Sherri Milliken stops me on the way out of class. Her small hand closes around my wrist with surprising strength. She blows a strand of dark stringy hair away from her face. Her chapped lips tremble. "Brianna, we need to talk."

"Later?" I'm not interested in whether she needs a fourth for the varsity math team.

"It's important." Sherri tightens her grip on my wrist.

"That hurts."

She lets go. "Sorry." She chews on a piece of dry skin on her lower lip, still waiting for a response.

I'm not in the mood for one of Sherri's rants. "I can't talk right now, okay? Call me." I scribble my cell number on a scrap of notebook paper in case she doesn't have it anymore.

She grabs the paper and stuffs it into the pocket of her jeans. "It can't wait much longer. It's important."

"Got it. We'll talk."

She finally disappears down the hall. When she calls on Saturday morning, I don't pick up. I'm not going back to the Mathletes. Not that it wasn't kind of fun, it's just that Sherri is one of those people who should only be taken in small doses, and I have a lot on my plate right now.

Saturday is the kind of perfect day that's easy to take for granted in Rancho Domingo. Warm but not hot, without a cloud in the sky. I stand in the center of the riding arena, clutching my vanilla latte and calling out encouragement to a trio of ten-year-olds whose ponies are probably worth more than the annual salary of the average American household.

I catch Parker Winslow's platinum hair blowing in the breeze at the far end of the arena. She manages to look perfectly styled, even at eight thirty in the morning, surrounded by horse dung and dirt. I'm not sure if it's genetic or just a money thing.

She raises her right hand in what might pass for a wave or something. Great. Seeing things again.

"Brianna!" No mistaking the wave this time. Parker climbs through the fence. Her beige riding breeches cling to her slender thighs before disappearing into a pair of custom-made boots that probably cost more than my car. Correction, definitely cost more than my car.

"Brianna Paxton, right?"

Since when does Parker even know my name? I sip my latte to ease my sudden case of cotton mouth.

"So you know Austin Montgomery?" Parker's voice is pure saccharine.

I almost do a spit-take. Seriously, it's all I can do to swallow my coffee without choking. So now my personal drama involves Parker Winslow?

"Do you know Austin?" Her impatience comes through this time.

"I guess so."

All trace of her smile vanishes. "Austin Montgomery?" She emphasizes the last name.

"Got it the first time. I know him. Do you?" It isn't like we hang in the same circles, but they do both go to McMillan.

Her eyes narrow sharply before she lets out a laugh. It's a laugh that doesn't invite company, more of a Cruella De Vil kind of laugh. "You really don't know?"

"Know what?"

"Austin and I went out for almost two years."

I try to process this bit of news.

"Don't pretend you didn't know." She's openly hostile now. So we're not going to be joining each other for mani-pedis anytime soon.

I lift my shoulders in what I hope comes across as a casual shrug. "He never mentioned it." I instruct my students to pick up a trot. I don't need to see Parker's face to feel the daggers her eyes throw at my back. After a few seconds, she sputters and goes to the rail. I look over just as she climbs through the fence.

"This isn't over." Parker glares at me.

A small laugh escapes my lips involuntarily. Parker's eyes widen before she storms off to her evil genius lair, or wherever it is she hangs out.

I probably shouldn't have laughed. It can't be good to have someone like Parker Winslow as an enemy. But she takes the drama queen thing to a whole new level. It isn't like Austin and I are going out or anything. I've met the guy twice. So he kissed me. It didn't mean anything. I instruct my students to bring their ponies to a walk and ride into the center.

"You know Parker Winslow?" Jenna Bowman, a skinny pale girl on a bay pony, asks.

"Something like that," I say, as the other two girls join us.

"Cool." Jenna looks at me with new respect, her blue eyes huge.

I don't know why I smile.

———

Haley and I have a late lunch at Christy's house. We make taco salad while Christy rehashes the details of the Jonah Timken disaster.

"What a prick." Haley is solidly in my camp on the question of whether Christy should see him again.

"I know, right?" Christy's eyes get all dreamy. "But he's really hot."

Haley looks at me and rolls her eyes. She might be on my side, but she won't try to stop Christy, either. Maybe I'm hopped up on guacamole, but I tell Haley and Christy about my strange conversation with Parker Winslow, even though Haley still hasn't said a word about Austin.

"Austin went out with an ice princess?" Haley looks thoughtful. "I don't see it. Austin's not like that at all."

Apparently, one hookup makes Haley the authority on Austin.

"She definitely said they went out. For almost two years."

"Well, he is hot," Haley says.

"True." A guy like Austin could go out with pretty much anyone. Someone like Parker wouldn't be out of his league, although he should probably aim higher. "I guess I thought he'd date someone nicer."

Haley laughs. "I'm sure she was nice to him. Is she pretty?"

"In a plastic, rich-girl way."

"Well, there you go." The question is settled as far as Haley is concerned. Throw in rich, and Parker's personality hardly signifies. "How do you think she found out that you know him?" Haley looks at me and lets the bigger question hang in the air.

Parker knows about *me*. Not Haley. Okay, there was that kiss in a dark bedroom, but Parker would be much more concerned if she knew Austin had been with Haley. Haley isn't rich, but she has the kind of looks that are perfect up close and don't require thousands of dollars in hair products or designer clothes.

"Maybe she heard about you and Austin," I say. A flash of anger lights Haley's turquoise eyes. I've hit a sore spot. No point dancing around it now. "It's probably the first time he's been with someone since they broke up."

Haley's expression softens. "That would explain a lot." I'm not sure what it explains, exactly. At least Haley isn't going to fly into one of her moods. She grins instead. "What do you think your buddy Sherri Milliken is doing tonight?"

I embrace the change in subject. "Probably at the library researching her essay on the psychology of peanut butter." I'm the worst sort of hypocrite, because no matter how boring a life I invent for Sherri, it's nowhere close to the string of social failures marking my current existence.

Haley throws her head back, her hair bouncing in time to her laughter. "Four out of five psychologists prefer Jif to Jung!"

"Even the chunky style is no match for a good old-fashioned Oedipal complex."

Christy laughs. "I don't even know what that means."

"Freud thinks every guy wants to screw his mother," Haley says.

"Gross!" Christy's mouth forms an O. "I don't know Freud? Is he a senior?"

Haley launches into a discussion of Freudian theory that goes far beyond the chapter in our Psych textbook. She's probably read Freud. She tends to read a lot since her mom doesn't allow Internet or television.

"Blake asked about you today," Haley says, changing the subject yet again. It's what I get for bringing up Austin.

"You saw Blake?"

"He came by Magic Beans." Haley raises her eyebrows and I know I'm busted.

I haven't said anything about my date with Blake tonight. Admitting to it will only make it that much harder when it doesn't happen. He hasn't called me all week. I know I should be the one to cancel, but I won't. Now that Haley knows, I have no choice but to fess up. "It's no big deal."

"Are you kidding? He's majorly hot! I can't believe you didn't tell us you're going out with him."

"Blake?" I can almost see the gears turning behind Christy's eyes. "Seriously? Omigod! Do you think it's the spell?"

"It's not the spell." I'm going to kill Christy's sister for giving her that damn book. "We're just friends. It's nothing."

"Friends with benefits?" Haley grins.

"No! He's just a major flirt."

"Well, he didn't flirt with me." I appreciate Haley's revisionist history, even if it's not entirely accurate. She looks over at Christy.

Christy shakes her head. "Me either."

"So it's just you." Haley pops a chip into her mouth and crunches with satisfaction.

I don't bother to recite the list of girls that Blake has flirted with over the last year, although I could. And that in itself is a huge problem.

It was the "other girl" thing that made me go crazy the first time.

Once I'd realized that Derek Kingston had another girl in the chemistry lab, I pushed him out of the way and ran to the back of the room. I had no trouble seeing in the dark then. I could make out every detail in the room, but my eyes were trained on the ball of girl huddled under the far table, her shoulders still rolling with laughter. Her blond hair practically glowed in the dark, and I wondered why I didn't spot her as soon as I walked in.

I could feel Derek behind me, his heart hammering in his chest as he followed, sputtering a string of pointless words. I dragged the girl out from under the table by her elbow. Cassidy Martin, the only girl in the band who played flute worse than I did. She wasn't even pretty enough to get invited to the same parties as Derek and me. But Cassidy was still laughing. At me.

Derek pulled her out of my grasp.

I spun on them both. "What are you doing with her?" I demanded, though the answer was obvious. "You're supposed to be with me." My whole eighth grade year was falling apart around me and it hadn't even started.

I never knew if Derek answered my question. All I knew was that I didn't deserve to be treated this way. These people didn't know who they were messing with.

Then the silver light was there, a bright flash that blinded me for a few seconds before everything went dark. It was as if everything happened in slow motion—I could feel the fire before it started. Not in the lab, but inside me, a heat that ran underneath my skin. My hands tingled with electric heat, arcs flowing between my fingers. A huge ball of fire floated in the palm of my hand, spreading to the tables until the whole lab was ablaze, engulfed in blue flames.

My fire.

I shouldn't be dating anyone, especially not Blake Williams. It's off-the-charts stupid. But there's a part of me that still longs for what I should never, ever allow myself to have, and I'm not going to be the one to cancel.

TEN

I change clothes three times before I settle on some vintage Calvins and a powder blue button-down shirt that matches my eyes. I am not above taking a pointer from the Parker Winslow makeover guide.

Haley calls and asks if I can give her a ride before I meet Blake at Magic Beans. Truthfully, I could use the distraction. I pull into her driveway and send a text, hoping Haley has her phone back. I wait a few minutes, fidgeting with the car stereo. Haley doesn't respond. I double check my phone, cringing at the thought of actually going to the door.

The Blue Box sputters and coughs as the engine shuts down. I wait another minute before I finally get the courage to go to the front door. I shuffle my feet on the doormat that says *Solicitors will be shot*. In case the message isn't clear enough, there's a giant picture of the barrel of a shotgun next to the words. I check my phone again for a reply. At this rate, I won't have time to drop Haley off at Kimmy's before I have to meet Blake. I ring the bell before I can stop myself.

A high-pitched screech comes from inside the house before footsteps approach and several locks turn. I put my hands at my side and try to project the fact that I am in no way soliciting. The door opens about two inches. Mrs. Marvell peers through the crack. "What do you want?"

"I'm here to pick up Haley." I hesitate, not sure whether she expects me to come in or wait outside. Outside is good.

The door opens just enough for me to get through. Mrs. Marvell stands to the side, a floral house coat hanging on her shoulders like a shapeless sack, the American fundamentalists' version of a burka. Her short blond hair is crimped into tight curls, a perfect complement to her pinched facial features. She never wears makeup, which somehow accentuates her hard lines. "Well, hurry up about it. You're letting all of the warm air out."

It's seventy-five degrees outside, so I can't imagine that her heater is running, but I don't argue. I take the two steps into the hall as fast I can, allowing her to close the door behind me. The blinds are closed, casting the house in artificial darkness. I feel Mrs. Marvell's stare as I pull off my shoes and turn down the hall. Even without shoes, my steps echo on the hard plastic that covers the floor. It's a miracle Haley ever manages to sneak in past curfew.

Haley opens her bedroom door as soon as I knock, closing it again behind me with a speed that comes from years of practice. I flop on the edge of Haley's twin bed, one of the only pieces of furniture in the house that isn't covered in clear plastic. Makeup is strewn around her dresser and her hair is still wrapped up in a towel. At least she's dressed, opting for low-rise white pants that hug her hips perfectly and a black scoop-neck top.

"I tried to text."

"I still don't have my phone." Haley reaches for a tube of mascara and applies it in the big mirror to her left.

"I'm meeting Blake in fifteen minutes."

Haley grins into the mirror, ignoring my not-so-subtle reminder that she's running late. "Are you excited?"

Before I can respond, Mrs. Marvell's shrill voice carries from the hallway. "Haley! Get out here!" Thank God she doesn't bother to make the short trip to Haley's room.

Haley rolls her eyes and then clicks down the hall. I glance again at my cell, trying to ignore Mrs. Marvell's screaming rant about folding towels into thirds. I don't know how Haley can stand living here. My own mother is a paragon of maternal love in comparison, nettle soup and all.

When Haley returns a few minutes later, a dark look crosses her face. "You should just go."

There's nothing I want more than to be out of this house. I'm just not sure I want to risk the trip back down the hall alone. "I'll just text Blake and let him know I'm running late."

"Thanks." Haley pulls off her towel and deliberately throws it on the floor. She twists her damp hair into a high ponytail that should make her look like a middle-school cheerleader but instead is fashion-model chic. She double checks her appearance in the mirror, adding some lip gloss. "Let's get out of here."

We hurry down the hall, our steps echoing in the dark. Haley stops in front of the kitchen where her mom stands over a pot at the stove. Mrs. Marvell eyes her. "I hope you're not planning on going out dressed like that."

"Of course not. I'm actually planning on stripping before I leave the house. Naked is the new black."

Mrs. Marvell's eyes squeeze closed, the only indication that she's heard Haley's reply. "Those pants make you look like a slut."

"Excellent! I was hoping to get laid tonight." Haley walks out of the room before her mom can respond.

I stand frozen in place, not sure what to do.

"What are you looking at?"

I mumble something incoherent and trace Haley's steps outside.

When I reach the car, Haley's smile is wider than normal. "Did you see her face? Priceless!"

I try to smile, but I'm sure it comes off as more of a grimace. I just can't see the humor in Haley's family life. But it's not something I can talk about with her. Haley doesn't mention my universal failure with guys, and I know better than to remind her that her mother is a mean witch.

Blake waits in front of Magic Beans, leaning against a large potted plant with his hands in the pockets of his dark jeans. His light hair contrasts nicely with a dark green polo shirt that does nothing to hide the lean muscle that lies beneath.

I'm painfully aware that the blue shirt and jeans ensemble I so carefully picked out seems completely lame next to Haley's crisp black and white outfit. Sure enough, Blake's eyes follow Haley's perfect form as we walk toward him.

"You mind if we drop Haley at Kimmy's?" I ask.

He doesn't look at me. "Do we have to?"

Haley smiles.

I do not smile. I don't even try to fake it. It's all I can do to keep from stalking back to my car and leaving them both to enjoy an evening of watery coffee and stuffed cows. No wonder Mrs. Marvell is such a cruel, bitter woman. It can't be easy to live twenty-four seven with Haley and her slutty white pants.

Blake finally makes eye contact with me. "Are you going to stop hiding from me?" he asks under his breath.

So we're going to play the what's-wrong-with-Brianna game again. I look away, not in the mood to defend myself at the moment.

"Your chariot awaits." He gestures to the giant SUV a few feet away. Haley has the decency to take the back seat, this being my date and all. Not that it matters. Mr. Schizo and I are hardly destined to fall in love. Not when he can't look at me.

Haley chats on about nothing as we drive, showing off her mastery of the art of small talk. Blake smiles and laughs at the appropriate places, but I've seen this episode of the Haley Marvell show before.

At Kimmy's townhouse, Blake lets the car idle while Haley goes to the door. We sit in silence for a while before

Blake leans back against his seat and closes his eyes, taking a deep breath. "I'm trying to figure you out."

Maybe I don't want to be figured out. I have a feeling that we're both better off not knowing. "What am I even doing here?" I say the thought aloud, not caring for once that I have.

He looks genuinely surprised that I'm not falling all over myself and swooning now that he's finally talking to me. "You think I'm crazy, right?" he asks.

"I'm obviously the crazy one for even thinking that this might be a good idea."

"Don't let that stop you." He flashes his perfect white teeth in a way that raises the hair on the back of my neck.

Haley opens the door and settles into the back seat. "She already left."

"Who?" I ask.

"Kimmy. I guess I missed her."

"Do you know where she went?"

"Not exactly." Haley leans back against the seat, at last looking like she might be troubled by the fact that her evening is not going as planned. "I can't go home. You saw how my mom was tonight. I have to wait until she falls asleep."

"Should we wait for a while? Maybe Kimmy just stepped out for a minute?" Even though this date may have been a terrible idea, it's still technically mine. I don't want a chaperone. More to the point, I don't want to end up becoming the chaperone.

"Is it okay if I just hang out with you guys for a little while?"

There's no way to answer that question truthfully without coming across as a complete bitch. It's not like I can send Haley back into that plastic-covered hell she calls home.

I look at Blake. He can.

"No problem," he says. "It'll be fun."

Best. First. Date. *Ever.*

ELEVEN

I lean back against the seat and stare out the window. I'm still not sure how Haley managed to invite herself along. She laments the lack of catchy tunes on the latest Rabid Monkey CD while we drive to some place that Blake says has the best steaks in the greater San Diego area. Haley doesn't complain, even though she went vegan six months ago. So much for meat as murder.

Blake doesn't look at me while Haley talks. Not once.

I interrupt Haley's music review. "So, where were you and Kimmy supposed to go tonight? Maybe we can drop you off there?" Or somewhere else. Anywhere, really. I hear Africa's nice. Haley will fit right in with the man-eating lions.

Blake looks straight ahead, pretending to concentrate on the road, but his cheek twitches in an almost-smile. He's probably hoping for a catfight.

"We were supposed to go to a movie or something. I never got all the details."

Blake finally looks in my direction, his eyes thoughtful, before he turns back to Haley. "You mind if I invite someone to join us?"

"Do whatever you want." She can't exactly complain under the circumstances. She runs her fingers through her ponytail.

I notice Blake doesn't ask me if I mind. Why should I? I never should have agreed to this. It's so much easier to be ignored when no one's noticed you to begin with.

Blake turns on his phone from a button on the steering wheel, hitting the speed-dial that flashes from the screen in the middle of his dashboard. The ringing that fills the car through the speakers is soon replaced by Austin's soft accent. "Blake, what's the word?"

Of all the people in the world he could invite on our date, it's Austin? I want to strangle Blake and Haley both. I try to gauge Haley's reaction. She stares out the window, her face a mask of indifference. She winds her ponytail tight in her right hand, the only indication that she's even aware of Austin on the other end of the phone.

"You up for a steak dinner?" Blake asks. "I'm buying."

"It's about time you spent your money on something besides cars and women."

"Oh, there's women." Blake glances back to Haley.

"Of course there are." Teasing laughter fills the car.

"Meet us at Hunter's in ten." Blake hangs up the phone and looks back at Haley. "I hope that was okay."

"It's cool." Haley winds her ponytail tighter and keeps staring out the window.

Wolfgang Hunter's is housed in its own building at the back of a shopping center I've visited a hundred times before without noticing the restaurant. It doesn't have any signs on the outside and the windows are too dark to see the inside. The hostess leads Blake and me toward a small booth in a back corner while Haley disappears to the restroom. Candles on every table cast shadows along the walls. A stuffed hawk glowers at me from a piece of dried wood next to our table. His glass eyes follow me as I slide into the booth.

"That's Pierce." Blake sits down next to me.

"He has a name?"

"They all do." He points to a deer head mounted across the room. "Hot Lips. The cougar in front is Klinger."

"You're making that up."

"I swear. My godfather owns this place. He names all his kills."

"Kills? As in he actually killed them?"

"That's generally how it works. It's not like the animals showed up one afternoon and applied for positions as decorative wall hangings."

"It's just . . . shouldn't those things be really old or something?" Killing and stuffing wild animals is something people did a hundred years ago. Before Safeway.

"Rush is an avid hunter. He's always adding to the collection."

I flip the menu open to a section describing multiple

cuts of beef. I turn the page as fast as I can. Maybe I'll join Haley with the vegetarian thing tonight.

"So this should be interesting," Blake says.

I look up from where I've just read the description for Caesar salad three times.

"Austin hasn't talked to Haley since they hooked up," he adds. "Twenty bucks says he doesn't remember her."

"You did this on purpose?"

"It was kind of obnoxious of Haley to crash our date."

Is it bad that for a second I think I might love Blake Williams? I'm a horrible, horrible friend. I compensate by jumping to Haley's defense. "It wasn't her fault."

Blake shrugs, like it hardly matters either way. He turns his attention to where Austin glides toward us, in a long-sleeved red tee that hugs his chest and arms.

Just as I'm wondering how I ever could have felt comfortable around Austin, he eases into the booth across from me and flashes a friendly smile that makes everything seem okay. "Hey, Juliet." He looks around the restaurant. "You said women, as in plural?"

"Don't worry. I've got you." Blake smiles, enjoying his private joke.

Haley struts up to the table, her hair now down and falling in long waves to the middle of her back. Her black shirt is pulled down so that the scoop-neck dips lower across her chest. She turns on her most brilliant smile.

Austin's face lights up. Having Haley show up has to be a bit like hitting the blind date lottery.

"You remember Haley, don't you?" Blake's voice is too innocent. "The girl from your party?"

We all know what Blake is implying. To her credit, Haley's smile doesn't falter, although her cheeks do redden, which makes her face glow attractively.

"How could I forget? You look lovely tonight, by the way."

Haley smiles. "You look pretty great yourself." It's exactly the kind of thing I could never say without sounding desperate and pathetic.

"Thanks." Austin looks right at me. "I was going for the Red Shirt Guy look."

I feel my cheeks redden. What is Austin doing? He shouldn't be referring to our kiss and looking at me like that. Not when we're both supposed to be here with other people.

I make eye contact with Pierce, the only creature at the table who has it worse than me. A jab on my side forces my attention under the table. Blake pokes me with a rolled-up twenty. I take the money, crumpling it into a tight ball in my fist before pushing it into the front pocket of my jeans. I hadn't realized how much I wanted Blake to be right until he wasn't. The mean, crazy girl inside me is alive and well.

A tall girl with porcelain skin comes by to take our order. I'm definitely going with a small salad, still fairly certain that I won't be able to choke down a meal under the circumstances.

"Blake! Omigod!" the server literally squeals, bouncing

up and down like a puppy until Blake stands up and gives her a quick hug. "Does Daddy know you're here?"

"Hey Portia," Blake says as he sits down, "do me a favor? Don't bother Rush right now, okay?"

Portia pats Blake's shoulder with her palm before pulling out a pad to take our order. She flips her chin so that her smooth chestnut hair falls just in front of her shoulder. She's pretty like a pond full of brown water, beautiful until you look too close. A dark cloud sits just beneath the surface of her gaze as she takes Haley's order.

When her eyes rest on me, the cloud rises all the way to the top, like someone's poked the water with a stick. "What are you?" she asks.

I want to back up. But there's nowhere to go in the booth next to the wall. The words echo in my head. Not who, *what*. "What am I having?"

"Right." Portia taps her pen on the pad in front of her. "What are you having?"

I fidget under her stare, rattling off my order. She doesn't write it down. It's not until she walks away that I realize what's made me so uncomfortable. Girls tend to treat me in a mostly normal way, but even they don't stare at me. Not like that. I put my hands in my lap and finger my bracelet.

Austin balls up his napkin and tosses it at Blake, hitting him in the chest. "Please tell me you didn't."

Blake grabs the napkin and throws it back. It just misses Austin's head before making contact with the wall and sliding down to the table. Austin grabs the napkin and stares at Blake, waiting.

"Okay, I didn't." Blake delivers the line straight, but his knowing grin tells another story. The scientist in me takes in the full implications of this exchange with detached interest. The crazy girl in me wants to strangle them both for even having this conversation in front of me. So Blake hooked up with Portia? Logically, I know his past is littered with girls. It's just not something I want thrown in my face.

I'm the last person they should be having this conversation in front of. I try to give Blake a pass. He doesn't know he's literally playing with fire.

"You're an idiot," Austin says.

I could think of a few more appropriate words. I bite them back.

Blake finally remembers I'm here. He makes an effort to turn his head in my direction. "It was no big deal. We went out a few times."

I twist the napkin in my hand into a knot. "It's really none of my business."

Austin raises an eyebrow at me from across the table, gauging my reaction.

A monster of a man with long black hair stands over our table, his large form casting a shadow across my plate. "Blake," he says, more command than greeting. Everything about the man is predatory.

"Rushmore," Blake says.

So this is the sportsman. I'm not completely crazy—

the guy is definitely scary. He curls his lips back to smile and I flinch before I can stop myself. "It's good you came," he says. "It's time you took your responsibilities seriously."

Blake laughs. "It's Jonah you should worry about."

Rush ignores the comment and finally looks from Blake to me, Austin, and Haley. I brace myself for his eye contact, but it never comes. He passes me over without so much as a glance, and I let out a breath.

"Enjoy your meal," he says before turning back to Blake. He lifts in his chin in a curt nod. "There's a new game. On Wednesday night. You'll be there."

Blake doesn't respond except to glare at Rush.

The two stare each other down for what seems like a full minute, neither willing to look away first. Rush finally breaks the stalemate. "You will learn your place."

"Family issues?" Austin says as soon as Rush is gone, breaking some of the tension that still fills the room.

"You could say that. Rush sets up my poker games. It's no big deal. The last couple of games conflicted with my schedule. Makes him crabby."

Austin straightens the balled-up napkin and sets it in his lap. "I don't know why you bother. The guy is a complete freak show."

I nod in agreement with the last part.

"I think he's kind of hot." Haley watches the hall where Rush disappeared. "What? I mean, for an old guy. If you're into the whole power thing."

My eyes meet Austin's across the table, and we both laugh at the same time.

Throughout the meal, Blake, Austin, and Haley chat easily while I stare at my plate, pushing cherry tomatoes in circles with my fork. Haley finishes her eggplant something-or-other, not bothered in the least that Austin is eating prime rib, while Blake enjoys a bloody-looking venison steak that may or may not have been one of Rushmore's recent kills. Hot Lips' glass eyes commiserate with me from across the room.

My attention is diverted by a shrill laugh. A couple of teenagers drink shots at a table just below Hot Lips, even though it's obvious they aren't old enough to drink. The girl's platinum-blond hair hangs down to her waist, much of it obscuring her face. The guy licks salt off her hand. I recognize his smarmy smile. "Isn't that Jonah Timken?"

Austin's face hardens to granite. "What's he doing with her?"

"Looks like tequila shots," Blake says.

"Don't joke about this. You know he's a bloody bastard." Austin gestures for Haley to slide over so he can get out of the booth. He strides to Jonah's table, his body tense.

The blonde looks up as he approaches. Parker Winslow eases her lips into a smile that's worth every penny spent on orthodontists and teeth-whitening products.

Blake laughs. "Looks like we're going to get a show after all."

"Who's that?" Haley asks.

"That's Parker, the girl I told you about."

"She's pretty."

Parker does look good. I've never seen her with her hair down, and the length in combination with the color is all kinds of fabulous. She giggles at something Jonah says to Austin. Jonah looks back at Parker and winks, sending Parker into fits of laughter.

Austin stalks back to our table. "I have to go before I hurt someone."

Haley blinks up at him. "Do you mind taking me home? I don't have a car." Or a license, but that's beside the point. Haley doesn't know how to do anything that requires lessons. Her mother probably wouldn't have let her go to school if she'd cared enough to bother with home schooling.

Austin looks down at Haley like he's surprised to see her there. "Fine. I'll meet you outside." He storms out of the restaurant without a goodbye, only glancing at the table where Parker and Jonah still giggle.

"I guess I'll see you guys later." Haley stands up and shakes out her hair. She tucks her shirt further into her white pants, drawing stares from most of the men in the restaurant. She stops and watches the table where Jonah and Parker each suck on a lime. When they feel her gaze and look up, she lowers her eyelashes, flips her hair back, and strides through the restaurant like a runway model.

Parker crinkles her nose like she smells something bad, creating unattractive lines on her forehead. A date with a needle and some botox can't be far behind.

Blake slides out of the booth and takes the seat across from me. "Alone at last."

"So what's the deal with Parker and Austin?" I ask.

"They went out for a long time. They'll probably get back together at least twice before it's really over. Double or nothing on my twenty?"

"No."

Parker drinks another shot of tequila, looking every inch the gorgeous heiress.

Blake rubs the top of his jeans with his palms. "Can we try this again?"

"What?"

"A real date. Just you and me."

I almost laugh. "You mean without my friend, your friend, your godfather, and your friend's ex-girlfriend?" I leave out the waitress he hooked up with, but he gets the point.

Blake grins. "Something like that."

The answer should be easy. I should insist he take me home right now. Everything about him and me is a bad idea. But I still want to ask about how he knew about Nana's nickname for me. At least that's what I tell myself. It doesn't hurt that his eyes light up when I say, "How's now?"

Blake throws a wad of bills on the table. "Let's go make some magic."

TWELVE

We sit in silence as we head toward the coast. The further we get from R.D., the more I start to question what exactly I'm doing driving off into the darkness with Blake. I almost tell him to turn the car around, but when I look at him, I stop myself.

He's staring out the windshield, lost in thought. Without the too-confident grin, he looks younger than his eighteen years. My stomach twinges with a familiar little ache of yearning before I can stop it. "I think at least one of us has to say something before we can consider this a real date."

Blake laughs at my comment even though he still doesn't look over. "I don't know. Some of my best dates involved very little talking."

"I'm not an expert or anything, but I think that talking about your dates with other girls is generally frowned on." Technically, he's done it twice now. The count's in my favor. One more strike and he's out. "Although I guess that explains your better dates."

He smiles, and for a second I let myself wish he'd turn that smile on me. He doesn't. He keeps staring straight ahead.

"Look at me." It's out before I can take it back.

To his credit, he turns his head in my direction, but his glance is so fleeting that it's hardly worth the effort.

"Nice try."

"Brianna." Blake's voice softens. "We're going to figure this out."

"I just want to go home." The only thing to figure out is how I managed to wind up alone in a car with a guy who can't even look at me. A guy who can only break my heart.

"We're almost there. I want to show you something that might put things in perspective. Then we'll talk." His angelic face is pleading.

I waver.

"You need to know the answers too."

Unless he's got a nice reasonable explanation to replace my pheromone theory, I don't want to know. "In case you're wondering, if this is some elaborate plot to get in my pants, it's not working," I say.

Blake laughs. "It's not, I swear. Right now that's the furthest thing from my mind. That's part of what we need to figure out."

"Is that supposed to be a compliment? If so, you really need to work on your moves."

Blake maneuvers his giant car into a small parking lot

above the beach. He comes around to the passenger side, opening the door for me. "Come on."

I follow him down a switchback path that leads to the sand. At the bottom, we head south, following the base of a rocky cliff. Moonlight reflects off the crashing waves, providing just enough light to see by. We go about a quarter mile until we come to the remnants of a fire still burning in a pit that's been abandoned by its makers. The small fire casts a golden glow along the cliff wall, and Blake stops. There's a narrow opening in the rock about six feet high. It doesn't look large enough for a person, but he disappears through it easily enough.

I stand next to the fire, not following.

Blake sticks his head out of the opening. "Come on, we're almost there."

I plant my feet in the sand. "I'm not going into some creepy cave with a guy I barely know."

Blake steps all the way out. "I know I shouldn't rush you." He looks up and down the beach. "No problem. We can do it out here."

I back up a step. "Excuse me?"

He laughs. "Not *that*."

"Right. I keep forgetting. I repel you."

He reaches for my hand, sending flashes of fire up my arm.

"You don't repel me, Brianna." His thumb traces a line along the chain that rings my wrist. "It's this."

The tingle that slides along my spine in time to the movement of his thumb is a study in contradiction. On the one hand, some primitive instinct screams at me to get away. Now. An even more primitive instinct wants to savor the riot of heat his touch sets off, urging me closer. I stand frozen, a victory of sorts for the part of me that wants to melt into him.

When his fingers brush the clasp of my bracelet, I jerk my hand away. "I won't take it off." Score one for self-defense.

"If you don't believe in it, what's the harm?"

I let out a breath. "You're not going to let this go?"

"Never."

I stare at my bracelet. The good luck charm Nana gave me three days after the chem fire.

Derek and Cassidy got out, but not before the flames had circled them, trapping them in the corner. The fire was right on my hands, between my fingers. And then it wasn't. The fire seemed to dance around me, like I could control it. That's how I knew I'd gone off the deep end. Cassidy's screams were what woke me from my psychotic episode. I walked right through the flames to get them out. They said it was a miracle no one was hurt.

After three days of the same questions went nowhere, the doctors prescribed me some heavy duty tranqs and sent me home. Nana came into my bedroom and sat at the foot of my bed. I was out of it, still in a sleepy haze that made everything seem like a fuzzy dream, but I was glad to see her. She put the bracelet around my wrist and told me that I should never take it off. That I would grow out of everything by the time I was seventeen, and then I wouldn't need it anymore.

I'm not seventeen yet, but I will be soon, and it's obvious I've grown out of exactly nothing. I turn to Blake. "So you think that this flower charm hides me. From who exactly? Guys?"

"Something like that."

"From all guys, or just players like you?"

Blake doesn't take offense at my calling him a player. "I don't know. I only know how it affects me." He looks back out at the ocean. "Austin doesn't seem bothered by it."

So he's noticed that too. "What do you mean?" It feels good to hear someone else say it. Like I'm not completely insane.

Blake runs a hand through this hair. "Just the way he looked at you tonight. You would know better than me. How do guys normally react to you when you're wearing that?" He says the last word with definite disdain.

"Same as always." I sit down in the sand next to the firepit. Before I can stop myself, I add, "Like I don't exist."

Blake sits down in the sand next to me. He forces his eyes to meet mine. "You can change that."

I should stand up and walk back to the car, end this now. With or without the bracelet, I'm still just me. Same crazy, blurting, pheromone-less me. It isn't like a piece of jewelry can change that. My hand clutches the silver flower, forming a makeshift shield. There is no way this little charm can change me. The whole debate is pointless.

And tonight I don't want any more proof of my complete lack of desirability.

But I don't get up. I'm alone on the beach with Blake Williams, and he's watching me. It's an outlier to the tenth degree. And I like it more than I want to admit.

I force myself to let go of the charm, letting my hands slide to the clasp. I fumble with it, my fingers shaking. When I finally manage to get it undone, I close my hand around the bracelet and lower it to my lap.

The firelight reaches out from behind me, casting shadows on Blake's face. He extends his hand, palm open.

"Just for a minute." I place my hand on top of his, my fist still closed tight. My hand shakes harder.

Blake puts his other hand on top, holding my hand steady. "Okay?"

I nod.

He rubs my closed fist. "You have to let go." His hands are gentle, his touch hot.

I close my eyes. The sound of the waves crashing against the shore amplifies. I listen to the water churning and falling, churning and falling. I can taste the salt in the air. My breath slows to match the rhythm of the rise and fall of the cresting waves. Slowly, I open my hand. At the same time, Blake's fingers close around the little charms. Then his hands are gone, and my own hand falls back to my side, empty.

I wait to feel something, anything. I don't.

It's official, Blake is a lunatic. I don't want to open my eyes. I don't think I can bear to see Blake's face.

"Yes! I knew it!"

My eyes open to Blake's smile. I look down to make sure that I haven't missed something. Same blue shirt and vintage Calvins. I grab a curl of brown hair, examining it closely in the firelight. The only thing that's changed is the way Blake looks at me.

And it takes my breath away.

Blake's eyes glow in the firelight. But it's the flames behind his eyes that make my whole body run hot. I can feel myself blush as he brings his hand to my cheek, branding me with his touch.

"Brianna Paxton." He lets his fingers rest against my skin, stroking just beneath my chin. "You are even more beautiful than I remembered."

My blood rises against his thumb. "You know you're crazy, right?"

He laughs. "Possibly. I still can't believe it. It's amazing. You're amazing." His eyes scan me from head to toe, full of wonder and admiration. I soak it in, reveling in the rush of power that comes with the certainty that he sees me. Wants me. He leans closer, so close I inhale a heady combination of vanilla and mint. His voice is low, his breath warm against my neck. "I've never seen anything like you."

The fire crackles and sparks, blue flames flickering in sync with the flame that rises along my skin. Blake takes a handful of my hair in his fingers and brings it to his lips. "Incredible," he whispers.

I breathe the word in, savoring it as my own breath comes faster.

Still clutching my hair, he pulls it back gently, tilting my head at an angle that invites him in. He brings his lips to mine. Just as our lips touch, a sharp ocean breeze swirls around us, blowing my hair and creating a small electric shock where our lips meet. I laugh, a little startled.

Blake pulls back, his hand still holding my hair. "What was that?"

"Static electricity? The imbalance of positive and negative charges caused by friction? For a guy who plans to be a doctor, you don't know much about science."

"You have an answer for everything, don't you?"

"Not this," I admit. I can't explain what's happening now. My theory is officially dead. And I don't even care. I just want him to kiss me again.

As if he hears the thought, he does.

"Zap," I say, my lips moving against his.

He laughs, sending warm vibrations against my mouth. His tongue licks softly against my lips. The hand that holds my hair pulls my head back further, allowing him to move deeper into the kiss, into me. The electricity in the air fills me completely. I would describe it as an out-of-body experience except that everything about it is so *in* body. My hands come up around his neck, pulling him closer. The wind swirls around us again, the cool air sending me further into his warmth.

We sink back into the sand. His fingers travel down my side, blazing a trail to my hip. The warmth of his touch sears through my jeans. His thigh comes between my legs as the kiss intensifies. He moves on top of me, his weight bringing him blissfully closer.

There's a brilliant flash of silver as his body pushes me into the sandy earth, a fact that barely registers as I urge him closer. My hands move down his back, clawing at his shirt. He breaks the kiss long enough to pull the offending polo over his head, and our eyes meet in the silvery blue glow of the fire. I smile as he puts his hands on each side of my head and leans down to rain kisses along my neck. My fingers explore the hard contours of his back.

And then his mouth finds mine again, and I'm pulled along on a tide of pure sensation. There's another silver flash, so bright I can see it with my eyes closed. When I open my eyes, we're surrounded by a dark mist, so thick I can no longer see the ocean. A thread of silver light dances in the fog, weaving in and out of the darkness, circling us.

In the silvery light, I see his face above mine, his green eyes ablaze, a half smile on his lips meant only for me. "*Mine*," he says softly.

Then he kisses me again, and for a second everything is black, so dark that I wonder if my eyes are closed again. A small sliver of light grows in the center of the darkness, moving just over us. The silver ribbon grows brighter, meeting the dark until the beach is a swirling mass of shadow and starlight.

Darkness and light together. Souls fused and melded. Forever bound.

THIRTEEN

The sound of crashing waves wakes me from sleep. Rough grains of sand scratch at my back. A damp breeze raises goose bumps on my bare skin. *Bare?* I sit up in a rush. My clothes are strewn around the sand. Blake is on his stomach next to me, mooning the moon.

I scramble to my feet and grab my clothes, not even caring about the sand that scratches my skin as I pull them on. Everything is a blur of silver light and darkness. Blake kissed me. I teased him about static electricity, and then he kissed me again, and then ... there is more, much more. It's all mixed up in the fog and mists. It doesn't make any sense. Was I on some kind of drug? I grab my bracelet from where it's still tangled in Blake's left hand and fasten it around my wrist. I kick his hip. "Wake up!"

Blake's eyes blink open. He looks groggy and out of it.

"Blake!!"

"What?" He pushes up on his arms and looks down at his bare chest. He spins around and grabs his jeans, pulling them on with record speed.

I look out at the ocean, not wanting to make eye contact. "What just happened?" I know I'm not exactly experienced, but I'm pretty sure that whole silver-light-and-mists thing was not supposed to be a part of it.

"I'm not sure." His voice is shaky; no sign of the cool, confident charmer.

I kick the ground, sending sand smattering across his legs. "You're not sure?"

"No." His face goes pale. "Oh God. What did you do?" He sits back down in the sand, putting his face in his hands.

"Me? Me?! What kind of drugs did you give me?" There's no stopping the tears now. They flow down my cheeks.

"Drugs? You think that was drugs?" He shakes his head. "This is bad."

"Bad? *Bad?* Shouldn't you at least wait until I'm not right here before you start declaring it bad?"

"Oh God," Blake repeats before he finally looks up. "Do you remember any of it?"

"Just the dream part."

"It wasn't a dream."

"How can you say that? You don't even know what I dreamed about."

"Brilliant light and blackest darkness? Melding of souls?"

My voice drops to a whisper. "You can't know that. Is that one of the side effects of the drug you gave me?"

He finds his shirt across a rock. "There's no drug,

Brianna. It happened. You should know better than me what you did."

What *I* did? Oh God, what did I do? I should never have come here. I should never have kissed him. "Take me home. Now."

Blake shakes out his shirt. All that's left of the fire are glowing embers, giving off just enough light that I can see the lines of his shoulders and back as the pulls his shirt over his head. Not that I'm thinking he's in any way attractive. Not that I notice how his casual good looks are almost heartbreaking when he's not flashing his cocky smile. I certainly don't feel any compulsion to put my arms around him and reassure him that everything is going to be okay. I don't want him to hold me and tell me the same thing.

I can't be that much of an idiot.

Our date ends the same way it began. We don't speak on the drive back to Rancho Domingo. I try to make sense of what's just happened, but I can't. It doesn't seem real, in the familiar surroundings of Blake's car, the radio playing in the background. It's all a hazy dream, another hallucination.

Except not.

Blake kissed me, and truthfully, it was amazing. I wanted to take it further. I wanted *him*.

This can't be good.

The Blue Box is the only car left in the parking lot in front of Magic Beans. There are light drops of moisture settling on the windows. Blake stops the SUV next to it but leaves the engine running.

I reach for the door handle, looking at Blake for the

first time since we left the beach. His forehead is creased. Beads of sweat form around his hairline. When he finally speaks, there's a measure of desperation in his tone. "There has to be a way to undo it."

I want to slap him, but I keep my hand fixed on the door handle. I open the door and jump out, not bothering to say goodbye. I climb into the Blue Box and slam the door, relieved to be away from him. The sputter and cough that accompanies the sound of the engine turning over is a welcome bit of normalcy. Blake's car still sits idling as I shift into gear and drive out of the parking lot.

When I turn onto the street, a pang rises in my gut, a sharp physical pain that almost doubles me over. As I get closer to home, the pain subsides to a dull ache. I recognize it all too well. It's the same pang that always comes when Blake ignores me. Only now it's constant, more pronounced. And there is no stamping it out. The ache is still there when I crawl into bed, a hollow reminder of his rejection.

The morning light filters through the blinds and falls across my face, waking me from what sleep I managed to find. I reach across my bed, half-expecting to be greeted by Blake's green eyes and warm smile, but grab only folds of comforter. I am alone. The realization is met with the same ache I've felt since leaving Blake. It isn't disappointment, exactly. It's more visceral than that.

I don't want to be one of those girls who thinks I'm in love with a boy just because we hooked up. So there. I am not in love with Blake Williams.

I just miss him is all.

By Monday, the pain is constant, and I wonder if I should ask my parents to take me to a doctor. I don't. It's too shameful to admit that I'm pining for Blake Williams. Worse, I don't want to tell my parents about the other part. If they find out I'm seeing things again, they'll make me go back to doing homeschool. Even the meager social life I've managed to find here will be over.

Haley and Christy wait on the curb in front of Christy's house when I pick them up for school. Haley's backpack is bulging with books, most likely the ones she borrowed from the library last week to gather historical data to augment our reading of Jane Austen in lit. Christy carries only a small blue denim designer purse.

"So?" Haley says before she is even halfway in the front seat. "You didn't return my calls. What happened with Blake?"

"You were there, remember?"

"I mean after I left."

"We hung out at the beach for a while."

Christy leans forward from the back seat, plainly interested in hearing the details. Not that there are going to be any. "The beach? That sounds kind of hot. And ....?"

"And we talked."

"And?" Christy giggles from the back seat.

I feel myself blush. "He might have kissed me."

"And?" It's Haley this time.

"And, that's it." I keep my eyes focused firmly on the road. I am definitely keeping the crazy part to myself. If I stay away from Blake, I might be able to stop the silver light from happening again. "What about you? What happened with Austin?"

Haley smiles. "He took me home."

"And?"

"He was sweet."

I'm happy it's working out for her. As happy as you can be for someone who's on boyfriend number thirteen. As happy as you can be for someone who's dating the boy who gave you your first kiss. "Did you ...?"

Haley just laughs. "It isn't like that with Austin. He apologized for the whole scene at Hunter's. He drove me straight home. It was just one kiss." Haley leans back against the seat and sighs. "It was really romantic."

What bizarre planet have I landed on? So Haley settles for a single kiss, and I lose it to the first guy to ask me out, after falling for some crazy theory involving my charm bracelet? I let myself be lured in, and then I couldn't resist the silver fire that lit up the darkness. *Oh hell.* Blake might be right about it being real.

"Haley said Jonah was out with that rich horse girl." Christy's voice carries from the back seat, shaking me from my daydream.

"He was." *Please, please, please* let Christy get over Jonah Timken already.

"I don't think it's going to work out with them." Christy holds up her cell phone in the rearview mirror. "He texted." She flips to the message and passes it to Haley.

Haley and I exchange a worried glance as she reads the

message aloud. "'Forgive me? I'll make it up to you Saturday. Party at Joe's.'"

"I told you the love spell is working," Christy says.

Haley passes the phone back to her. "Are you going?"

"Will you come with me, Brie?" Christy asks. "I don't really know Joe."

Like I do. Near as I can tell the guy is mute.

"You can see Blake," she adds.

The dull pang flares to a sharp sting at the mention of his name. I try to ignore it. "Please don't do this. That Jonah guy is serious trouble." Plus, there is no way I can stand watching Blake flirt his way around a party.

I don't have to see Christy's face to know she's pouting. "Fine. Don't help me. It's not like I wouldn't do it so you could see Blake. And I'm sure he's perfect boyfriend material."

I can't really disagree with her. And I can't let her go see Jonah on her own. Someone has to be there to watch out for her. I feel myself start to surrender. For Christy. It has nothing to do with an overwhelming wish to see Blake. Just see him. "Fine. I'll go."

The school day drags by in a haze of distraction. I try to look forward to my AP biology and calculus classes, where everything will have an explanation. A right answer. When I was kicked out of middle school and put on independent study, math and science were my only friends. They helped me make sense of the world again. Today, they're no help. There's no comfort in the Pythagorean theorem, no solace in the Punnett square.

To make things worse, Sherri Milliken corners me again after calc. "It can't wait any longer. We have to talk."

Time for the direct approach. "I'm sorry, Sherri. I'm not interested in joining the math team."

Sherri's face twists. I forgot how she sometimes gets kind of scary when she doesn't get her way. "Just hear me out."

Back to Evasion 101. "Can I call you later?"

"This can't wait much longer." She steps aside and lets me escape from the classroom. "You need to be ready."

I'm saved by Haley, who meets me in the hall and drags me away. "What's with her?"

"She wants me to join the Mathletes again. Like I need that kind of social suicide."

Haley smiles and puts her hand through my elbow. "You really think anyone would care if you were still on the math team? I think it's cool how you can do those problems in your head. Besides, it would be fun to see you pummel the geeks from McMillan Prep."

"Seriously?"

"Sure, why not?" Haley can still surprise me. "Besides, isn't Blake some kind of medical student? I bet he'll be drooling all over himself when he finds out you're on the team."

"Pre-med, and I'm pretty sure that my being on the math team doesn't qualify as foreplay."

Haley laughs. "I thought it was just a kiss? Is there something you're not telling me?"

A lot, but I don't know where to start. Haley knows I was homeschooled before we moved to R.D.—she just doesn't know why. I should've told her, but it's one of those conversations that's so much easier not to have. There's never a good time to bring it up.

Braden Finley approaches just as we get to Haley's locker. Haley rolls her eyes when she sees him, but I know for a fact she deliberately takes the long way around the science building so she'll arrive at her locker at the same time as Braden.

She leans back against her locker and smiles, waiting for Braden to turn toward her. I know the ritual by heart. Braden tosses his math book into his locker and grabs a key ring holding a small wooden baseball bat and the keys to his yellow Camaro. Next he turns to Haley just as he shuts the locker door.

"You look hot today." Braden dangles the keys in front of Haley. "Want to come to lunch?"

Haley bats her eyelashes and says no, even though Braden is by far the cutest guy at R.D. High. It's the same every day. It doesn't matter if Braden has a girlfriend or if Haley is seeing someone. It's all a pointless game. So why do I want so badly to be invited to play?

At home, I sit at my small desk to do some homework, irritated that I haven't managed to finish it at school. I tap my pencil, watching the charms on my bracelet move in time to the tapping. I set down the pencil and stare at the charms.

I've always loved the little horse the best. Then the horseshoe. It's the good luck part of the bracelet—the whole reason I have it. I never thought much about the monkshood.

Such an odd-shaped little flower.

I pick up my pencil and go back to my book, staring at it until the numbers run together. I finally give up, reaching for a volume on botany on the bookshelf.

I flip the pages to the monkshood entry before I can change my mind. The purple flower is eerily familiar. *Wolfsbane ... an extremely poisonous flowering plant with a history steeped in myth and death.* Beautiful, but deadly. It resonates in me in a way that it shouldn't.

Deadly.

Like me.

FOURTEEN

I find Mom in the den going through the Multiple Listing Service on her computer. She's surrounded by color signs and mock ups. *Cyndi Paxton sells dreams!*

I sit down on the loveseat next to the desk. I don't say anything at first, not sure where to start. But there's no point beating around the bush.

"What am I?" I ask.

Her face twitches, just for an instant. She still doesn't look at me. For a minute, I think she's not going to say anything at all. Then she says, "You should know better than to fish for compliments. It's unbecoming."

"That's not what I meant." Now that I've put the question out there, I'm not leaving until I get a straight answer. Mom has avoided me long enough. She's avoided *this* long enough.

"Fine. You're a smart, beautiful girl I'm proud to call my

daughter. Is that better?" It's exactly what moms are supposed to say to their kids. Probably something she heard on a talk show.

I'm not going to let her off with generic platitudes. "I'm some kind of freak." I hold up the wrist with the bracelet. "That's why Nana gave me this, isn't it?"

Mom's nose crinkles up at the corners, the same way it does when a seller is unreasonable about a listing price or when an escrow falls apart. She doesn't like any bumps in her perfect suburban world. "Nana gave that to you because it's part of your heritage."

"Please. I need to understand what's happening to me." I wonder if she hears what I don't say. *It's happening again. I need for you to talk to me.*

Her face relaxes. "Honey, you're just growing up. Your body is changing." She pats my knee, her Clinique Happy perfume filling the air with the movement. "Didn't you read that book I left in your room?"

Mom's idea of a good talk consists of discretely placed books and magazine articles. "This isn't about sex," I say. At least not entirely. "Something else is happening. Like before."

She can't hide the wrinkles that cross her forehead. She takes a deep breath. "Honey, nothing happened before. The fire was caused when a few of the vials of chemicals broke."

"Then why did you ask me about the wildfire? Why did you think that was me?"

Her lip quivers. "I was wrong to think that. You weren't even in town." She looks away. "I shouldn't have asked."

"Stop it." She's not going to ignore it anymore. I can't pretend that nothing is wrong. "Nana knew something about it, but she's not here. I have to know the truth."

Mom weighs her response. After what seems like forever, she finally speaks. "I don't know." She lowers her voice, almost to a whisper. "There were stories. I never paid much attention to them. It all seemed kind of silly."

I'd thought the same thing about Nana's talk of faeries and witchcraft and vengeful men. Once. Now it's all I can do to keep from hurling all over the laminate floor. "What do you know about my bracelet?"

"Not much. Nana made me promise to make sure you always wore it. But you always wore it anyway."

"You thought I took it off last fall. Why?"

Mom pats her hair, making sure every strand is perfectly in place, as if being well-groomed will somehow prevent the truth from coming out. "The flames," she finally says. "They were blue."

Blue fire. The color of my fire. But it was a chemistry lab, and gas burns blue. It's an unusual color for a brush fire, although possible if the fire is hot enough. "Why does the color matter?" I ask.

Last night at the beach, when Blake kissed me, the fire turned blue.

Mom shifts in her chair. "It was just one of your Nana's superstitions."

"Then why did you think I took off my bracelet? When you thought I started the wildfire?"

She puts her hands in her lap, wringing her fingers together. "You know Nana believed in the old legends."

I wait, silent, until she takes a breath and goes on.

"She believed our family was touched; that every seventh generation there would be a daughter with great beauty and power."

Nana believed a lot of things that had no application to our real lives. "What does that have to do with me?"

Mom's hands shake now. "Honey, I don't believe it and you shouldn't either."

"Believe what?"

"The stories."

"Tell me."

"Nana's great-grandmother's grandmother. She was supposed to be a seventh-generation daughter."

"What about her?"

Mom takes a breath and then closes her mouth before she says anything. "She killed a lot of people." She balls her hand into a fist. "Nana said she burned an entire village to get revenge on the man who broke her heart. With blue fire."

I try to rationalize what my mother is saying. Does mental illness run in my family? Some recessive gene that manifests every seventh generation? I add up the generations between myself and my grandmother's great-grandmother's grandmother. Seven. "Am I going to go crazy?"

Mom shakes her head. "I don't know. Nana said the bracelet would protect you."

"From what?"

"From men who would burn you as a witch. From yourself. At least until your seventeenth birthday."

"What happens on my seventeenth birthday?"

Mom looks down at her hands. When she finally looks up, her eyes shine with tears. "I don't know, honey. You tell me."

I can't imagine my mom believing in anything beyond the power of a beautiful smile and firm handshake. I think back to my fire. The blue flames on my hands. The feeling that the fire came from inside me. That I could control it. It seemed so real. Am I going to go so crazy that I might really hurt someone?

I put my hands over hers. "I don't know what to believe."

We sit in silence, holding hands, for a long time. When I finally stand up, she turns back to the computer without saying a word.

I go into my room and crawl into bed, pulling a pillow over my head and crying until I fall asleep. I don't even wake up for dinner.

The next day goes by in a haze. My gut aches again as soon as I wake up, hollow and empty. I want desperately to go back to being the science geek whose main role in life is to serve as witness to Haley's string of true romances. I don't want to be the nut case who disappears in mists or imagines guys speaking to me during frozen moments in time. I don't want the pain of knowing that Blake hasn't even tried to contact me since Saturday. I don't want to wonder what it means that my seventeenth birthday is only ten days away.

As I drive to Bridle Oaks after school, I try to focus on the preparations for the Del Mar National. At least Dart loves me no matter what kind of freak I am. But when I get to the stable, Dart's stall door is wide open and empty. His halter's gone too, so it's unlikely he managed some great barn escape and ended up on the highway. Still, I don't like not knowing where he is.

Marcy's school horse, Hershey, grazes alone in the pasture where we turn the horses out. There are no horses in our riding arena. I walk over to the larger arena where Sam's students ride. A beautiful chestnut is going through a set of jumps. It takes a second before I realize it's Dart. The jumps are at least half a foot higher than anything I've taken him over. He clears them with confidence, his form textbook.

Parker Winslow guides Dart to each jump with the timing and skill of a professional. Marcy and Sam smile and talk in the center of the arena. I lean on the rail, awed that this amazing horse is really mine. I can't take credit for his natural talent or excellent breeding. Even so, I had a little to do with spotting the potential in the skinny track reject with high withers.

Jenna Bowman comes up next to me, her eyes wide as she watches Dart sail over a four-foot oxer. "He's perfect."

"He is, isn't he?"

She nods, her eyes still following Dart around the arena. Jenna is horse crazy in the way only ten-year-old girls can be.

"You want to ride him sometime?"

Jenna's eyes grow even wider. "Really? Can I?"

"Sure."

Both her feet leave the ground as she squeals. I laugh and make a mental note to ensure it happens soon.

Parker brings Dart down to a walk and lets the reins go slack. She smiles and pats him on the neck. Dart's ears flick back toward her, his breath fluttering through his nose in contented snuffles.

I'm grooming Hershey in the barn aisle when Marcy catches up with me a half hour lather. "You're not going to believe this!" She grins. "Parker Winslow is thinking of buying Dart."

I flinch. It's irrational, I know. I don't like the idea of Dart becoming the equivalent of the latest Prada bag in Parker's closet. Sure, he would have the best grooms, supplements, and trainers that money can buy. But who would love him?

Marcy must see the expression on my face. "You know that Parker wouldn't dream of owning a horse that cost less than two hundred thousand, right?"

"Dollars?"

Marcy laughs.

A groom leads Dart into the barn and puts him away. He munches a chunk of apple from his feed bin. The light scent of lavender shampoo fills his stall. He doesn't even look up to greet me when I slide under the chain.

"*Et tu*, Dart?" It's just as well that it's a rhetorical question. Dart roots in his bin for another piece of apple. He has so moved on.

By Wednesday night, the dull ache in my gut has grown to a sharp, relentless throbbing. Blake still hasn't called, a fact I can no longer ignore. I check my phone for messages with increasing frequency just in case. Haley has already made plans to go out with Austin on Friday, and even Jonah the slimeball made the effort to text Christy again. So while Christy and Haley come up with endless plans and speculation about the upcoming weekend, I bury myself in my pillows and fight the urge to call Blake myself.

At midnight, I sit straight up in bed. I know where Blake is. Rush set up a poker game for tonight.

I throw on a pair of jeans and a sweatshirt and am in my car before I can think enough to talk myself out of it. Within ten minutes, I'm in Wolfgang Hunter's parking lot, my headlights pointed at Blake's black SUV.

This is definitely crazy-stalker territory. I don't care. We have to face what happened eventually, and I need to figure some things out—soon. My seventeenth birthday is a week from Friday, and Blake might be the only person who can understand what's happening to me. He said he saw the silver light too. Besides, just knowing he's here makes me feel better. At least I know he's safe.

Safe? R.D. doesn't have much crime beyond the occasional car burglary or drunk driving arrest. It's a shock to realize that a good part of the discomfort I've felt since leaving Blake is some primitive concern for his well-being, especially since I, psychotic stalker girl, probably pose the biggest threat to his safety.

There are a surprising number of cars in the lot given

the late hour. I debate whether to go in. One glance in the mirror is enough to keep me firmly rooted to the driver's seat. My hair is even wilder than usual, curling out in all directions. I instantly regret my rush to get out of the house. I turn on the radio and wait.

I'm not sure how long a poker game is supposed to last, exactly. It's almost an hour before anyone walks out of the restaurant. A gray-haired man in a long coat glides through the parking lot and climbs into a large Mercedes. He drives off without ever looking toward the Blue Box.

It's another thirty minutes before a short round man in a baseball cap walks out and gets into a red Porsche. Definitely compensating for something there.

Another hour goes by. The air temperature drops at least ten degrees while I sit in my car waiting for a glimpse of him in a dark parking lot.

At three o'clock, I make up my mind to go home before I embarrass myself completely. When I turn the key in the ignition, the Blue Box sputters but doesn't turn over. Perfect. How am I going to explain this one to my parents? I doubt they'll believe that I woke up with a sudden craving for venison.

I'm about to try the engine again when I hear laughter across the parking lot. Four people exit the restaurant. I know Blake is with them even before they cross into the light of one of the lampposts. His blond hair stands out in contrast to the darkness that surrounds him, creating a glowing halo. Endorphins ricochet around my brain. It's all I can do to stay in my car.

In contrast, Blake's walk is relaxed and casual. Two girls flit around him. The taller one brushes her hand against his arm.

I pull the key out of the ignition and curl a fist around it, imaging how I could use it as a weapon if she touches him again. My hand shakes with rage.

What is wrong with me?

The group crosses under the light just as Blake walks ahead. Portia rushes to catch up with him. The other girl is Fishnet. She drops back to where Joe walks a step behind, her shoulders slumped in defeat. Joe leads her to the right, away from Blake and Portia. Perfect wingman.

I watch with morbid fascination as Portia leans into Blake, trying to get his attention. He pulls her into an embrace that has me reaching for the door handle. He says something in her ear and then abruptly lets her go, stepping back. She glares at him, crossing her arms over her chest. I can almost feel the frustration as Blake runs his hand through his hair. Hell, I *do* feel it. And then Blake turns and walks away. Portia starts to follow him, but seems to change her mind mid-step, spinning on her heel and marching off to a blue VW.

Blake approaches his car, and I swear I feel his mood lift a little now that Portia is off his back, or maybe that's just my mood lifting.

Mine. I try to squash the thought. One stupid date does not make him mine. Still, it takes every ounce of self-control I can muster to keep myself in the car. I want to run to him, to throw myself in his arms, wrap myself in him. Pathetic.

As he reaches for the handle of the SUV, he stops and turns his head, zeroing in on the Blue Box. His eyes, burning silver, find me in the dark. I can feel his mood shift again, even from across the parking lot. He's not happy to see me.

I glare back. Did he think that after what happened I would just disappear? Fine. If Blake Williams wants a fight, I'm more than ready to take him on. I push the door open as hard as I can. The door swings out, but stops abruptly before it opens halfway.

A dark figure looms over my car, blocking the door. I stop pushing and try to pull the door back. It holds firm.

"Brianna," Joe says in a calm voice. "We need to talk." He smiles, an unlit cigarette hanging from the corner of his mouth.

FIFTEEN

I shrink lower in the seat of my car.

"Mind if I join you for a minute?" Joe steps back, letting the car door come toward me so fast I have to push against it to stop it from slamming.

Blake climbs into his SUV, wasting no time. He starts his car and drives out of the lot. As the car gets further away, the pain in my stomach returns.

Joe walks around to the passenger side of the Blue Box and opens the door. He curls his long body into the seat next to me. His James Dean pompadour smashes up against the roof and his knees press up against the glove box. I laugh.

"What?"

"I don't think you'll be buying one of these beauties anytime soon," I say.

"You got that right. For starters, it's Japanese. All these newfangled imports have been hell on our economy."

"This thing is older than both of us."

Joe pulls the cigarette from his lips. He rolls the filter between his thumb and forefinger. He concentrates on the movement for a few seconds before he looks at me again. "You and I haven't talked much, have we?"

Try at all. I don't say anything. My eyes search the street where Blake's car disappeared. Joe sits quietly, staring out at the darkness with me.

"Let me be frank." Joe's voice pulls me back. "You seem like a nice girl. So why the hell are you chasing down a rat bastard like Blake?"

I smile at the description. "I thought you were his friend."

"Can't help liking the son of a bitch." He squirms in the seat, trying to find a comfortable position. "Pardon me for saying so, but you don't seem like his type."

What is that supposed to mean? So I'm not dumb, snobby, or slutty ... *Oh.*

Joe fills the silence. "See, guys like Blake will always have their minions, stray puppies that follow them around begging for the smallest scrap."

"It's not like that." The words sound hollow now. Even if I could justify my behavior as a science project to test my pheromone theory, it doesn't explain why I'm sitting in a cold parking lot in the middle of the night. But it's not like I'm about to beg Blake Williams for anything. Last time I checked, I was getting out of the car to kick his ass.

"Blake and his kind are nothing but trouble for girls like you."

"Thanks for the advice, but if Blake sent you here to let me down easy, you can forget it. There's nothing going on." Unless you count the weird hallucinations or the fact that I'm sitting in this now-empty parking lot. Minor details.

"This isn't about Blake. It's about you. See, where I'm from, there's two kinds of girls, the kind you screw and the kind you marry. And Blake's got no interest in the second group. Got me?"

Joe has officially taken this retro thing too far. I've been on one ill-advised date. "You think I want to *marry* him?"

"Nah," Joe shakes his head. "I know you aren't ready for that."

"So you're saying I'm a slut?" Probably true, at this point, but no way am I going to stand for Joe insulting me in my own car. It's bad enough that I'm never going to get the hair gel off the ceiling.

"Nah, you're not that kind of girl either. It's just that if you take up with Blake, one of two things will happen." Joe opens the door of the car and stretches out his right leg. "Either Blake Williams is gonna break your heart..." He stares outside.

"Or?"

"Or you become the other kind of girl." Joe pushes his head outside the car and unfolds his tall body one part at a time, our conversation apparently over.

"Joe?"

"Yeah?" He bends over and sticks his head back into the car.

I nod to the cigarette still dangling from his lips. "You ever light that thing?"

"Nah. Stuff'll kill you." He winks. "Don't press the gas so hard when you start 'er up this time. Sounded like you flooded the engine there." He closes the door with a soft thud and walks down the lot until he reaches a vintage white Buick.

I turn the ignition, tapping lightly on the gas, and am relieved to hear the whining of the engine as it coughs to life. Joe's car cruises behind me, following me all the way to my driveway. He idles outside until I've unlocked the front door and am safely inside.

It's not the least bit creepy. It's kind of nice.

I'm still half asleep when I grab a granola bar from the kitchen and head off to school in the morning. But the hair on my arms stands at attention almost as soon as I open the front door, jolting me awake better than a triple-shot latte ever could. The pain in my gut is replaced by a satisfied hum.

His black SUV is across the street. Blake is out of the car, leaning against the door.

I storm up to him, still furious that he's ignored me for the last four days. With every step that brings me closer, my traitorous body celebrates, making the combination of pleasure and pain almost unbearable. I try to read his expression. There's no trace of emotion in his face. He barely spares me a glance.

I want to put my hands around his neck and kiss him, right here on the street. No. I don't need *that* humiliation. When he finally lets his eyes slide to mine, there's anger, yes, but something else too. A fear that claws at my neck. A sadness that floats up from nowhere and pulls me along. Desire, so strong that I want to fall into him.

My anger flees, taking any trace of courage and self-respect with it. I bite my trembling lip, fighting back the tears that threaten to escape at any second.

Blake starts to run a hand through his blond waves, stopping halfway through. There's no point trying pull off relaxed or casual, not with me. "Let's get this over with."

Is he breaking up with me? Panic courses through me. We aren't exactly together, so he can't really break up with me, right? I bite down harder on my lip. I start to wipe away a tear. Before I can, his hand is there, his thumb lightly rubbing my cheek. The soft touch sends flickers of heat to my stomach.

"Can we go somewhere?" Blake's voice is softer now.

I nod, my eyes closed, not wanting to see how he doesn't look at me, not wanting the touch to end. It does anyway. When I open my eyes, he's already sitting in the car, his eyes facing straight ahead.

Once I'm in the car, Blake drives in silence. The current of emotion that mixes with my own becomes increasingly hostile. It's like I can feel his anger from the inside.

"*You're* pissed?" I shout, even though I'm only inches away. "I'm the one who was manipulated and used, then thrown away like I never mattered." The tears flow freely now. There's no stopping them. "You are such a jerk."

Blake's cheek twitches. A vein on the right side of his throat pops out, creating a ridge that travels into the collar of his yellow T-shirt.

I feel the violence that simmers just beneath the surface—my own. I lean against the window of the car, putting as much distance as I can between us. I can't afford to lose control.

We drive into the Heights, a neighborhood of mini-mansions that was hit hard by last fall's wildfire. After about a mile, he turns up a meandering driveway that leads to a tree-filled lot, although half the Eucalyptus trees are dead. As we get closer to the top, it's clear that there is no longer any house, just a bare slab of blackened concrete and an empty swimming pool. It's desolate and depressing. The perfect setting for our little breakup. Especially since he thinks I'm the one who started the fire.

"Is this your house?" I ask.

He rolls down the windows before turning off the ignition, letting the smell of charred and rotten wood fill the car. "Was."

I choke a little as the stale air fills my lungs. My eyes travel out across the lot to a ridge with an expansive view. I can see almost all of R.D. from this angle, a sea of tract homes with tile roofs. The view is a stark contrast to the rotting waste of the American dream that surrounds us.

Blake finally looks at me. And I wish he wouldn't. His

eyes hold nothing but anger. I press back further against the window, my right hand clutching the door handle.

"Let's get one thing straight," Blake says, his voice a growl. "If anyone has been manipulated, it's me. I didn't ask for this, and I don't want it. So just do whatever hocus-pocus you need to do to undo it, and do it now."

I stare back. He's still putting this on me? "If I remember correctly, you're the one who kissed me. I'm not the one who tried to pretend like nothing even happened."

Blake barks out a laugh. "Nice try. So I kissed you. You unleashed the power of the bandia." The last word rolls off his tongue with undisguised venom. "You did this to me, and you will *undo* it. *Now.*" The vein on his neck pulses and flexes. His hands ball into fists.

I jump from the car, walking fast, putting distance between us with every step. I stop only when I reach the ridge at the end of the barren lot. I cross my arms across my waist, hugging them to me. I remind myself to breathe.

The cars move along on the roads below. People go about their morning routines, heading to the gym, work, playdates, school. Just another Thursday in R.D. Lucky bastards. Even listening to my lit teacher dissect every line from *Paradise Lost* would be better than standing in this dead yard waiting to be dumped. And that's only half of it.

He said it again. Bandia. Nana's name for me. My name. I don't trust myself not to lose it. At least there are no chemicals handy.

After about ten minutes, I finally hear the footsteps I knew would come, slow and resigned. His breath teases my neck as he steps behind me. If I lean back just an inch, I could rest my head against his chest. He could fold his arms around me and hold me to him. Or he could push me off the edge of the ridge. I turn to face him. Whatever happens, I'll see it coming.

"I'm sorry," he says. "I didn't mean to scare you."

"You know what happened." My voice breaks. "On the beach."

"I have an idea."

"You know what I am?"

"You still don't?"

I rub the poisonous flower that hangs from my wrist. "It's nothing good, is it?"

He actually laughs, a sound that warms me from the inside. "I'm sure that depends on who you talk to."

Taking my hand, he guides me to a retaining wall abutting the ridge. We sit and stare out at the view for a few minutes. I don't let go of his hand.

Blake is pre-med. Maybe he just recognized the symptoms of my psych issues. Maybe there's a diagnosis somewhere I haven't found. I could just be a pyromaniac schizo. It's beyond pathetic that this is sounding like a good thing.

"What am I?"

He's silent for a few minutes before he answers. Finally, he takes a breath and looks right at me. "You're a living, breathing bandia." He swallows. "But it's not like I've ever seen one before. I didn't think there were any of you left."

SIXTEEN

I'm more confused than ever. "There are others? With my nickname?"

"I don't know." Blake's hand squeezes mine. "I mean, you ... they ... it's just stories. No one has seen a bandia for generations. Then there was the fire, but even then, I didn't believe you really existed until you walked into that kitchen."

"Without this." I hold up my wrist, ready to release the clasp.

He eyes the bracelet. "Don't. It's hard enough as it is, now that we're ... just don't."

"What does 'bandia' mean?" I brace myself for his answer.

"It's a word from an old story, like a fairy tale. It means goddess."

I want to laugh. I was ready for something like witch

or fire monster, but goddess? He's really reaching here. So it's definitely crazy. Crazy I can understand, at least.

"You know the fairy tale? Are there horses?" I ask.

"Not that I remember."

"A handsome prince?"

"Just listen, okay?" Blake scoots closer to me so that I feel his body heat along my side. I turn my face up to the sky but Blake's warmth is a hundred times stronger than the sun on my face. "So, a long time ago . . . " Blake starts.

"In a galaxy far, far away?"

"Close. A small village in Ireland." Blake finally makes eye contact. "Will you let me finish?"

I shift, pulling my knees to my chest, trying to ignore the word that echoes in my head at his mention of Ireland: *home.*

He starts again. "This girl named Danu lived in a small village. She was hot, and all the guys noticed, but the villagers feared her as much as they wanted her. She was a creature of dark magic, with power over fire, earth, air, and sea. Yet lust won out over fear. The men fought for her attention."

Okay, definitely not me. There has to be an evil stepsister.

"Danu ignored them all, except for the one man she couldn't have, a young warrior named Killian, a leader in the Crusade against dark magic. Danu represented everything he was sworn to bring to an end. And even with her dark powers, she couldn't make a man fall in love with her."

I stifle a snort. Maybe I can identify with this girl after all.

"Danu would not be denied, so she seduced Killian and lured him to the spirit realm, where she bound him to her soul, creating a connection that couldn't be broken. When they returned to Earth, Killian discovered that Danu had not only taken a piece of his soul, but cursed him with dark powers. He rejected her, even though it hurt him physically. He swore that she would never have his heart. Killian married the daughter of a neighboring landowner, even with his soul all tangled up in Danu. Her heart broken, Danu disappeared."

"What about Killian and the girl next door? Did they live happily ever after?"

"Hardly. Killian was cursed with the very powers he'd vowed to banish from the earth. The evil he fought against now lived deep within himself. Even as he struggled to live life as a simple man, his soul still ached for the loss of Danu."

Nice story. "What about Danu?"

"She appeared again, many years later, still young and beautiful, and hell-bent on destroying Killian and his family. Unlike his father, Killian's son Brom found it impossible to resist her. Brom ran away with Danu, abandoning his own wife and child. Then Danu burnt Killian's land to the ground and forbade the sea from giving rain, creating a famine across all of Ireland."

The fire thing hits a little too close to home. "Isn't there supposed to be a happy ending?"

Blake smiles. "You believe in happy endings?"

He has a point. "For fairy tales."

"Not this one. But there's more." Blake looks at me then, really looks. "Brom and Danu had children. And their children had children. It's said that every seventh generation, Danu's daughters become more than just carriers of her DNA. The Seventh Daughters are said to embody the power and beauty of the bandia herself." Blake closes his eyes, lost in his own thoughts.

My breath stops. "And you think that's me?"

Even as I ask the question, I can feel the surge of adrenaline that comes with positing a new theory that might actually work. The scientist in me is already checking off the boxes. The nickname Nana gave me... my connection to Ireland... the woman in the field with flowers... the seventh generation thing Mom told me about. My fire.

Hell. What if the monster in me isn't something I can chase away with scientific theory or antidepressants? What if the monster in me is really some dark goddess who won't hesitate to kill to avenge her broken heart?

Blake opens his eyes. "I've seen you when you aren't hiding behind that bracelet." He stares out at the view. "We were together in the spirit realm."

I'm trembling. "At the beach?"

Blake nods. "That was all you, sweetheart."

Except I'm not sweet. "Can you not call me that?" I push his shoulder.

Blake pushes me back. "I wish I didn't like you so much."

There's a darkness behind his eyes that makes me uncomfortable.

"Why?" Maybe it has something to do with the fact that I'm a raving lunatic who burns things. Who may or not be the descendant of a crazy goddess.

"It would make it easier to end this."

Oh. I'd almost forgotten that we're here for some big breakup scene. Yet another way that I'm like Danu in the story. I can't make a guy love me. Not Derek Kingston, and certainly not Blake Williams.

"You're shaking." He lifts a curl of hair away from my face and tucks it behind my ear.

"When we were together, something happened. We were joined somehow. It hurts to be apart." I run my fingers along the bare skin of his arm, marveling at the little electric shocks that play at the tips of my fingers. "Do you feel this?"

He stares. "Even with your bracelet on."

"It's why I came to see you last night." I look out at the view. Blake knows more than he's saying. He knows the story of the bandia; he knew it before we even went to the beach. "How do you know all this?"

"My godfather likes to entertain us with stories about Ireland. I never believed it before."

"Wait. Your godfather? The scary hunter guy? He's from Ireland?"

Blake nods. "My whole family is. Well, my great grandfather moved to the States after World War II."

Okay, this is starting to feel a little weird. "So, what are you doing for Beltane?"

He laughs. "I wouldn't mention that word around my family if I were you. It's not a holiday we're particularly fond of in my house."

"And you call yourself Irish?"

"Aye. As Irish as they come."

"But you don't celebrate Irish holidays? Not even as an excuse to drink whiskey?"

He squeezes my hand a little tighter. "We celebrate enough. St. Patrick's Day, for one."

"That doesn't count. Everyone celebrates St. Patrick's Day."

"Even your family?" He looks skeptical.

He's dead right on that one. For all Nana's insistence on keeping old Irish traditions, she hated St. Patrick's Day. One year I made the mistake of pinning a shamrock to my sweater before going to school and was branded a traitor. "How'd you know?"

"Lucky guess. Beltane's an ancient pagan holiday. St. Patrick's Day is basically the celebration of the death of paganism." A cloud sits behind his eyes. "They're not exactly compatible." I can almost feel the remorse as he says the last part. I *can* feel it.

"Why does it matter to you?"

He looks back out over the view. "It shouldn't. Let's just say that your family's Ireland and my family's Ireland are two different places."

"How'd your family end up in this town? It's not like Rancho Domingo has a huge Irish contingent."

"You'd be surprised." He laughs. "My grandfather came here for college and never left. What about you?"

I kick the wall with my heel. "My dad got an offer he couldn't refuse."

"Sounds mysterious."

"Yeah, the dark world of life insurance is full of secrets." I feel a hum in my stomach as he smiles, a combination of my reaction and his. "Do you think we're bonded? Like Killian and Danu?"

He lets out a sigh. "I don't know what else this could be."

So we're tied to each other somehow? Then the pain when we're apart isn't just my overreaction to his not calling—it's a physical reaction to being apart from him. This could be a problem. It's not like I can follow him around everywhere. Worse, it's not like he wants me to.

"Didn't Killian break the bond and marry someone else?" I ask. "There must be a way."

Blake shakes his head. "Killian could never break the bond. He rejected Danu but spent his life suffering for it."

I should be upset at the idea that Blake is bonded to me against his will, but some perverse part of me likes the idea of Blake being tied to me. I can't say I'll mind the suffering he'll endure if he tries to be with someone else. Wow, I really am sick. "So I'm keeping you from a neighboring farm girl, is that it?"

"No." He looks back out across the valley. "I don't know.

I'm eighteen. I haven't thought much beyond next week." Blake's expression doesn't change but his mood shifts. He doesn't expect any happy endings. "I want my life back. You have to try to end this thing."

Logically, I know he's right. But I can't say I want to go back to the way things were before. Even if he never really wants me again, he *sees* me now, and that's something. Of course, Blake seeing me and not wanting me is going to be worse than his not seeing me at all.

Still, it isn't like I can snap my fingers or wiggle my nose to fix something I don't even understand. "I wouldn't know where to start," I tell him.

"I have an idea." Blake takes my wrist and rubs his thumb across my bracelet, reaching for the clasp. "Maybe we can get back to the spirit realm and undo it."

I don't try to stop him when he takes the bracelet off. I don't want to. The feel of his fingers on my skin is electrifying. Addictive.

His hand closes around the chain, his fist shaking against his leg as he stares at me with a hunger in his eyes that I feel in my bones. "God, Brianna. I thought it was bad before. I'm not going to be able to hold back."

I reach across the short distance, setting my hand on his thigh. "So don't."

He grabs me by the waist, lifting me onto his lap until I'm facing him, my legs straddling him as we sit on the retaining wall. His arms come around me, simultaneously shielding me from the sheer drop of the ridge below and pressing me against him. His mouth covers mine, his tongue thrusting in and out, leaving no doubt where this is headed.

I move against him, desperate to be closer. I run my hands down his back and pull the back of his shirt up. My hands dive underneath, eager to explore his muscled back. He groans as my fingernails graze across his bare skin. I feel his desire build alongside my own. But there is no flash of light or swirling mist. This is purely physical.

He pulls back, his breath coming fast. "This isn't working."

I lean into him, letting my hands drop lower. "Isn't it?"

His lips move closer to mine, so close that I can feel his breath mix with my own. He hesitates there, and I can feel the war he's fighting with himself, trying to harness a desire that's so strong, so *there*. He's with me, and his lips brush mine for a second before he rips them away.

He lifts me off his lap with such force I almost lose my balance as he sets me down next to him. He throws the bracelet in my lap, his breath coming hard. "Put it on."

My fingers clasp the charm.

"Better." His breath is still labored. He turns away from me before he stands up and stalks back to the car.

I hold the charm in my fist tighter, fighting back tears and the biting sting of his rejection. There's no consolation in being right. Having him see me and still not want me is so much worse than being invisible was. I wait until I'm sure I'm not going to cry before I walk back to the car.

Blake turns the engine over before I can shut the door. "You should go to school," he says as we drive back toward my house, as if it isn't entirely his fault I've already missed my first two classes.

"What's your problem?" I blurt, tired of holding it in.

"At the moment?"

"I'm sorry, I should've realized that I would have to clarify, given the multitude of problems you undoubtedly have."

"My problem," he says, still looking straight ahead, "is *you.*"

I don't have to feel the nauseating mix of anger and anxiety that rises in my stomach to know he tells the truth. But it's there anyway.

SEVENTEEN

Christy is already fifteen minutes late. I pull my jacket tighter as I lean against my car. I glance at my phone again. Maybe she'll change her mind about going to Joe's party, but the odds are overwhelmingly against it. It's far more likely she's waiting for Haley. It always amazes me that it takes Haley so much time to get ready; it isn't as though she needs the help.

Haley's thing with Austin must be going well, since she decided she's definitely coming to Joe's tonight. Not that Christy would let me out of it. I can't even come up with a good argument—we both know that if Austin is there, Haley will disappear within minutes of our arrival.

My one consolation is that it's Christy's turn to be designated driver. If she doesn't drink, she might think twice about hooking up with Jonah Timken. And if she still wants to get with him, I figure I can come up with a reason for her to take me home in a hurry.

My pocket barks loudly. It's not Christy, it's Sherri Milliken. I hit the ignore button, even though I'm starting to reconsider. The math team might be just the distraction I need right now. Something logical and sane.

She leaves a text when I don't answer. *Time is running out.* Just as I finish typing out a response, the headlights of Christy's Mustang come around the corner.

Haley opens the passenger door. She doesn't bother to get out of the front seat. She pulls the seatback forward, leaning her body with it, so I'm forced to suck in my gut and twist to make it into the back seat.

By the time we get to Joe's, the party already has a buzz going. Most of the crowd is outside, milling around a custom pool and spa. The girls wear dresses and heels. The guys wear pressed dress pants and button-down shirts. Not a swimming suit in sight. Not even a pair of jeans other than mine. Not that anyone notices.

"Look who's missing her weekly Scrabble tournament." Haley points toward the patio.

A pretty girl with long black hair stands next to three guys. She twists a piece of hair around her finger while she talks. I don't recognize her until she turns her head so that I catch the profile of her roman nose, less pronounced than I remember it. Sherri Milliken throws back her head and laughs.

"Is that who I think it is?" I ask the question even though I know damn well who it is.

"Ohmigod!" Christy's mouth drops when she realizes who we're looking at. "Did she have some kind of extreme makeover?"

It looks that way. Sherri's hair is straight and sleek. Her face looks almost the same, but somehow her features now work together to form a striking whole. The curve of her nose draws attention to her large eyes and full lips. Cheekbones that once seemed too sharp now appear high and delicate. I would never have thought it possible, but Sherri Milliken is hot. The guys that surround her seem to agree.

"Good for her," Haley says, not the least bit threatened by Sherri's transformation. She turns to a group by a large firepit and flashes a smile at Joe.

Joe lifts his hand slightly, acknowledging Haley with a curling lip. His dark hair is teased high, fully recovered from its run-in with the Blue Box. A white tee peeks out from underneath a crisp blue oxford shirt.

I know Blake is there before I see him. The ache in my stomach is replaced with a gooey warmth, marshmallows melting into hot chocolate. My eyes find him, honing on his pale hair as light and shadows dance across it. Portia stands next to him, too close. Her burnt-orange sundress clashes with her chestnut hair. At least she got the memo about the dress code. She whispers something in Blake's ear, but he doesn't smile.

As we step closer, Blake turns his head. His eyes meet mine and everything else fades away. I hold my breath, and I think he does too. In this moment, everything slides into place, filling me with a peace I haven't felt in the two days since I last saw him. This is what I've waited for ever since he first walked into Magic Beans over a year ago.

He sees me. Even with my bracelet.

He looks away, and the moment is gone. I feel the churning emotions that swirl around in him as he pushes me away. Then it's as if he's walled me off completely, erecting a barrier that leaves me alone to wallow in my own pain.

I look away, determined not to let him see how much he's hurting me. I can't keep it up for more than a few seconds. When I look back, Portia has her hand on his arm. The impulse to rip her away from him is strong.

No. I can't let myself lose control. Not with all these people here. But my eyes are drawn to the fire beside them. I can almost feel it calling to me.

I spin away, abandoning Christy and Haley without any explanation. I head for the side of the house, as if putting stucco, glass, and wood between myself and Blake is all I need to do to change the direction of my thoughts, to keep from doing something that I can't take back.

I rush right into a pale green dress-shirt.

Austin's hands come out to steady me as I bounce from the impact with his chest, which is every bit as solid as it looks. "Juliet, take it easy."

"I'm sorry. It's just ... " I rub my palms on my jeans and glance back to where Portia laughs and leans into Blake.

Austin follows my gaze. "Right." He grabs my forearm and pulls me in the direction I'd been walking. "Follow me."

I fall in step beside him, around the side of the house and down a narrow gravel path. The path ends at a three-tiered fountain that's lit from the bottom by round lights. The little garden surrounding it is in full bloom. Yellow and purple flowers cling to the perfectly manicured bushes that frame a half circle behind the fountain. The splashes of water falling from the top bowl into the pools below cover the sounds of the party in a blanket of white noise.

"You okay?" Austin asks, still holding my arm.

I exhale, taking inventory. The crazy feeling is gone. For the first time in a week, there's no pain. None. It's odd to feel so normal. "I think so."

"Good." He lets go of my arm and puts his hands in his pockets. He stares for a few seconds without saying anything. "You want to talk about it?"

I can't begin to explain any of it. Not my jealousy-induced pyromania in eighth grade, not this bonding thing with Blake. "It's not a big deal, okay?"

"You don't know how badly I want to believe that."

"But you don't?"

Austin steps closer to me. A smile plays at the corners of his lips. "You could convince me otherwise."

I sit down on the cold bench, moving away from him. "I doubt it."

"Ye of little faith." Austin sets his foot on the bench and leans forward.

I feel trapped. Something about the way he's watching me, his body blocking my way back to the path, is unnerving. I realize he's waiting for me to say something. "I just need some time."

"I'm afraid you have less than you realize. Your fate will find you whether you hide from it or not." He leans closer still, like he might kiss me. I don't know if I want him to, but I'm not doing anything to stop him, either. I'm frozen, like something is keeping me here. His eyes grow darker, even as the gold flecks in his irises get bright. I'm lost in them, pulled toward him on an invisible current, my lips moving toward his.

A loud crunch pulls our attention to the gravel path. Austin moves away, putting distance between us, and I feel like I've been woken up from a dream too soon—fuzzy and instantly alert at the same time.

Blake moves forward, a shadow in the setting sun, his footsteps quick and determined.

The light of the fountain dances across his face as he stops at the path's end. His spine is rigid, making him look even taller than his six-foot frame. I feel his barely contained aggression, not only from his posture, from the inside. It flares up in me.

Mine, but not mine.

EIGHTEEN

"What exactly do you think you're doing?" Blake's voice is a roar.

I stand up and step around Austin. "What does it look like, Blake? I'm obviously having wild sex on a cement bench with my best friend's boyfriend fifteen feet from a yard full of people."

"Do you two want to be alone?" Austin steps around me. "You don't have to leave."

Austin moves a few steps away from me anyway. As soon as he does, the now-familiar warm hum and angry stomach pain converge on my abdomen like bad carne asada.

Blake comes closer, standing directly in front of me.

"You have to end this now." His voice is soft but he can't keep the menace very far below the surface. "I'm going to kill someone if you don't." He glances at Austin, just in case I haven't gotten the hint.

"So you get to completely ignore me and hang out with whatever girl you want, and I can't even talk to another guy?"

"Don't pretend you don't want him." He lowers his voice so only I can hear. "You want him so much that half of me wants him too."

That is so not an image I want to have. And he's wrong. I don't want Austin. I moved away when he tried to kiss me, didn't I? It's still all fuzzy.

Blake runs a hand through his hair. "You have to end this."

I take a step closer to him. The warmth in my gut swallows the pain as I get closer. I take another step, stopping only when I can feel the heat from his chest against my collarbone. "I don't know how." I let my hands come up to his shoulders. He doesn't back away. I take one more tentative step, so that my feet are touching his. I let my head rest against his chest.

His arms curl around me. "You have to find a way. I need my life back."

I don't argue, although at the moment the last thing I want is my life back. I just want him to hold me like this.

Steps crunch on the path as Austin turns and walks back to the party.

Blake's hand moves in spirals down my spine. I sink further into him, emboldened by the swirls of pleasure that follow the trail of his hand. His mood lifts. His pleasure becomes my own and the adrenaline that flows through me feeds a craving I didn't know I had. I'm helpless to do anything but wrap my hands around his neck, closing my fingers in his hair.

When he kisses me, I'm completely lost. Nothing matters except his lips on mine. His fingers moving along my back. His chest pressing into mine.

He breaks the kiss abruptly. "Damn it."

My breath comes in ragged, shallow gulps. "Blake, please..." I feel the pain that tears him inside. It slices through me, sharp and jagged. I want to fall over from it.

"I can't do this, Brianna. You have to figure out how to fix this before it's too late. You don't understand what it means." The anger and hurt and worry all bleed together.

"So tell me!"

He shakes his head. "I can't. Just trust me, okay? I don't want this."

"You're lying." I pound my fist against his chest. "You wanted me on the beach. And I can feel what you're feeling now. You *do* want this. You can't pretend you don't."

He grabs my wrist, stopping me from continuing to hit him. "Let's get one thing straight, bandia. You're a cold, evil creature who would just as soon see me burn as kiss me. And I can't ever forget it."

He knows.

He knows exactly what a jealous lunatic I am.

The thought fills me with raw panic that is one hundred percent mine.

He lets go of my wrist so suddenly that my hand falls to my side. "Stay away from me. Just stay the hell away."

I step back, hiding my face in the shadows so he can't see my tears as he walks away.

Falling back onto the bench, I clench my stomach, trying to control the stabbing pain before I die of internal bleeding. I don't bother trying to keep from crying now. At least the sound of the fountain drowns out my sobs.

Blake is bringing out the monster in me, but it's even worse than that. He knows. He knows exactly what kind of crazy I am. No wonder he thought I burned down his house. No wonder he hates me.

And the sickest part is how much I need to be near him. I've turned into an obsessive stalker while he seems to be able to just walk away, even though I know he feels the same connection I do. He complains about it enough. Joe was right about one thing—a relationship with Blake Williams will only lead to heartbreak, and that's the best-case scenario. It could be far, far worse.

I twist the charm hanging from my wrist. I don't want Blake to ignore me. God knows, I should, but I don't. I unclasp the bracelet. I sniffle and wipe my nose. Oh yeah, he's going to fall all over himself now.

I drape the little chain across the top of the fountain, letting the water run over it. As the water runs over my fingers, I feel a surge of energy. The water not only flows across my skin, but *underneath* it. It pumps through my veins, cold and strong. I draw its strength to me, closing my hand around the stream. It crackles and freezes. I open my fingers to a perfect flower blossom formed in ice.

The odds are about seven billion to one that water

would freeze into just this shape. And no law of nature can explain how water could freeze at sixty four degrees Fahrenheit. I close my hand around the flower and let it melt back into the fountain.

There is no flash of light, no electric shock or rustling of wind. Nothing to indicate that any magic is in the air at all. Because it isn't. It's *inside* me. All of it. The earth, wind, water, and fire. I laugh, giddy with power. I don't have to look at my reflection to know that I'm beautiful. I feel it; the power that can possess a man, body and soul. That already has.

"Freeze," I say under my breath, and the water in the fountain is instantly frozen, a solid block of ice. Icicles hang where the water spilled over only a second before. I squeal with excitement.

I step onto the small lawn, kicking off my sneakers and socks and letting my bare feet sink into the grass. The earth is solid and strong, waiting for me to command it. I laugh again as I hold the power of the earth between my toes. I dance on the grass, spinning and laughing.

"I knew I heard something."

I stop and turn toward the male voice in the darkness. The tone is light and friendly, but there's some other indefinable quality to it.

"Keep going," he says from the shadows. "I like to watch."

The emphasis on that last part makes my skin crawl. I put my arms around my chest, wanting to cover up even though I'm fully clothed. Jonah steps out of the shadows and walks toward me, the outline of his body lean and strong. I back up as far as I can, until I'm pressed up against a large juniper bush, its rough leaves clawing at my back.

"You can run if you want," he says, as if my fear is entirely expected. "I like the chase too."

I freeze in place as he comes closer, not sure whether to run or scream, and seemingly unable to do either. I reach for the power I felt only seconds before. There is no trace of it. Nothing but damp grass beneath my feet and the frozen water in the fountain, mocking me.

He bears his teeth as he smiles. "You really are something," he says, his voice still calm. "Better than I ever imagined." He grabs my arms, hard, hauling me against him. I try to bring my knee up to his groin but barely make contact with his thigh. He squeezes my arms tighter, laughing at my feeble attempt to fight back.

"Jonah," I say, finding my voice at last. "Don't do this."

NINETEEN

"Don't do what?" Jonah holds me against him. He traces his index finger down my cheek. The motion is eerily soft.

Bile rises in my throat.

He cups my chin in his hand and tilts my head up so that I'm forced to look into his dark eyes. "I never in a million years would have suspected Brianna Paxton. Hiding in the shadows of her hot little friends." He laughs to himself.

I manage to lift my foot and come down hard on his instep.

He doesn't flinch. His left hand grabs my neck. "You wanna fight?" He squeezes, cutting off my breath, letting up only when I gasp for air. "Don't tempt me to end this early."

"From what I understand, you can't help ending early." My voice is raspy and dry, but my meaning is clear.

His eyes widen and his grip around my neck tightens.

"You have nerve even showing up here, at the home of a giolla."

Giolla? "Where's Blake?" I rasp, hoping to buy some time. I hear laughter from around the corner. We're not far from the party. Someone might hear us if I can get him to let go long enough to scream.

"You think Blake will help you?" Jonah's hand tightens, making me gasp again. His thumb presses hard where my pulse throbs. "He'll be first in line to rip your heart out."

He pushes me backward, thrusting his foot behind my knee and sending me sprawling to the grass. He does nothing to slow the momentum of my fall. My back hits the ground fast and hard. I want to scream at the shock of pain, but I can't get a breath. He's on top of me before I can do anything, his fingers back around my neck. His body is a dead weight, trapping me against the grass and dirt. The earth is cold and unforgiving. I try to find some connection to it. There is nothing.

Jonah's leg pushes between my legs. I try to kick. I can't move beneath his weight. My arms are pinned to my sides by his body. My stomach heaves. I'm going to puke.

"Brianna!"

At the sound of Austin's voice, Jonah freezes. "This is none of your business," he growls, still pushing against me.

"Help!" I try to scream. The word comes out in a whisper. Austin is there in a second, pulling Jonah off me. I scramble to my feet as soon as I can, grateful to be off the ground. I shudder, my hand coming up to rub my neck.

Jonah is on his feet too, glaring at Austin, his eyes wild. "Stay out of this, Montgomery."

Austin stands his ground, turning his shoulders to block me from Jonah's line of sight. "Go home, Jonah."

Another set of footsteps comes around the corner. Joe takes in the scene and marches toward us, shaking his head.

Jonah steps closer to Austin, appearing larger and more menacing. His entire body is tense, and there's no mistaking the threat he poses. "Last chance, Montgomery. If I have to go through you to get to her, I will."

"Have you gone mad?" Austin responds, with no trace of the fear that pulses through me. I shrink back from Jonah.

Joe lays a calm hand on Jonah's shoulder. "Time to go."

Jonah doesn't move. "You see what she is. I have to finish this."

Joe looks around Austin, searching me out. "You okay?" he asks smoothly, his hand still on Jonah's shoulder.

I'm pretty sure I'm not okay. I mean, the guy just attacked me. I don't want to think about what could've happened. My stomach lurches again. There is no stopping it now. I move over to the hedge and puke.

I wipe a trail of saliva with the sleeve of my jacket. "Keep him away from me."

Joe grabs Jonah's arm with a strength that belies his skinny frame. Jonah stumbles to remain upright. "Time to go," Joe says again, still cool and smooth, leading Jonah away.

Before they turn the corner, Jonah looks over his shoulder and silently mouths, "Later." He kisses the air, sealing the promise.

I tremble. Jonah is not going to let this go. Whatever this is.

"Are you okay?" Austin asks, his eyes searching.

I shake my head and run to him. I bury my head in his chest; his arms come around me, holding me to him. He rubs my back, gently stroking my hair. "It's okay."

I nod, wanting desperately to believe him.

"Let me take you home," Austin whispers. His breath is on my neck, too close. I back away, but his smile is so innocent that I'm sure I must have imagined the invitation in his tone.

He leads me toward a gate in the side yard. I'm glad we aren't going back toward the party. I'm not ready to face anyone yet.

But as we pass the fountain, something isn't right. I stand taller and walk faster, pulling Austin with me. "We need to hurry."

He resists. "Don't worry. Jonah's just a bad drunk. Joe can handle him for now."

We're isolated in the side yard. A cold breeze comes off the fountain, raising the hair on the back of my neck. I regret not going out through the party now. "We need to go back." I turn around and pull on Austin's arm. The water in the fountain is no longer frozen. It churns and laps, spilling over the edge of the basin. "Now."

Austin doesn't move to follow me. "Brianna." The

quiet way he says my name is more terrifying than if he'd screamed it.

I turn around slowly. Austin doesn't move, his eyes focused on something in the shadows in front of him. A flash of silver glows in the darkness, growing a blinding white light. An onyx shimmer appears in the center of the light, sucking the light to its center like a giant black hole. Then the light is gone, except for a silver glow that illuminates the dark figure.

"Bloody hell." Austin backs up a step.

I'm unable to do anything but stare. Jonah stands before us, bathed in the light of a thousand stars. He wears only a tartan cloth draped around his waist, with a long swath of cloth across one shoulder, accentuating his bare chest. Silver light dances in his eyes. He's a living oxymoron, simultaneously beautiful and scary as hell.

Austin moves in front of me.

Jonah laughs, a melodic sound that rides the wind blowing around us. "You shouldn't get involved, Montgomery."

A glint of silver draws my eye to Jonah's right hand. He raises his hand, revealing a hideous serrated knife. The handle is covered in jewels, making it look more like a ceremonial relic than a weapon of war. He wields the jagged blade with smooth strokes.

As he steps closer to Austin, Jonah's eyes get bright with a cold, harsh light. He lunges, a movement that's barely perceptible. The knife slashes at Austin's chest.

Austin laughs as he steps back, nearly crashing into me.

Then Jonah disappears. Vanishes, throwing us into darkness. I blink, waiting for my eyes to adjust. Before I can acclimate, there's a flash to my right. Jonah appears directly behind Austin, the knife poised to slice his neck.

"No!" I finally scream, a true scream, high and loud.

Austin swings his arm, knocking Jonah off balance. He twists away and grabs Jonah's wrist.

Jonah recovers quickly, turning the knife to graze Austin's shoulder with the sharp edge. Austin lets go with a curse. Blood spreads across his ripped shirt sleeve.

Jonah steps closer, grinning. He raises the knife to strike again.

"Get back!" I yell. A swirl of wind grows around me as I move forward. "Back!" A rush of air flies away from me, straight at Jonah. It picks Jonah up, sending him flying into the fountain. His right leg hits the base hard, pitching him forward. He lands in a heap on the ground, his silver eyes closed.

Austin falls to the ground, grabbing his shoulder.

I kneel beside him. "Are you okay?" The question of the night.

Austin grins at me. "About bloody time." He sits up, still holding his arm. His shirt is torn. Blood spreads along the fabric.

I take off my jacket and press it against Austin's shoulder.

A bright flash of light forces our attention back to the fountain. Jonah is on his feet. He limps toward us, his right leg barely touching the ground.

"We need to get out of here." I tug at Austin's arm.

Austin curses and falls back down on the grass. I wrap my arms around his chest, trying to help him up.

Jonah fixes his silver eyes on me.

"Stay back!" I try yelling again. Nothing happens. I try to remember what I did before. I put my arms out. "Back!"

Jonah curls his lips in a smile. Then he disappears again. I spin around in the dark.

"Get out of here, Brianna." Austin sits up, still holding his arm. "I'll be fine."

I reach for the knife, still lying in the grass next to Austin. The jeweled handle is hard to grasp, and the blade is heavy. It takes both my hands to lift it. Silver light flashes to my right, and then Jonah is next to me.

He grabs my arm with such force that I'm pulled off my feet. I fall toward him, turning away from the teeth of the blade in my hands.

The wind whips harder around us, and for a second I wonder if I'm doing something. There's another burst of silver light and I'm pushed away from Jonah, the knife falling to the ground between us. I land in the grass beside it.

"Stay out of this." Jonah's honey-laced voice has a sharper edge to it.

I turn to see Jonah fly back against the house.

When I finally look over to where the silver light appeared, it's almost too late. I only catch a glimpse of him, bathed in the same otherworldly light as Jonah, his blond hair glowing white.

"Blake?"

Then he's gone, leaving no trace he was ever here. I see Jonah's glowing body slumped in a flowerbed next to the house; then Jonah disappears too.

Before I can say anything, Jonah appears again in the same spot, surrounded by perennials. Not the bright, beautiful version of Jonah, just the plain old petulant jerk, in dress pants and shirt, his hand pressed to a bloody wound on his leg.

Austin sits up on his elbow and tosses me a cell phone. "I suppose you'll want to call an ambulance."

TWENTY

Wild dogs. That's what we tell the paramedics. A couple of wild dogs jumped the fence and attacked Austin and Jonah. The jagged cuts look enough like bites that the story seems to hold up. The ambulance takes both of them to the hospital. Austin still has my jacket, leaving me in a white tee splattered with his blood. I nurse a glass of orange juice in Joe's kitchen. As if the natural sugars can stave off shock. No hope of that.

Christy watches me from across from the table, worried.

Haley sits next to me, her eyes holding nothing but accusations. "So are you going to tell us or not?"

Is it that obvious that the dog thing is a lie? I hold the glass tighter, swirling the orange liquid. "I told you what happened." The familiar dull ache in my stomach has returned with a vengeance.

"Dog attack, whatever." Haley leans forward. "That's not what I'm talking about."

I have no idea what her problem is.

"I can't believe that I fell for it when you said you didn't know it was Austin, that night you disappeared with him." Haley's tone is cold.

Are we really going to get into that? Now?

"And then you were going out with Blake, and I was glad you finally had a boyfriend." The emphasis Haley puts on the word "finally" is not flattering. "Just because Blake dumped you or whatever, it's no excuse for what you did tonight." The knives flying from her eyes are even sharper than her words.

I hold my glass up like a shield. "He didn't dump me. We were never together." Unless you count that whole soul-bonding thing. I'm not sure how to begin explaining that one. Okay, so Blake dumped me.

Haley's blank stare tells me that my relationship with Blake or lack thereof is of little concern to her. "So it didn't work out. You don't have to be a skank about it." She pats Christy's arm. "And you had to involve Jonah too?"

Christy's lower lip trembles. "I thought you were my friend."

"I am."

"Right. That's why you went off with both Jonah and Austin? Because you're such a great friend."

Leave it to Haley to assume that the only possible reason I could have been alone with two guys is to broaden my sexual horizons. They can't seriously think that I went off with Jonah and Austin for some kind of weird orgy. And anyways, *Jonah?* Totally gross.

"It wasn't like that."

Haley's eyes narrow. For the first time, I can see the resemblance between her and her mother, and it scares the crap out of me. "You think I haven't seen the way you look at Austin?"

Christy's hand is over her mouth. Her eyes are huge and wet.

The glass shakes in my hand. "I … " I want to deny it. I shouldn't have to deny it. But I can't exactly deny it, either.

Haley stands and turns to Christy. "Come on. Brie can't even come up with a decent story this time."

They walk out of the room, leaving me with my half glass of orange juice. Not that I will drink anymore. It might be the only friend I have left.

"You shouldn't frown like that." Sherri Milliken saunters into the room like a fashion model. "It'll give you wrinkles."

"Hey." I know I should comment on how great she looks, but I'm not really in the mood to chat at the moment.

Sherri sits down in one of the wood chairs, leaning back until the front legs are off the ground and the back hits the wall behind her. She puts both her legs up on the table, crossing her ankles. "You never called me."

"I texted you tonight." Not that joining the Mathletes is at the top of my priority list right now. "I've been busy."

Sherri laughs with the kind of confidence of someone who is gorgeous and knows it. It sounds strange on her.

"That's a bit of an understatement, don't you think?" The shakiness in her voice is completely MIA.

"What do you mean?" Has the speculation about me and Jonah and Austin already made it through the entire party?

Sherri lets her chair fall back to the floor, leaning in until her face is just a few inches from mine. "From what I can tell, you've already started to access your power even though your birthday isn't for another week. And you've managed to engage a Son of Killian and survive." Her full lips curve into a gorgeous smile.

"What?" I whisper.

"Oh, get over it already. Is this awesome or what?"

"But," I stammer, my entire vocabulary apparently now that of a two-year-old.

Sherri reaches into the front pocket of her shirt, pulling out my bracelet and dangling it in front of me. "Lose something? It's much better than mine. It doesn't alter your appearance at all, it just makes it irrelevant. I was always so jealous."

"Yours?"

"My talisman. I hated the way it made me look. Like a total geek. It did its job, but you have to admit, the last four years sucked for me."

I reach over and take the bracelet from her. Once it's back around my wrist, I rub the flower charm between my thumb and finger. "You're?" I'm still struggling for words. "Like me?"

"We can't talk here." Sherri stands up. "Follow me."
Sherri leads me outside to a gray hatchback.

I've always felt guilty about abandoning Sherri the way I did. She never seemed to hold a grudge about it, but somehow that made it worse. Then Haley took me under her wing and that was it. No pheromones required.

We get into the car. "Where are we going?" I ask as we head south on the freeway.

"It's time for you to meet Sasha."

"Who?"

Sherri just smiles and turns up the radio.

We get off the freeway in Mira Mesa and pull into the empty parking lot of a nondescript office building. There are no locks on the main door. Inside, a large atrium with planters and sparsely lit floors opens to two hallways on either side of an elevator. Sherri leads me to a plain brown door with a sign that only says *Suite 111*. She punches a series of numbers into a keypad on the door. When a light on the panel goes green, the door clicks open. She flips a light switch, revealing a dark walnut receptionist desk in a bland office.

I pick up a *People* magazine from about six months ago. The address label has been blacked out with marker. The office is devoid of anything that would indicate who works here or what type of business it is. There are no signs, no framed diplomas, no personal photographs.

We move to a conference room in the back. It's just as sterile, with an oval wooden table, eight leather chairs, and a plant in the corner. Sherri walks to a small mini-fridge and pulls out two Diet Cokes.

A beep sounds from the front room, and within seconds a young woman bursts through the door. Her white-blond hair flows past her shoulders and sets off her luminous blue eyes perfectly. She's not thin, but voluptuous in a way that says pure sex. No one, not even Parker Winslow, would call this woman fat.

She frowns at us as she closes the door, her lips forming a seductive pout. "So this is her?"

"Brianna, meet Sasha Westley."

I hold out my hand to shake, but Sasha grabs my left hand instead, turning over my palm to stare at my bracelet. I pull my hand away.

"There's nothing to worry about." Sherri pops open her can of soda. "Sasha's on our side."

Our side of what?

TWENTY-ONE

"Show me," Sasha says, still eyeing my bracelet.

I set the bracelet down on the table and fold my hands in my lap.

Sasha takes a seat across from me and grabs the bracelet. "Amazing!" She holds it in her hands and closes her eyes, then lets out a squeal. "Ohmigod!" She sounds like a sorority girl.

"What?" Sherri stares at her.

"It's hers," Sasha says.

Sherri's mouth falls open.

"I know it's mine." I reach over to take the bracelet back, but Sasha leans away from the table, keeping it out of my reach. "Give it back," I say.

She ignores me, staring at the charm, turning it over in her hands. "It's not possible. Gwyn's line is supposed to be dead."

"Give it back!" At my words, the silver chain flies from her hand and sails across the table, landing in front of me. I close my hand around it and pull it against me.

Sherri laughs out loud. "I told you."

"How old are you?" Sasha asks.

"Sixteen," I answer automatically, although I'm not sure I owe this woman anything.

"Impossible," Sasha says to Sherri.

"She does have the charm."

"What about it?" I tighten my grip.

"That charm," Sasha says, "was made by Danu herself. For her oldest daughter Gwyn."

"You're a Seventh Daughter," I say to Sasha.

"Your family told you, then."

"Sort of. And a boy."

Sasha inhales. "A boy?"

Something keeps me from saying Blake's name. His secret isn't mine to share. "He just told me the story about Danu. It wasn't hard to figure out the rest, given the weird stuff that's happened to me."

"Who is this boy?"

"Just someone I talked to at a party." Not a complete lie. "I told him about the weird stuff, and he told me he knew a fairy tale about women with powers." Less true.

Sasha's expression doesn't change. I have no idea if she believes me or not. "What was his name?"

I take a breath. "I was pretty wasted." A total lie.

A shadow passes across Sasha's face. She tries to cover it with a brilliant smile, and I'm reminded of Blake. The smile is a mask. "I'm sure you'll remember it in time. Perhaps when your powers are more fully in your control. For now, it's important that you understand that the 'fairy tale' you heard is a lie. The true story of Danu is known only by her ancestors." She leans back in her chair. "Danu was a goddess, but she was born on Earth, the descendant of a human mother who had enchanted a god."

Sounds like the same story to me, but I keep my mouth firmly shut.

"When the Milesians banished the gods to the underworld, the demigods were the only hope to bring the gods back to their rightful place on earth."

"The Milesians?" The men who would burn me as a witch.

"Mortals who came to Ireland speaking of one true God. The gods had ruled Ireland and its human inhabitants for centuries, but the Milesians fought against them. After our gods killed their leader, they retaliated, tricking the gods into sharing Ireland equally. The Milesians divided the earth between the underworld and the corporal world, taking the top half for themselves. Effectively banishing the gods from the earth."

"Where does Danu fit in?"

"The gods left a legacy. Demigods, like Danu, who might someday conquer the mortals and set the gods free. But there was no tolerance of magic in the human world, and the Milesians hunted down the demigods, killing them when they were young, before they had the power to strike back." Sasha leans back in her chair. "Danu let her heart get in the way of her fate. She fell for one of the killers, so much so that she brought him to the spirit realm, intending to bind him to her for eternity. It worked too well. Killian claimed a piece of her soul, and with it something even more precious. Magic."

She purses her lips. "Even after Danu made Killian a demigod in his own right, he didn't love Danu. He confessed his plans to marry another woman, and vowed to do so despite the magic that bound him to Danu."

I might know something about Killian's rejection. I keep my head down and let her keep talking.

"Danu ached for the loss of the part of herself that Killian carried. His absence left her feeling physically ill."

I almost say something. I bite my lip hard instead.

"Danu returned to the spirit realm, seeking a way to break the bond."

I can't keep quiet now. "Was there a way?"

Sasha raises her eyebrows at me, not appreciating the interruption to her story. "No. They were tied to each other until death. When Danu returned to earth, it was many years later. She was still a young woman and she still ached for Killian. But it was Brom, Killian's son, who lived on Killian's farm then. When Brom smiled at Danu, the pain seemed to disappear."

"Because she loved him?"

Sasha ignores my question. "Brom and Danu fled together, starting their own life in a village far away from Killian and his bride. They had children of their own and lived a peaceful, quiet life for many years."

"So there was a happily ever after." I don't add that Sasha has left out some important details, like Danu burning Killian's land and causing a drought over all of Ireland.

"Hardly. Killian's rage only grew after Danu ran away with his oldest son. He used the power he stole from Danu to hunt down and kill the remaining demigods in Ireland. All that remained was Danu."

So Blake left out some important details too.

"With the bond, Danu could feel Killian's rage, and she knew that he would pursue her. She created protective charms to keep Killian from discovering her and her children." Sasha's eyes find my bracelet. "In the end, it wasn't enough. It was Gwyn who found her mother's body, laid out in a field, her heart cut from her chest."

So much for happily ever after. "Killian murdered her?" I can't keep the shakiness from my voice. The whole heart-ripping thing hits a little close to home.

"It's been that way ever since," Sherri jumps in. "Killian's descendants exacting revenge every seventh generation."

"What do you mean?" I ask.

Sasha shakes her head vehemently. "Not now, Sherri. It's too soon."

"There was an attack tonight."

Sasha's pale skin goes whiter. "Tonight?"

"They came after Brianna. I saw the flashes of silver light. Two humans were hurt."

The anger that Sasha masked earlier returns to the surface, hardening her features to a point. She's even more beautiful when she's angry. "So it's true. The Sons are here."

"And they're hunting." Sherri takes a sip of her Diet Coke, not the least bit fazed by the direction this is going.

"Hunting?" I ask.

The gleam in Sherri's eyes is somehow more disquieting than her words. "For us."

So it isn't enough that I'm the lucky number seven in my family who gets saddled with crazy powers, not enough that I'm bonded with a guy who wants nothing to do with me or that my two best friends think I've morphed into some kind of disloyal skank. Might as well throw in the fact that a bunch of demigods want me dead.

Sasha explains that the Sons of Killian have mastered their powers over the centuries, using them to increase their prowess as crusaders against magic. They've hunted and killed Danu's descendants, nearly succeeding in eradicating magic from the earth. Except, of course, their own.

I half-listen while Sasha talks about the rumors that the Sons of Killian have increased their powers through selective breeding, deliberately seeking out women who have some ancestral link to the gods and goddesses. Over the centuries, the Sons have been extremely successful. And as far as Sasha can tell, the three of us represent the last of Danu's direct descendants. The last of the Seventh Daughters.

It all seems a little coincidental. "Don't you think it's strange that we're all here?" I ask. "The three of us? And the Sons?"

Sasha practically rolls her eyes. "It's inevitable. We're drawn to each other. To magic."

Even as I listen, my mind keeps wandering back to Blake bathed in silver light. He didn't attack me—not on the beach, and not when we were alone together in the Heights. I'm pretty sure that tonight, he saved my life.

The lecture over, Sasha walks over to the mini-fridge, her hips swaying. "We can't launch an attack until we know which ones are the Sons. And Brianna isn't seventeen yet."

"She's got powers," Sherri replies, as if I'm not sitting right next to her. "I say we nuke 'em!"

"Nuke?" Sherri has my full attention now.

"Spontaneous combustion." Sherri says the words slowly, drawing out the syllables as she twists a piece of gum around her finger. She snaps the gum back into her mouth, flicking her hand toward the plant in the corner so casually it might be an afterthought. The plant bursts into blue flames, dark smoke rising against the wall.

"Sherri!" Sasha waves a hand at the plant with more haste. The fire is doused with a surge of water that materializes out of thin air. All that remains is a charred pile of ashes and the thick smell of damp briquettes. "You'll set off the fire alarm."

"You get the point," Sherri says to me.

I do get the point. And more—the blue fire sends off alarms in my head. "The wildfire," I say. "That was you."

Sherri shrugs. "It wasn't like I planned it. I was having a bad hair day."

I understand all too well how it could happen. What I can't understand is Sherri's nonchalance. "Those were people's homes."

Sherri laughs. "They're just humans."

"How can you say that?"

Sherri glares at me. "The humans are meant to serve the gods, and they need to be put in their place. When the gods return, the humans will pay with more than a few possessions."

"When the gods return?"

Sherri rolls her eyes. "Have you been paying attention at all? Maybe I should put it in terms you understand. Earth minus the Sons of Killian equals the return of the gods. It will be amazing. We'll rule alongside them. And you can help us."

At the mention of me, Sasha brushes a piece of lint from her jacket. "She's not ready. We need to keep her hidden until she turns seventeen. You can continue your efforts to infiltrate the Sons."

Sherri shakes her head. "Like that's going to be easy now that they know about her?" The way she says "her" is not exactly flattering. "They'll be looking for us now."

Like the blue wildfire wasn't a giant clue? Still, there's no denying that I've compromised the Seventh Daughters. It might have helped if I'd known the danger ahead of time.

Sasha sighs. "They must be surprised to find even one of us. They won't suspect there are others. There's no reason to change our plans."

"What are you planning?"

Sherri's face twists into an expression that reminds me of her former self, hard lines and distorted features. "To hold hands and sing 'Kumbaya.' What do you think? We're going to stop them from killing us and finally end this thing."

"How?" For some reason I need to hear her say it out loud.

"The blazing inferno wasn't enough for you? I forgot how slow you can be sometimes."

The last vestiges of shame and guilt I've carried since dumping Sherri freshman year float away on a cloud of indignation. "You can't kill him."

"Him?" Sherri narrows her eyes.

My pulse quickens in my throat. I've said too much. "The Son that attacked me and Austin." At least Sherri doesn't know there were two.

She blows a strand of her newly straightened hair off her face. "I'm not going to sit around and wait for the Sons to kill me. You of all people should understand why we have to do this. You should be dead right now. Why aren't you?"

I can't let them find out about Blake. I stare down at my can of soda. "He never got close enough." I slow down my words before I blurt something that will reveal too much. "Austin got in the way. Then I sent the Son flying into the fountain and he passed out."

Sherri watches me with the intensity of a sniper, keeping me squarely within her scope. I want to go back to being invisible. "But he got away."

How does she know that? "Right." I stumble on the word. "I was helping Austin and he disappeared." I'm not sure why I don't out Jonah as a Son. It would serve him right to have Sherri after him.

Sasha tries to mask the look of skepticism on her face and fails. I wait for her to call me out. She saunters back over to the table with a can of Coke, full sugar. "I'll keep her at my house until her birthday," she tells Sherri. "It's safe there."

Sherri nods. "Fine. It'll be easier without her around."

"I can't just disappear for a week."

Sherri grabs my arm when I try to get up. "Don't be stupid. They know who you are now. And they won't be happy. Not only did you get away, but there were humans hurt. It's way too public."

"So they can't risk another attack for a while." I hope I'm right. Besides, some of us have priorities that do not include fighting over something that happened a thousand years ago. I have no intention of getting involved in this battle.

Sherri and Sasha exchange another look. Sherri finally lets go of my arm. "It's your funeral. Just don't mess this up any more than you already have." The threat hangs in the air. Way to make new friends.

"We'll be in touch." Sasha flashes a gorgeous smile that's meant to charm me and comes nowhere close. I rush out of the conference room before they can change their minds about letting me go home.

I'm halfway down the corridor of the dark office building before I realize I don't have my car. Waiting for Sherri is not an option. I need to get as far away from her as I can. Unless I want to enlist in her blood war.

I keep walking, not stopping until I reach a gas station several blocks away. There's only one person who will understand any of this. I wait until I'm inside the mini-mart before I dial the number.

Blake answers on the first ring. "Are you okay?"

I wish people would stop asking that. I don't even know the answer anymore. "I need a ride."

"I don't know if I can get away."

"I wouldn't ask if it wasn't important."

"I'll try," he hedges, but I know he means yes. I don't even stop to question how I know.

TWENTY-TWO

I feel Blake before his SUV pulls into the parking lot. The anger that's simmered underneath the surface is gone, replaced by something stronger. Resignation?

He stares straight ahead as I climb into the car, but there's a wave of relief that mixes with my own. It matters to him that I'm safe. We don't say anything for the first few minutes of the drive. Somewhere along the I-15, the silence becomes unbearable.

I look at him. "Are we going to talk about this? 'Cause I'm a little freaked."

Blake doesn't answer. He sets his hand on the top of mine and squeezes. I close my eyes and relax into the artificial warmth. It's weird how danger feels so much like safety. His thumb rubs my wrist, brushing the silver chain.

When we get to R.D., he doesn't drive toward my

house. "Where are we going?" I ask. I finally feel the wariness I should have felt when I first got in the car.

"The Heights."

"I think I just want to go home."

"Not yet." Blake finally turns toward me and I have to suck in a breath. I might never get used to the fact that Blake Williams is Looking. At. Me.

"The Sons don't ask questions, Brianna. If there's a threat, it'll be extinguished. End of story. The only thing that's kept them from hunting you down so far is fear of exposure. It won't last long. You need to be prepared."

"Them? More than Jonah?"

"Jonah's a punk. He's the least of your worries at the moment. Most of us don't even care about the old wars, but Rush and his group are another story. Jonah's got them fired up. You need to be prepared to fight."

"Fight?" I have a different plan in mind. It consists of going home and burying my head under my pillow until this all blows over. Not exactly proactive or realistic, but better.

"It's fight or die." Blake pauses. "So what were you doing in Mira Mesa anyway?"

I search for an answer. "I left the party with a girl from school and she brought me there." Not a lie. Not the truth either.

"To a gas station?" Blake isn't buying it. Of course he's not. He can feel my discomfort.

I can't tell him the truth. I may not want to be part of Sherri's blood war, but that doesn't mean I'm ready to throw her to the wolves, either. "We aren't exactly friends. But it's not like I could stay at Joe's."

Blake pulls into the vacant lot where his house once stood, driving up the charred driveway to the concrete pad. He lets go of my hand but doesn't move to get out of the car. "Why didn't you leave with Christy?"

"She's kind of mad at the moment. She thinks Jonah and I ... " I let my voice trail off. I can't finish the sentence. I rub my neck where Jonah's hands squeezed it. I have to remind myself that I can still breathe.

"I shouldn't have left you there." Blake's eyes are soft, and I'm struck by the difference in him. In the quiet moments when he's not smiling or flirting, he's almost another person. This is a boy that a girl could fall in love with, if he ever gave her half the chance.

"It's not your fault."

"He could've killed you."

"You stopped him." I can't resist reaching across the car to let my fingers trail along his shoulder.

He shakes his head. "You don't understand. I almost didn't come."

My hand slides down between his shoulder blades. "You did."

The air is still, crackling. He leans toward me, his breath on my neck. "What is this, Brianna?"

I don't dare move, for fear he'll pull away.

"This wasn't supposed to happen this way." He kisses me. Soft. Warm. Not nearly enough. He stops, leaning back against his seat. He runs his hand through his hair with such force that he ends up looking slightly crazed, his blond layers sticking up and out at odd angles.

Maybe Sherri was right. Maybe I'm a little slow on the uptake. *This wasn't supposed to happen this way.* What does that mean?

"What wasn't supposed to happen?" I ask. He just sighs and looks out the window, ignoring my question.

What? Blake wasn't supposed to like me? Of course not—he was supposed to kill me. I grab his arm, forcing him to look at me again. "Should I be dead right now?"

His eyes are sad, resigned to the truth even if he won't come right out and say it. "It's complicated."

"But I should be dead, right?"

He doesn't say a word, which is as much of an admission as a full confession. He's every bit as thick as Sherri and her little death squad.

"I am not Danu," I state. "I don't care if she burned down a farm or caused a drought or stole someone's husband. She's been dead for a thousand years or more. And I have no intention of dying over something my great-grandmother to the hundredth power did or did not do."

"I know you're not her." Blake's eyes are a swirling mix of emotions that barely hint at the spin cycle of anger and grief that rises inside me. "You've done what she could never do, haven't you? You've bound me to you in a way I can't escape. Made me feel things that go against everything my family stands for."

"Your family? Is that what this is about? What about *you*? What does Blake Williams stand for?"

He stares outside of the car. The charred trees outside look almost alive as the shadows of their bare branches weave and twist around each other. "Can this wait? I'm trying to help you here."

"I'm still getting over the fact that you regret saving my life."

He spins to face me. "Let's get one thing straight. I've let my family down in every possible way. I've attacked one of our own, and now I'm about to deceive the entire Circle." Blake's lips curve up gently in a smile that's at once sad and imperfect. "But I don't regret saving you. That's the problem."

My mouth is dry. "Oh."

He flashes a grin, armor securely back in place. He even manages to quell the spinning in my stomach. "Besides, letting you die would be a bit like losing a piece of myself, wouldn't it? No way in hell I'd let that happen."

I want to grab him and wipe that stupid smile off his face. "Can you be real for more than thirty seconds at a time?"

He laughs. "Trust me, you don't want real. Real is a pretty twisted place. You've seen the blackness that fills my soul, remember?"

I turn away. It should be obvious that the black soul was mine. Blake practically glows with silver light even when we're not in the midst of some bizarre soul bond. And I didn't need to see my soul to know the darkness inside. I've kept it at bay for the last three years. Sasha may think that Danu just wanted to live in peace, but from what I've seen, Blake is right. Having power is dangerous when your heart wants vengeance.

"Hey," Blake says, his hand rubbing my shoulder. "I didn't mean to upset you. Was it that bad?"

I shake my head. "What if it's not you?"

"What are you talking about?"

"The black soul. What if it's me? What if I'm some kind of evil, vindictive, psychotic killer?" There. I've said it out loud. What I've feared since I was thirteen. Since I almost killed two kids in a fire. For what—disappointing me?

Blake laughs. Not the reaction I expected. "I hate to break it to you. You're all of those things."

"This is where you're supposed to tell me I'm imagining things. That it's all going to be okay." That I can choose who I want to be. That I can change my nature.

"There's a reason my kind has hunted your kind for a thousand years."

It's my turn to look away. "It all seems so pointless."

He takes my hand in his, letting his fingers weave in between my own. "It's just the way it is. Kill or be killed. For all I know, at some point you'll come after me, and one of us will have to kill the other."

"I won't kill you," I say, too quickly and too loud. It doesn't sound like the truth even to me.

"You don't know that. For now, you need to understand what you're up against. It'll make it easier to keep you—and that little piece of me inside you—alive. There are seven of us who are Seventh Sons. Jonah you know, and you've met Rush. Micah and Jeremy are my cousins. They're good guys."

I raise my brow, not masking my skepticism.

"It's the old guard you have to watch for," Blake continues. "Rush, Levi, and Dr. McKay."

"The geneticist?"

Blake nods. "He's actually not as rabid as the other two. They're kind of extreme in their beliefs. I always thought they were a little nuts, believing in the myth of the bandia. But now … " He lets his voice trail off.

"Now what?"

Blake grins. "Now I know better."

I want to bottle that smile and keep it with me.

"Anyway, Micah and Jeremy are nothing to worry about. They've been hoping to meet someone like you for a long time, but they won't hurt you. You'll understand when you meet them. It's the others who are dangerous. The breeders, too. They're human, but in some ways they're the most bloodthirsty of the lot."

"Breeders?" If I wasn't creeped out before, I am now.

"Humans who have been recruited into the Circle because of their genetic ties to Killian. First through sixth generation carriers."

Whoa. It seems Sasha has some good intel. "Do the breeders know what they are?"

Blake nods. "Too much knowledge has been lost because the demigod power only manifests every seventh generation. The Sons didn't know the secrets of the Seventh Sons that came before them. The giollas helped, but even they had their limits."

The familiar word sends a new wave of fear through me. What had Jonah said? "Giolla?"

"Servants to our kind, like Joe."

"What does he do?"

"He's kind of a historian. He passes down information from the Sons that came before. There's less use for the giolla now, since we're able to isolate the Killian gene and test humans who might be carriers. Now that we can pinpoint the carriers to a specific generation, we can use selective breeding to create Seventh Sons in almost every generation."

"How? If the power only manifests every seventh?"

"By combining carriers of the Killian gene from different generations. My dad's a fifth generation carrier and my mom's a sixth generation carrier, so I'm both a sixth generation carrier and a seventh generation Son. Since I have the sixth generation gene, my own sons will be sevens and manifest the demigod power too. They'll be both Seventh Sons and first generation carriers."

"Okay, that's not confusing."

Blake grins. "It gets more complicated. If I breed with a fifth generation breeder, my children will also carry the sixth generation gene, which means that my *grandsons* will manifest the seventh generation power. Dr. McKay wants us to breed with the more remote generations, so that eventually we can breed all seven generations of the Killian gene into one person, ensuring a line of Seventh Sons in every generation."

"It's not that different from how thoroughbreds were created from a mixture of other breeds," I say.

"Kind of sick, right? But it works. We can pass down information directly to the next generation of Sons, so Joe mostly babysits the younger Sons. He makes sure we don't do something stupid that will get us discovered before we learn how to control our powers."

"You said that someone like me hasn't been seen for generations." I let the unspoken question hang in the air. Why are they breeding for more Sons if they think the main threat is gone?

"I always assumed the bandia legend was a common enemy to bring us together, or a folk story made up by generations past to explain our kind."

"Where exactly are we supposed to have gone?"

"We thought we'd broken the curse."

"How?" The big SUV feels altogether too small. I lean against the passenger door.

"By ripping out the heart of every last bandia." Blake smiles then, teeth gleaming in the dark. "I guess we missed one."

TWENTY-THREE

We stand on the concrete foundation of what had once been his house. "You want to see my bedroom?" Blake asks, eyebrow cocked. How can he even look at me when he still thinks I did this? He doesn't wait for an answer. "My parents can't agree on what to rebuild. Dad wants the same floor plan. Mom wants a completely new design."

"What about you?"

He shrugs. "Nothing will bring back the old house."

I wait for him to accuse me of destroying his home again, his life, but he doesn't. "I didn't do this," I say.

He takes my hand and brings it to his lips. "You don't have to deny what you are. Not to me. I'm going to show you how to defend yourself. But you're going to have to trust me." He gives my hand a little squeeze. "Are you ready?" he whispers. Before I can answer, he disappears.

And then I know I'm not ready. I'm not ready for any of this.

The flash of silver is blinding. I want to turn away, but I can't. A dark circle grows in the center of the light, larger and larger until it takes the shape of a man. Not a man. Something far more potent. Holy crap. Blake is there. Not Blake, *Blake*. Bathed in starlight, his eyes shining silver. His lean legs are visible beneath the cloth that ties just below his waist. His chest is bare. And when he smiles, my stomach does enough double back-handsprings to make the varsity cheer squad.

"Wow." Not exactly articulate, but it pretty much sums it up. I move forward, aching to touch him. When I see the jeweled sword in his hand, I back up. It all comes back to me at once: Jonah's knife at Austin's neck; the cuts on Austin's arm and shoulder; the blood.

Blake doesn't advance. "You're right to be afraid." His voice is warm honey. I want to melt into it in spite of my fear. "We're warriors first, Brianna. Don't forget it. In this form, we're lethal, and you'll have to catch us off guard to have a chance."

He slashes the sword in the air. Then there's a burst of light and he's gone. The world is darker without his light, and I struggle to see. Then the flash is behind me. I spin to meet it, but it's already too late. Blake pulls me against his chest, his sword raised to my heart.

"Checkmate."

I'm too terrified to move. I can feel the sharp edge of the blade through my shirt.

He laughs and then vanishes again.

When he appears again, there's no light. He's just Blake, relaxed in a pair of black pants and a striped shirt. "If we disappear, you can't attack us," he says. "And we can appear again anywhere within our line of sight. If I wanted to kill you, you'd be dead before you even realized I was there."

I don't answer right away. I'm trying to remember to breathe.

"You need to know what you're up against." He rubs his hands from my elbows to my shoulders and back again. The gesture is meant to calm me, but my pulse is picking up pace with every touch. One hand slides down to my wrist. "Now take it off."

My heart pounds in my ears. I blink up at him.

"The bracelet."

I knew that. "Are you sure that's a good idea?"

"The bracelet hides you, and it hides your magic. Taking if off will help you access your powers. You could have done more to hurt Jonah. You could have killed him. You need to learn how."

Blake isn't thinking clearly. It can't be a good idea to teach someone with a dark soul how to kill.

Blake's hand moves from my wrist along the underside of my arm. "You need to practice." He grins as if he knows exactly what I'm thinking. "You're not going to make this easy, are you?"

I step back from him, away from his distracting touch. I unclasp the bracelet and hand it to him.

The way he looks at me is a miracle. I've seen Blake

Williams look at a hundred girls, but never like this. His eyes shine, not with starlight, but with fire. And then he is here, standing in front of me, his chest nearly touching mine. So close. His finger lightly traces the bruises on my neck; his lips brush my ear.

"I'll kill him if I have to. I won't let anyone hurt you again," he whispers.

I want to believe him. I think I even do. But something in the back of my brain won't let me relax, a niggling feeling that his protection doesn't matter at all. That the threat isn't something we can fight together.

Behind Blake, someone clears their throat. Blake spins around, forming a human wall between me and the shapes in the distance.

"Is that her?"

"Jesus, it's true."

Joe walks toward us, between two very tall guys who are identical except for their hair. "Settle, boys. Blake, you might want to—"

"Got it." Blake pushes the bracelet into my hand.

"No way." The guy on Joe's right steps closer. His long hair brushes his shoulders in thick dark waves that Christy would kill for.

"What the hell?" The other twin's hair is much shorter, closely cropped in a buzz. Funny—now that I know about the Sons, it's almost impossible not to see that they're something more than human. They move with an almost impossible grace that doesn't fit their large, muscular frames. Their eyes sparkle, even in the dark. Their very maleness is on display in perfectly fitted clothes that accentuate slim waists and broad shoulders. They puff out their chests like peacocks unfurling their plumage. I would laugh if I weren't so intimidated.

"Glad to see you're okay," Joe says to me.

"Thanks." I manage a smile. "How's Austin?"

If Joe notices that I don't ask about Jonah, he doesn't show it. I feel Blake's blood rise at my mention of Austin.

Joe nods in my direction. "Already released from the hospital. He's just fine."

I'm grateful for the update. I don't know if I could forgive myself if anything else happened to Austin because of me. It doesn't seem fair to drag him into the middle of this disaster.

Blake steps to the side, reaching for my hand. "Micah, Jeremy, meet Brianna Paxton."

The one with long hair smiles in the darkness. "Seriously? Where did the other one go?"

Blake laughs. "It's still her. She's protected by magic at the moment. So you can't see what she is."

Buzz Cut sniffs the air. "Total fail."

Blake lets go of my hand. "Show them again."

Is he serious? He wants me to reveal myself to more of them?

Blake feels my uncertainty. He floods me with a sense of confidence that is definitely not my own. "Micah and Jeremy are against the war. And against Jonah even more. They won't hurt you."

Easy for him to say. He watches me expectantly.

Long Hair, who I think is Jeremy, grins. "We don't believe in destroying magic."

Micah nods. "We should be hooking up, not killing each other."

Blake laughs.

Joe takes a pack of cigarettes from his pocket and taps it lightly against his wrist. "Let's just say that none of us would be too upset if you knocked Jonah down a peg or two. We're here to show you how."

"All of you?"

Joe nearly smiles. "We aren't all bad."

I unclasp the bracelet, setting it in Blake's palm and stepping away.

"No way!" Jeremy steps back. "No effing way!"

Micah laughs. "Jesus, no wonder Jonah went all psycho-spaz."

"Dude, Jonah is always going psycho-spaz. It's a permanent condition."

"Check her out. He must've freaked."

"He's still a douche."

So apparently Harold and Kumar go to the spirit realm.

Blake grins at them. "You guys want to help her learn to kick Jonah's ass?"

"Does a baboon's ass need Rogaine?" Jeremy high-fives Micah. And then they're gone in a flash of light.

I take the opportunity created by their disappearance to confront Blake again. "Are you sure about them?"

Blake laughs. "I trust them. Not as much as Joe. But more than you."

Micah and Jeremy reappear to my right. Still identical in every respect except their hairstyles, right down to the red and green plaid that drapes their bodies. And they're huge. Built like linebackers, with wide chests, arms, legs.

Joe walks beside us. "Sparring rules: Light contact, no cuts." He looks at me. "No fire. And if you kill someone, all bets are off. Break the rules, pay me later."

Jeremy twirls a huge broadsword in his hand like it's made of plastic. It's not. I probably couldn't pick that thing up with both hands.

Blake puts my bracelet in his pocket. "Remember. Keep moving. Catch them off guard or you'll be firing at air." He disappears at the same time that Jeremy and Micah do. I spin around in the dark, not sure which way to go, or what weapon I'm supposed to be firing.

Joe nods at me. "Anywhere but right where you are would be good."

I run a few steps forward just as Micah and Jeremy both appear in the exact spot I was standing. They bump into each other, jostling for position on the same small patch of concrete.

Blake appears to my left, nodding toward the twins. "You're missing your chance. It might be your only one."

"What exactly am I supposed to do?" I concentrate on the air around me but nothing happens. I start to panic, but then water is there, flowing through my blood. Not my first choice when the twins are grinning at me with swords drawn. I send a geyser of water at Micah, but he disappears before it can make contact. Jeremy shakes his head as some spray lands in his direction.

"Dude! Watch the hair!"

I laugh. Too late, I see the flash of light out of the corner of my eye and Micah is next to me, his sword poised at my neck. "Point."

Joe nods and Micah drops his sword.

Blake walks up behind me. "The count's 0 and 2. You better start swinging."

All three disappear at once. I don't hesitate. I run toward Joe as fast as I can.

Blake appears ten feet in the other direction. Micah appears right where I was standing, like I would be stupid enough to stay in the exact spot this time. Jeremy guesses better. He's only a few feet in front of me. I have to move to the left to avoid contact with his sword.

I don't wait for him to come at me. A deluge of water rains down on his head as soon as he appears. He drops his sword and runs his hands through his hair. "Dude! This is not a water balloon fight!"

"Point," I say to Joe.

Micah disappears and I start to run again. He appears on my right. I send a wave over his head, but it doesn't faze him. He still runs next to me, wiping water from his face. "Water? Really?" Then he grabs my arm and throws me down on the ground with such force that the breath is knocked out of me. He falls on top of me, pinning me to the ground with his body.

Panic. Every nerve in my body is screaming. I'm screaming, kicking, and punching at Micah's solid form as hard as I can. My fists bounce off his chest as he raises the sword above me.

Blake comes behind Micah, grabbing his wrist and pulling him off me. "Not cool."

With Micah's weight gone, my panic recedes. I pull myself to my feet. The fire that fills me is a welcome relief. I am not weak. I am not powerless. My fingers tingle with white heat.

Micah spins to face off with Blake. "Jesus. Chill. She's not even hurt."

Blake's intervention is exactly what he told me to look for. A distraction.

The fire inside me grows, begging to be unleashed. When I look at them this time I see only monsters, men with swords drawn to kill. I won't be their victim. Not now. Not ever. Not again. A ball of fire ignites in my hand, blue flames licking at the air, searching for fuel. I can end this now. I *want* to.

A hand brushes my shoulder, startling me. "Point," Joe says, raising his eyebrows at the dancing fireball in my hand. He turns his chin toward the crumbling remains of a chimney.

My eyes dart back to Micah and Blake, still arguing. Jeremy walks up to my right, his sword poised to strike. I've missed my chance. It's still an effort to beat down the desire to light them up, and for a second I'm not sure I can. Only Joe's hand on my shoulder keeps me grounded.

I turn and throw. The fireball explodes with a shower

of color as it hits the blackened bricks of the chimney. Blake and Micah turn to stare at once.

Micah looks lost. "I thought he said no fire."

"Game's over." Joe pulls a cigarette from the red pack and places it between his lips. "Time to go."

Blake hands me back my bracelet without saying a word. His eyes tell me everything. He knows how close I just came to ending this, to ending him.

Of course this isn't a threat we can fight together. The threat is me.

Blake waits until the others have gone before he walks me back to his car. "Better. You'll be ready for Jonah if he tries anything else."

My eyes go to the blackened pile of bricks. "I'm not sure that's a good thing."

"We'll find a way to get the Sons off your trail. For now, it'll have to be enough for you to know you can beat them if you have to."

Them. He's shown me how to kill them—not just Jonah, all of them. Even himself. "Why are you doing this?" I ask.

"To keep you alive." He smiles. "Can we drop it for now? For the moment, I want to pretend you're just this really cool girl I met."

"Pretend?"

"You know what I mean."

I try to imagine Blake as just an ordinary boy. Me as a regular girl. It's a fantasy I've never believed in. "Fine. I'm going to pretend that you called me after the night on the beach."

"I wanted to." His buries his hands in my hair and pulls me closer. "You have no idea how much."

When we kiss, the warmth that fills me isn't an all-consuming fire. The spiritual bond and strong physical connection are there, but my heart flutters just a bit, and there's something between us that doesn't feel like magic.

Something a little bit real.

TWENTY-FOUR

After only four hours of sleep, even a triple-shot latte isn't enough to make me feel halfway human. I order a second drink from Kimmy and find a table on the patio of Magic Beans, still trying to manufacture the energy to get to the ranch.

A flash of honey highlights is the first thing that draws my eye to where Haley walks across the parking lot, her blue apron in hand. She doesn't see me, but it's too late to get up without her noticing. She has buds in her ears, and her head bobs along with whatever song is cued up. She's almost to the sidewalk when she finally sees me. She raises her hand partway and wiggles her fingers in a tentative wave.

I can't decide whether to be relieved or pissed. I mean, she did abandon me at a time when I really could have used a best friend, leaving me alone at a party teeming with dark creatures, at least some of whom wanted me dead. Okay, so she didn't know about that part. Still, she knew I'd just been through an ordeal. And she accused me of lusting after her boyfriend. Okay, that part might have been a little justified. But thinking I lusted after Jonah Timken? Unforgiveable.

Her smile doesn't reach her eyes as she takes the chair next to me. She lets go of the apron just long enough to pull the buds from her ears. "I'm sorry," she says, her hands twisting the apron in her lap.

I can't let her off that easy. So I wait.

"I know I shouldn't have jumped to conclusions last night. Austin explained everything, and ... "

Everything? Just how much of everything did Austin mention?

"I'm sorry," she says again. "It's just, Austin's different. I *really* like him. A lot. And when you and Austin are together, the way you joke around, I don't know. I guess I feel a little invisible sometimes."

I choke on my latte. Literally. I cough and sputter for what feels like a minute before I can talk. "I don't understand."

Haley shrugs. "I'm jealous?"

"Okay," I say, drawing out the two syllables. "Since when have you ever had a reason to be jealous of me?"

"I know I shouldn't be. And I totally trust you. I do. It's just hard sometimes, keeping up with you. You're so smart, without ever having to study. And you act like you don't know you're beautiful, but you are. You just send off this vibe that keeps guys at a distance. But I'm really happy about you and Blake. And now, with Austin, it's just weirder than I expected, you know?"

Crazy goddesses I can almost deal with. Bloodthirsty warriors? Learning. But I can't even comprehend a world where Haley Marvell is jealous of me.

I wait for the teasing laughter, for the final nail to sink into the center of my heart, for a hole to open up in the earth and send me into the fiery pits of hell. I stare at the ground for what seems like minutes. When I finally look back up, Haley's eyes are big. Her apron is bunched into a tightly wound ball.

"Haley, you're the most beautiful girl in this town. You can't walk two feet without getting asked out. And talk about smart. You're the one who always reads classic literature and studies ancient cultures. *For fun*, I might add."

"So I've dated a lot. It's not like it ever turns into anything serious. And I read because I don't have a TV or computer in my room. What else am I going to do? Hang out with my mom? The one time I tried to read a Harlequin, she found it. Ever been to a book burning? It's horrifying on so many levels." She lets go of the apron and sets her hands on the table. "And look at you. If it weren't for your body language, which is very ice queen, you'd have guys crawling all over you."

I rub the flower charm. Haley had her own theory—I am just unapproachable. It's not too far from the truth.

"Austin told me that you and Blake had some kind of fight and then Jonah tried to take advantage of the situation. I mean, we knew Jonah was a creep, right? At least he was the only one to get hurt when those dogs came."

I remember my bloody jacket pressed against Austin's shoulder and the stains on my shirt. "What about Austin? He isn't hurt?"

"No, he's fine. You didn't know?"

"It all happened so fast." I don't sound convincing to my own ears. I saw the blood. Austin had been hurt.

"So what about you?" Haley asks. "Are you and Blake okay?"

"I guess so."

"So is he like your boyfriend now?"

For once, I don't deny it. Last night Blake and I seemed to have come to some kind of understanding. Too bad I'm not sure exactly what that understanding is. I try to ignore the twinge in my stomach. I should know better than to let myself hope when it comes to Blake Williams.

"What about Austin?"

Haley squeals, her signature smile back. "Amazing! Last night was the best night of my entire life." She explains that Austin showed up outside her bedroom window after midnight. He took her to the beach, where they shared a bottle of wine under the stars until almost dawn. Haley smiles again, practically bouncing in her seat. "I think I really like him." She glances at her phone. "Shoot! I have to work. So we're good?"

I nod. I don't know how long I sit, not moving, long after Haley has gone into the shop.

By the time I get to Bridle Oaks, I can't feel any trace

of caffeine in my system. The two lattes only make me feel bloated. I grab my brush box and slip into Dart's stall. Sundays are normally my favorite, since I don't have to give any lessons and can focus on Dart. I pick up a curry comb and rub Dart's neck in large circles. He leans into the pressure, enjoying the gentle massage. I make patterns in his coat, big swooping loops that crisscross each other as I let my mind go blank for a blissful ten minutes.

I'm shaken from my peace when Dart startles. His muscles tense as he lifts his head, his ears pricked forward. He snorts and paws the ground with his hoof.

I pull the comb away and pat his neck. "Easy, boy." He paws the ground again and sidesteps closer to the wall.

My own body tenses when I hear the approaching voice. "Honestly, Parker. I don't know why you bother with prey animals."

"Jonah, you are so bad!" Parker Winslow laughs as they stop in front of Dart's stall. "Look at this one. He's my newest acquisition."

I step to the side, making myself visible to Parker and Jonah. "Excuse me. Last time I checked, Dart was still my horse."

Parker blinks but otherwise appears nonplussed. It's Jonah's face that changes. His slightly bored expression transforms into a wide smile. *The better to eat you with, my dear.* He leans forward on crutches.

I stand up taller and lift my chin, meeting Jonah's gaze head-on. Even though my legs tremble underneath me, I don't back down. But I don't conjure any flaming balls of fire either. I'm trapped in a void of indecision, vacillating between fight and flight.

Dart snorts and stomps the ground again.

"I think I'll name him Ulysses," Parker says. If she's aware of the tension that surrounds us, she ignores it.

Jonah's eyes water with the effort it takes to keep looking at me, his creepy smile widening until I can count all of his teeth.

"Come on." Parker is already bored with this. "You still haven't seen Tristan."

Jonah leans back down on his crutches and winks at me before following Parker down the aisle.

It takes at least a minute before Dart relaxes again. I'm not so resilient. I sag against the wall and shake for another ten minutes. I don't leave the stall for thirty, and only when I'm certain that Jonah and Parker are no longer in the vicinity.

I resist the urge to call Blake. Jonah Timken is a fact of my new life. And he can't hurt me now. It's too soon for him to try something. At least that's what I tell myself.

I find Marcy in the tackroom. The smell of seasoned leather hangs in the air around us.

"What's the deal with Parker Winslow?"

"She loves Dart!" Marcy is full of enthusiasm.

"She's serious about buying him?"

"I'm almost certain we'll have a check when her dad gets back in town next week."

"Before Del Mar?" I can't keep the disappointment from slipping out.

"The whole point of going to the show was to get him seen by prospective buyers. It's not like it matters now."

The show would be the culmination of two years of training. It was never just about finding a buyer. It was Dart's coming out.

"Maybe I don't want to sell him." I say it before I can think not to.

Marcy sets down her pen. "What?"

"I don't want to sell him." I believe it this time.

"It's a lot of money."

"It's not about money."

Marcy's eyes widen. It always comes down to money for her.

Before she can respond, there's a brilliant flash of light, so bright I have to close my eyes. A shrill scream carries through the air. Not a human scream—a screeching whinny that communicates an animal's fear and pain on a level that language never could.

I run out of Marcy's office and into the barn aisle. All the horses are reacting, stomping and snorting as the high-pitched crying continues. The screams are so loud they seem to be all around, making it impossible to pinpoint exactly where they're coming from. Then, just as suddenly as it started, the screaming stops. The silence that follows is terrifying.

I run faster, glancing into the stalls as I go by. I smell the blood before I get to Dart's stall, taste the salty tang in the air. I duck under the stall guard before I can bring myself to look.

Dart is lying on his side, eyes wild. He struggles to keep his nose raised, just above the puddle of dark blood that pools around his head. He's trying to breathe, but he's getting weaker by the second, and his nose keeps falling back into the puddle. He coughs as he inhales the liquid. He'll soon drown in his own blood.

I fight a wave of dizziness and kneel beside him, holding his nose in my hands and moving beneath him until his head rests in my lap.

I have to force myself to look at his injuries. He might not live long enough to drown after all. Two deep gashes run along his neck, open and gaping so that muscle and bone are exposed beneath the skin. The majority of the blood pools below his throat, which has been mangled and sliced so deeply there's nothing but chunks of bloody meat hanging in shreds under his chin. It's a wonder he can breathe at all. He thrashes his head in my hands, still looking for the monster that attacked him.

Marcy stands in front of the stall guard. "Did you see it?"

"It?"

"The mountain lion," Marcy says.

I shake my head. Of course there was no mountain lion.

"I'll call Dr. Snow." Marcy runs back down the barn aisle.

I stroke Dart's cheek, speaking in a low whisper. He lays his head down in my lap. Whether he is too weak to fight or calmed by my presence, I'm grateful for the peace that settles in his eyes just before they roll back into his head. There's nothing left to do but reassure him the monster is gone.

The monster. The monster with the silver eyes and the sharp knife.

I don't know how long I sit there, whispering to Dart's lifeless form, but my jeans are soaked through with blood and my leg is asleep when I hear Austin's soft voice outside the stall. "Brianna?"

I don't answer. Austin climbs under the stall guard and holds out his hand. "Come on."

I shake my head. I can't leave Dart, not like this. And Austin shouldn't be here with Jonah on the loose.

Austin moves closer. "There's nothing you can do at the moment."

I know he's right, but I hesitate. "The vet's on her way." It's a stupid statement. There's nothing for the vet to do. But I'm still holding on to an irrational hope, and I'm not letting go. It's like none of it will be real until the vet makes an official pronouncement.

Austin steps closer. "You can't help like that." He holds out a hand. "We should get you cleaned up before the vet gets here."

I don't know why this sentence makes sense to me, but it does. I take his hand and let him help me up. We move some shavings under Dart's head, covering the pool of blood. Austin guides me out of the stall to a wash rack at the end of the barn. He fills a bucket with water and shampoo and helps me clean my arms and face. My jeans are black with blood. I run the hose over them, watching as swirls of dark liquid slip down the drain.

Neither one of us says anything until I turn off the hose.

"Who did this?" Austin asks. Not what. Who.

"Jonah." When I say his name, it doesn't matter that I'm wearing the bracelet. My power starts to simmer, flowing through my veins and rising to the surface. The heat that fills me is welcome, reassuring. I'm not helpless. Far from it.

Austin meets my gaze. "He should pay for this."

"He will."

It's an understatement. Forget spontaneous combustion. Jonah's death will be slow and painful.

Austin's lips curve into a crooked smile.

TWENTY-FIVE

Austin just stands there smiling. I can't let it go. "Why are you smiling like that?"

"Like what?" Austin steps toward me, not stopping until he is too close for polite conversation. His crooked grin doesn't falter.

"Like that. Stop it." I wrap my arms around my waist, hugging myself.

"I'm sorry about the horse," he says. "But I think you're right to go after Jonah. He deserves it after what he did. They all do."

"All?"

So Austin knows. I don't know why I didn't realize this sooner. I mean, it's not like he didn't see Jonah with his own eyes when he attacked us last night. But how does he fit into all this?

"They won't stop until you're dead." He reaches out

and takes my hand, pulling me the short distance to him. I'm too drained to do anything other than fall against his shoulder. "It's okay," he whispers. "We'll take care of it."

We. I nod, glad that I am not alone in this, relieved to have someone else who understands exactly what kind of monster Jonah is, someone who might be on my side.

He tilts his head until his lips are so close to my skin they're nearly touching. "For God's sake, Brianna, let me take you home." There's no ambiguity in his meaning as he whispers in my ear.

The same ear that's covered with dried blood.

I push him away. "I need to go." I back up a step, putting more distance between us.

He follows, closing the gap. I hold up my hand. "Please. I need to be alone."

Austin finally stops, his body tense. There's a flash of darkness in his eyes, but it disappears so quickly, I question whether it was ever really there. "You shouldn't be alone," he says. "It's not safe. I tried to find you last night. I went by Joe's as soon as I got released from the hospital, but you were already gone. And then you weren't at home."

"You went to my house?" Since when does Austin even know where I live?

"I didn't wake up your parents or anything. You're okay?"

Of course I'm not okay. "I guess I lived," I finally answer.

"I was hoping you might." He lifts his arm to rub the back of his neck, and I realize there's not even a bandage where he was cut. Not even a *cut* where he was cut.

"What about you? Your arm? Your shoulder?"

"I'm fine. He can't hurt me."

I remember the blood that soaked through to my jacket. And Jonah's knife looked like it could do a lot of damage. "It looked pretty bad."

"It looked worse than it was."

I stare hard at him, searching for any signs of injury. He pulls down the collar of his shirt so I can see his shoulder. "See? No harm done."

I back up another step.

His eyes do darken now. Not a fleeting thing at all; a shadow that grows. "Why are you so skittish? Is it Blake?"

I'm not sure how to answer that. It's Blake. It's Haley. It's the fact that his shoulder doesn't have a scratch. I have no idea who Austin even is, let alone what he has to do with the Sons of Killian.

Austin laughs. "You're not exactly good for him, are you? Perhaps it's time for you to end it once and for all. You were never meant for him, not in the way you want to think."

"You have no idea what I think."

Austin's eyes are nearly black. Except for the shining bits of gold. I can't stop staring at them. But I have to get back to Dart.

"The vet will be here. I need to go."

Austin grabs my arm, holding me. "Stay."

The single word stops me in my tracks. I'm frozen in place, staring into the abyss of his eyes. The pull is strong, and I feel myself leaning toward him. It's hard to remember why I shouldn't.

"Stay with me." His voice is a soft whisper this time, but I hear it as though he's shouted it. More so. His voice resonates inside me like a deep bass. I try to fight it, though I'm not sure why I bother. It would be so much easier to fall into his arms. Into him. I take a tentative step closer.

He smiles and I stop. Everything's fuzzy, but I know something's wrong. He shouldn't be smiling.

Why not? There's just him and me and this magnetic pull, like he's the sun and I'm circling in his orbit.

I hear a whinny in the distance. I can barely make it out, but it's there, like a far-off dream. And then I remember: Dart. Jonah. Blood. So much blood.

I spin away from Austin and run.

I run as fast as I can back to the stall. Dart still lies on the ground, unmoving. I throw myself on his chest and cry, finally letting it out. I don't know how long I lie there before Austin climbs in behind me.

"You really love the horse?"

What kind of question is that? I want to yell at him, but I'm too exhausted to do anything but bury my head in Dart's mane.

Austin kneels beside me and strokes Dart's bloody neck. "I might be able to help."

"You can't."

"You shouldn't doubt me." His voice is soft, but there's no mistaking the warning in it.

I instinctively move away from him.

Austin shakes his head. "My kingdom for a horse."

I choke on a sob.

He smooths his hand along the largest cut. "*Draiocht leasaigh*," he says quietly.

Dart's right hind leg kicks out involuntarily. I jump back.

Austin's hand continues its path along the jagged cut. "*Draiocht leasaigh*," he repeats. When he removes his hand, the cut is gone, the skin perfect. The only thing that remains is the dried blood that still clings to Dart's fur.

I don't move. Austin brings his hands to the mangled area below Dart's throat. "*Draiocht leasaigh*," he says again. Dart's eyes open and his head lifts off the ground with a snort. Austin backs away, waiting as Dart gets his legs underneath him and rises to his feet.

"My God." I mouth, more than say, the words. Dart shakes out his mane, which is still clotted in dried blood.

Austin is some kind of healer? But he did more than heal. Dart was *dead*.

"What are you?"

Austin leans back against the wall, ignoring my question. "I left a small wound for the vet to stitch up. He should be fine now. He won't even remember the attack."

I throw my arms around Dart's neck, but it's not until he nuzzles my pockets in search of treats that I really believe he's going to be okay. "Thank you," I murmur.

"Let's just say you owe me one."

I don't have to see Austin's face to know he is smiling.

TWENTY-SIX

I should know better than to let Christy talk me into going out tonight. She claims to be over Jonah, but I know that part of her is still hoping he'll call. At least she's finally convinced that he's not going to be the great love of her life. That doesn't stop her from wanting him to want her, if only so she can be the one to walk away. That's the explanation she gives me anyway, as we pull into the parking lot of Magic Beans. We both know that if Jonah calls her she'll be rushing out to meet him, her memory conveniently lapsed until his next indiscretion.

Here's the thing. I'm probably more anxious to see Jonah than Christy will ever be. Every time she mentions his name, I feel a jolt of fiery rage mixed with ice-cold certainty that I can't let the attack on Dart go unchecked. The hot-cold dichotomy creates a fog that obscures rational thought; everything is blurred but the razor-sharp clarity that Jonah will pay.

But I can't tell Christy any of it. Just like I can't tell Haley that Austin is some kind of powerful creature who can bring back animals from the dead. I wouldn't know where to start.

Christy reaches under her seat and pulls out a thick volume with frayed edges, and I'm brought back to the moment.

"Tell me that's not what I think it is."

She smiles for the first time since she picked me up. "You're not still freaked out about the whole witchcraft thing? It's not like I'm going to make you do the spell, after you fainted and everything. I can do this one by myself."

I grab the book from her, my hand shaking slightly. It's not like the last spell worked. I mean, Christy and Jonah weren't exactly a match for the ages. And I know I wasn't imagining Austin flirting with me today; Haley's romance can't be going anywhere good. And then there's me and Blake. Talk about a disaster.

The book is heavier than it looks, and I nearly drop it.

"Careful!" Christy reaches between us. "Delia will kill me if something happens to this. She swears it's the real deal."

"She probably bought it at a swap meet for ten bucks. I wouldn't worry about it too much if I were you."

Christy snatches the book back. "Just because you don't believe in magic doesn't mean it's not real."

I almost laugh. Christy uses the occult the same way I

use science, as an escape from the truth she's not ready to face.

I trail after Christy as she walks through the coffee shop. Matt grins at her from behind the counter. "Sunshine. Light. A face that brightens a room with a smile."

Christy waves and walks right past him. Matt fumbles with a carton of soy milk, splashing some on his blue apron. I don't bother saying hello. He may be a dork, but he's still a guy. My invisibility doesn't discriminate.

I follow Christy to a table in the corner. She already has the stupid book open and is flipping through it in earnest.

Haley comes out of Kimmy's office and walks toward us. "Cracking a book twice in three weeks has got to be some kind of record, right?" She gives me a hug, silently confirming that we're still okay.

"I found the perfect spell for Jonah." Christy looks up, eyes shining.

"Don't tell me you're even thinking of trying to get him back." Haley looks like she's ready to tackle Christy, if that's what it takes.

"Not even close." Christy points to the open page in front of her. "I'm going to banish him."

"What?" Haley and I say it in unison.

"There's a spell to banish your enemies. To trap their souls in the underworld."

Haley twists a long lock of blond hair. "Doesn't that seem a little extreme?"

Christy doesn't waiver. "After he hit on Brianna?" Her voice shakes a little on my name, and I know she wants revenge for more than just me. It's an effort not to tell her I've got it covered. But who am I to stop her from getting her own peace of mind? And if his soul is banished in the process, it's a bonus.

I take a seat next to Christy. "Let's do it."

Haley's eyes widen until she looks like a manga version of herself. "Seriously? I thought you didn't like this whole witchcraft thing. Aren't you the one who fainted last time?"

Christy brushes back a black wisp of hair from her eyes. "It's not like Jonah's soul had a chance anyway. He was already an evil bastard when we met him."

Haley sits down. "I thought you were only going to do white magic."

"This is white magic. We're ridding the earth of some serious evil." Christy shifts in her chair even as she tries to sound confident. "That's as good as it gets, right?"

Haley flashes me a skeptical glance. "You're not going to pass out again, are you?"

"No," I say, but I have no idea what to expect. Nana believed magic in my hands was dangerous, but I doubt this spell could be more dangerous than what I have in mind for Jonah. If there's a chance that Jonah could be banished with magic, it would be better for everyone.

Christy takes my hand and reaches out to Haley with the other. We hold hands in a circle. Haley squeezes my hand as Christy reads from the book.

"*Bane of all that is true. Come out of the weeds. Make your last strike. Your time on earth is at an end. A thousand years of otherworldly night.*"

I don't feel dizzy. At first, nothing is out of place. It's not until I realize that I can no longer hear Matt cleaning up behind the counter, or even Christy as she repeats the spell, that my pulse kicks into overdrive. The fact that the room is devoid of sound is the only warning I get before the entire room goes pitch black.

Crap. It occurs to me, too late, that *I* might be considered an evil creature who should be banished from earth, and I wonder if the spell really did work. But then the room comes back into focus, everything and everyone immobile, lost in silence.

I wait for something to happen. For someone to move in the stillness. At first there's nothing, just a frozen moment in time, stretching into a hollow void.

The movement comes from behind me. I let go of Haley and Christy's hands and get up from the table. When I turn around, everyone remains still. Matt's hand hovers over a notepad, his eyes locked on Christy even as his pen presses the paper.

There's a flash of silver dancing in the air to his left. Then the fairy tale princess is there, her indigo eyes sparkling.

"Are you Danu?" I ask as she walks toward me, her arms outstretched.

"So you know me now, do you? A short-lived peace, then."

"What do you want from me?" It comes out as a stutter.

"That is the curse of being both beautiful and

powerful, isn't it? Everyone wants something from you." Her smile is sad. I notice that she doesn't deny she wants something. "Come with me."

She takes my hands and there's another flash of silver light. The coffee shop falls away, and we stand in a damp green field. An icy wind blows around us, and I recognize the large, moss-covered rocks that seem to grow right out of the ground.

"Better," she says, turning her face up to the gathering clouds. Thunder rolls across the sky in the distance.

"Why are we here?" I ask.

She sighs. "You are the seventh generation of the Seventh Daughters. Your destiny has been foretold."

I'm not sure how to tell her that I've never really believed in destiny. I try anyway. "I'm more of a 'from chaos comes order,' logic-and-reason kind of girl." As I say the words, I almost believe them.

She laughs. "You don't believe in fate?"

My answer is quick. "How can anything be fated when there are infinite choices? The mathematical probabilities are against it." It's a perfectly rational thought, but sounds hollow even to me. What if I can't stop what's coming?

"Perhaps your choices are just different paths, all leading to the same place."

I wait for her to say more. She doesn't.

"So what's my fate, then?" At least I'll see it coming.

Her eyes are weary. "The war with the Sons ends with you."

That doesn't sound so bad. Promising, even. "That's good, right?"

Danu looks off into the distance. A huge wire-haired dog lopes down the hill toward us. She eyes it warily. "Not necessarily."

"Since when is the end to a war a bad thing?"

She takes my hand again. "When you're on the losing side."

As the dog gets closer, I see it's some type of wolfhound. It's even bigger than it looked from a distance, its lips curled back to reveal sharp teeth. A long line of drool hangs from its lower lip.

Danu squeezes my hand just as a flash of lightning streaks across the sky. I blink, and then I'm back in the coffee shop, still sitting at the table, hands joined with Christy and Haley.

Christy finishes the spell, smiling across the table from me. "See? It's no big deal, right?"

I laugh. I can't stop.

"What?" Christy lets go of my hand, not hiding her hurt expression.

How do I begin to explain the bizarre series of events that is now my life? Me, the girl for whom every question had a rational answer. "I'm sorry, Christy. I'm not laughing at you." I struggle to come up with a credible lie. "I was just imagining what Jonah was doing when he got zapped."

Christy smiles. "I hope we ruined a date with that Parker girl."

Haley doesn't laugh. She's watching me closely, still holding my hand. "Did something feel weird to you?"

"When?"

"During the spell. For a second, I don't know, it just felt weird. And I thought I saw something. Like a bright light. Did you see it?"

I shake my head, but the movement feels transparent even as I do it.

Haley takes the book from Christy and starts flipping through it.

Christy stands up and stretches. I don't have to look to know that Matt is staring at her from across the room. "I feel better already."

"What do you think of Matt?" I ask Christy.

She shrugs. "He's cute. Kind of like a bohemian puppy." This sounds like a compliment, but coming from Christy, it's the death knell to any future romance. Christy doesn't date puppies. She prefers wolves.

Haley looks up from the book. I know I should say something about Austin, but I'm not sure what I should say exactly. It's not like I can tell her that her boyfriend has some kind of freaky powers. But since he brought my horse back from the dead, there's probably nothing to worry about.

Then there's the part where I'm pretty sure he wanted to hook up with me. There's no good way to tell her that.

"What?" Haley's turquoise eyes look right through me, like she knows I'm keeping secrets and she's just waiting for me to cave.

"Can I see the book?" I take it from her and place it in my bag. Maybe Christy will forget about it if it disappears for a while.

I head over to the counter. I have to tap Matt on the shoulder to get his attention. He's about to look away, but I grab his arm. "You know Christy, right?"

"Huh?" His eyes find her automatically, though it's got to be hard for him to see through his combed-forward and sprayed layers of hair. "Why? Did she say something?"

It's weird to hear Matt talking in English as opposed to Haiku. "Not exactly. Have you ever broken a girl's heart before?" I don't know why I bother asking. It's pretty unlikely that Matt has even had a girlfriend. Girls like tortured artists and all, but somehow I don't think there's a large pool of spoken word groupies.

He's still watching Christy. "What kind of question is that?"

"I don't know. Could you try being more of an asshole?"

"Why would I do that?"

"I'm trying to help you out here." I don't know how to explain it. "Just forget I said anything."

I'm about to walk away when Matt stops me. "Wait. Are you saying that Christy would like me better if I wasn't so—"

"Nice." We both say at once. He actually looks at me then and for a second it feels like he might even see me.

His lips curve into a goofy smile. "I might be able to do the whole bad-boy thing."

Christy and Haley walk up behind me. "Did you order the usual?" Haley asks.

Matt's expression changes when he sees Christy. For a second his eyes go all googly, and then I can practically see him remember. He glares from across the counter. Well, he tries to glare. Mostly he narrows his eyes and looks like he's going to throw up.

"Are you okay?" Christy asks.

"Who's asking?" Oh God. Matt does a bad New York accent. Like he's seen one too many mafia movies.

Christy steps back. "Why are you talking so weird?" It's saying something that Matt's gangster voice is stranger than speaking in verse.

Matt curls his upper lip. "If you don't like it, you can go screw yourself."

Christy's jaw drops, her lips curving into an O.

I try not to laugh, but a snort comes out anyway. Haley steps behind the counter and starts making our drinks, since it's obvious that gangster Matt isn't going to do it. Christy grabs my arm and guides me over to the stuffed cow.

"Omigod," she says, her voice a hurried whisper. "Remember how you were asking me about Matt earlier?"

I nod.

"Don't you think he's kind of hot?"

This time it's my mouth that falls open.

TWENTY-SEVEN

I call Marcy twice to check up on Dart while Christy flirts
with Matt at the counter and Haley gets stuck making coffee for a group of U.R.D. students who come in for the
two-for-one lattes.

For now, I have a moment of peace. No crazy attraction to boys who can only cause me heartache, no homi-
cidal demigods, and not a drop of blood in sight. If it
weren't for the pang of emptiness in my gut, I could almost
believe that the world is normal.

The pain in my stomach eases and I know I'm not
alone anymore. I stare down at my coffee, wanting to pre-
serve the illusion of normalcy for just a few seconds more.
The warm thrum that fills me isn't entirely unwelcome,
but it also means that I have to stop pretending.

Blake sits across from me without saying a word, casting a shadow across my coffee.

"How'd you find me?" I ask, still not looking up.

"It's not so hard these days. Like having built-in GPS."

I meet his gaze then, struck by his perfect bone structure and seductive smile. Not that I'm complaining. I mean, if I have to be wrapped up with someone like this, it doesn't hurt that he's beautiful. And I might even like him a little bit. Something else to torture myself about if I end up killing him.

"So you can find me? Just like that?"

He shrugs. "I'm here, aren't I?"

"Can I do the same thing?"

He sits back in his chair, his knee touching mine under the table. "I don't know. Have you ever tried?" I shake my head, trying to ignore the rush of longing that accompanies the contact with his leg. Blake runs a hand through his hair. "I guess we should talk."

Does he know about Dart already? About Austin? Does he know I plan to kill Jonah? Maybe he's here to talk me out of it. "Can it wait?" I ask. "I kind of like pretending that my life is completely normal."

Blake crosses his arms and very deliberately pulls his leg away from mine. "You shouldn't bother. There's nothing normal about you."

I take a sip of my latte. "You really do need to work on your moves."

His answering smile is meant to placate me. "You keep saying that, but I think I'm doing all right."

"On what planet is calling a girl abnormal considered smooth?"

He sets his chin in his hands. "When I said you aren't normal, I meant that you are extraordinary."

"Oh." Our eyes hold for a minute, and I have to stop myself from reaching out to touch him again.

Blake stands up, rubbing his hands across the denim that covers his thighs. "You want to get out of here? There's something I want to show you."

I glance back to where Christy is laughing at something Matt said. My work here is done.

We drive toward the beach. "Back to the scene of the crime?"

"Something like that."

I keep sneaking glimpses of Blake. I don't feel the rush of heat and anger that I'd expected. Maybe it's because Dart is alive. Maybe it's because Blake isn't Jonah. Still, I know better than to trust that I won't find myself consumed with a heady mix of power and rage at some point. It's like there's a bomb ticking away somewhere deep inside me. Too bad there's no digital readout of the countdown, so I'll know when it's going to detonate.

We get out of the car and walk along the base of the cliff. The firepit is a dark pile of ash, barely visible in the moonlight. We stop in front of it.

"Do you trust me?" Blake asks.

"I'm not sure. I want to."

"I wanted to show you this when we came here before." He blushes. "We got a little distracted." He walks up to the small crevice in the cliff and sticks his arm inside. He ducks and disappears into the side of the cliff.

"Blake?"

"Just try it," he says from somewhere on the other side, though he sounds far way.

I inspect the cliff more closely. The crack can't be more than six inches wide at the widest point. And it doesn't appear to go anywhere. I can't see anything but rock. "How did you do that?"

"You just have to trust it."

I tentatively stick a hand inside the crack. It fits well enough. I push my arm in further, stopping when I feel Blake's fingers close around my wrist.

"Close your eyes," he says.

He pulls me to him, letting his arms close around me.

The air changes. The heavy ocean breeze disappears altogether, chased away by a bone-chilling wind. I hear water, but it's no longer the rhythmic sound of waves crashing against the beach—it's the steady pounding of a rushing river.

Blake steps behind me, his hands clasped around my waist. "Whenever you're ready," he says.

I open my eyes, fighting a wave of nausea. We're standing on a stark bluff, flat gray rock under our feet. The cliff we came through is a barren wall of rock behind us. At least fifty feet below, water rushes over rocks and stones, moonlight reflecting off the surface. Across the river is another rocky cliff, and behind it, more stark walls of rock, with waterfalls that carry more water down to the river. It's a bleak and unforgiving landscape, and it's breathtaking.

"Where are we?"

Blake leans over my shoulder. "I have no idea."

"You don't know?"

"I've been here a hundred times, and I'm not any closer to figuring it out than the first time I discovered it."

"How did you find it?"

"Promise not to laugh?"

I nod.

"I come to the beach a lot. I run in the dark along the cliffs, as fast as I want. One night I ran right up to the cliff and couldn't stop in time. I thought I was going to eat it. Instead, I went right through."

"It's amazing. Why did you want to show me?"

"I guess I just wanted someone else to see this."

"It's beautiful." It's true. Stark, cold, barren, but all of it works together to create a sense of awe.

We sit down on a large flat boulder and watch the river rush by for a while. I fold my knees up to my chest. "We need to talk."

"Do we have to do this now?" he asks, not as eager as he appeared at the coffee shop.

"Dart was attacked today."

"Dart?"

"My horse. His throat was cut."

"You're sure?"

He can't hide the shock in his eyes. He didn't know. I let out a breath. There's a certain relief knowing that Blake wasn't involved in the attack. As if I couldn't be sure until now.

"Marcy thought it was a mountain lion."

I feel the hope rise in his chest. "Was it?"

I shake my head. "It was Jonah."

"You're sure?"

"The cuts were jagged, like Jonah's knife. And Jonah was there, with Parker." I feel tears welling up as I remember Dart lying on the floor of the stall. "I know it was Jonah." And I'm going to kill him.

Blake reaches out to rub my shaking shoulders. "I'm sorry, but let's think about this. Jonah's a hothead, but it still doesn't sound like something he would do. He attacked you because it's what he's trained for. He believes in the war against magic. He wouldn't have any reason to hurt your horse, unless your horse is some kind of magic creature. He's not, is he?"

I pull away from him. "Don't defend Jonah. I saw him just before it happened. He meant to hurt me. It was in his eyes." My anger mixes with Blake's emotion, which feels something like compassion. It doesn't help. I don't want Blake's sympathy. I want to be angry. I need to be, to do what I have to do.

"I won't defend him, Brianna. Don't you get it yet?" Blake's eyes sparkle, not with otherworldly silver but with something far more potent. "I will always choose you. I already have." His lips curve into a melancholy smile and my heart feels like it will break in two.

I finally loosen my grip on the dark emotions I've held so tightly since this afternoon. I let myself feel what he feels. The certainty. I grab onto it for dear life. It's the only thing keeping me from being sucked into a pit of Dart's crimson blood.

He brushes my cheek with his fingertips. "I know you haven't made up your mind about any of this." My skin heats beneath his touch. It's a stark contrast to the cold air that moves around us.

"What if I can't stop it? What if I end up killing you? It feels so much bigger than me sometimes. I don't know if I'll even have a choice." I finally admit the truth. To him. To myself.

"You always have choices, Brianna. No one can take that from you. You're the only one who can decide *how* this ends."

How, not whether. "It has to end though, doesn't it?"

I hate that I even think this now. What if no matter what I choose, all paths are taking me to the same place?

Blake doesn't say anything at first. He leans forward and presses his lips to my forehead. Gently, so I feel just the lightest sweep of his lips against my skin. Then he lets his head fall until his forehead rests against my own. "Not if I have anything to say about it."

I bring my hand to his mouth, tracing the line of his lips with my fingertip. His mouth opens, just enough for the tip of his tongue to tease the pad of my finger, sending a shock of fire through my skin until every part of my body is heated through. I trail my finger down his chin to his neck, to the opening at the collar of his shirt. His breath is coming harder, mirroring my own.

Then his hand closes around my wrist, stopping me. "Are you sure?" he asks, as if he can't feel the answering desire that rages inside me, mixing with his own.

I cover his hand and reach for my bracelet. I undo the clasp and let it fall on the rock. "What do you think?"

His sucks in a breath. "You have no idea how beautiful you are, do you?"

I close the tiny distance between us until our lips meet. His mouth covers mine, and then we're lying back on the boulder. The cold stone against my back only serves to intensify the fire inside as we kiss.

I pull Blake closer, my hands wrapping around him, every touch calculated to bring him nearer. I curl a leg around his thigh, pressing, pulling, pushing against him.

The heat of his skin comes through his shirt, and the fabric becomes an intolerable intrusion. He helps me pull the shirt over his head, and it's my turn to gasp. My fingers slide from his neck to his belly button, forging a tentative path along his stomach. "You know you're kind of beautiful yourself."

"You think so?" A dimple appears on his cheek. He kisses me again. A deep kiss that spreads through me until I'm not certain where my craving stops and Blake's begins. We are of one mind, pushing each other forward, so that for a few minutes at least, we might both be blissfully whole.

"Ahem."

We both sit up and spin toward the sound. Austin stands just in front of us, his hands nestled casually in the front pockets of his jeans, his lips curved up in a crooked smile. "Mind if I join you?" His perfect accent makes the question sound almost innocent.

Almost.

TWENTY-EIGHT

Blake grabs his shirt from the rock beside him. "How did you find us?" Is it my imagination, or do Austin's eyes travel along Blake's torso as Blake pulls on his shirt?

"Quite by accident, I assure you."

"How did you get here?" Blake's emotions shift from a mix of surprise and anger at being interrupted to a more cautious suspicion.

"Same as you, I expect. Through the crevasse."

"No one knows about this place."

"You might want to reevaluate that." Austin looks at me and winks.

I scoot closer to Blake. I haven't told Blake about Austin, about what he can do. Austin looks completely relaxed, perfectly at home among the rocks and rushing water. Even the cold wind doesn't seem to bother him.

"You've been here before?" I ask. What *is* Austin?

"You could say that. It's my home."

"I thought you were from England."

He laughs at that. "That's probably a crime in some parts. Ireland, actually. Although I have spent time in England." His eyes meet mine, so dark they're nearly black. "So, does all this small talk mean you're not interested in my joining you?"

Blake stands up, stepping in front of the rock. "You could say that. Or do we have to spell it out for you? She's not interested."

I stand up. "I can handle this."

Austin laughs. "Yes, by all means, let the girl make her own decisions. She might surprise you." As he talks, his eyes bore into me, drawing me in.

Blake reaches for my arm but I shake him off.

"Good girl." Austin's voice is sticky-sweet caramel.

Everything is a blur. Like I'm walking in a thick, hot fog. Austin holds out his hand. The pull is strong. My hand moves toward Austin's on its own volition. It's not a choice. It's a necessity.

"Brianna?" There's a voice in the distance, far, far away. I almost don't hear it but it's there, tugging at the knot of confusion in my heart.

Austin's low voice thumps through me again. "That's it. You're almost there."

I hesitate. "No." The word echoes in my head, and I'm not even sure I've really said it. But the fog in my head dissipates and I can feel Blake again—a sense of relief that's mine and his both.

My hand drops to my side. I turn around and run the short distance to Blake. He pulls me against him, part protector and part possessor.

"What the hell was that? Can you use Compulsion?" Blake glares at Austin.

Austin laughs, but his eyes are angry. "Trust me, half-breed, you don't want a demonstration of my powers." His hard gaze slides to me. "You're a feisty one, aren't you? No wonder he's keeping you alive."

I want to repeat Blake's question. And *what the hell is Austin?*

"Leave her alone." Blake's voice is strong, but I feel his wariness as it swims through me.

"Easier said than done, I'm afraid. Magic practically spills out of her. It's quite a turn-on, isn't it?"

Blake starts to move forward but I grab his shoulder, holding him back. Blake glares at Austin. "You're more than a breeder."

I turn to Blake. "He's a breeder?" Blake hasn't told me everything by a long shot. I feel like I don't know either of them.

Blake nods. "He has the Killian gene, but we weren't able to pinpoint a generation."

"The Killian gene, is that what you call it?" Austin steps closer to us. "What a piece of work is Man. Always looking for a natural explanation for the unnatural, aren't you?"

He's just summed up the last three years of my life. I've spent them looking for a rational explanation for things that never had one, trying to overcome my birthright by pretending it doesn't exist.

I don't want to contemplate what other secrets Blake has kept from me, so I turn on Austin. "What are you?"

"I imagine that depends on whom you ask." Austin's smile is eerily sweet.

"I'm asking *you*."

"I'm just like you, Juliet."

The nickname holds no magic for me. If anything, my stomach feels slightly queasy. "You're a demigod?"

"God, warlock, angel, demon. Would not a rose by any other name smell as sweet?" He puts his hands back in his pockets. We might as well be talking about the weather. "Of course, you're only half god," he adds. "I'm the real deal."

He turns away and walks toward the cliff wall, his back to us. "Enough about me. It's clear you want to be alone. Might I suggest you take yourselves elsewhere?"

"What is this place?" I call after him. I'm not nearly satisfied by Austin's answers.

"Avernus," he answers, just before he disappears through the crack in the wall.

Once Austin is gone, the cold wind stops. The sound of the river below grows louder.

Blake pauses. "Something's not right."

There's a sound from behind a large rock by the edge of the bluff. The growl is so low I almost miss it.

Blake disappears from my side and for an instant I am alone in the wilderness, looking around for the creature that made the sound. A thick fog rolls in, covering the ground so quickly that I'm disoriented. I can barely see the cliff behind me, the gray rocks fading in and out through the fog. I can't see to the edge where the little stretch of land falls away to the river below. The ground just melts into the mist.

The bright silver light flares next to me. Blake reappears, illuminated in silver. I want to touch him. I back away instead, my instincts recognizing my natural enemy even as my brain registers that it's Blake.

The growl is louder now, and much too close. I reach for any bit of magic, trying to call back the chill wind that blew earlier. The wind is long gone. I try again, focusing on the water that condenses in the fog, but the fog continues to churn around me with a mind of its own, so thick that I'm nearly blind. I stomp the ground, assuring myself that I am still in the here and now, not lost in the mists of magic. Not that there is any magic here for me. I'm on my own.

I feel the beast's approach before I see anything. Blake does too. His adrenaline combines with mine so that I'm even more anxious. He leans against me, urging me backward as a large shadow appears in front of us.

I reach behind my back, searching for the solid wall of the cliff, not finding anything but empty air. In front of us, the fog dissipates enough for me to make out the silhouette of three massive heads pushing toward us. Not one, but three creatures. Blake pushes with all his weight, forcing me back faster as I try to get my bearings.

My back hits the wall of the cliff hard, which

momentarily knocks the breath out of me. I run my hands along the rock, feeling for the crevice that will take us back to the beach. Blake urges me to the left, and I continue to move as the shadowy figures draw closer.

The three animals snap their teeth and all bark at once, in perfect unison. As they emerge more fully from the fog, I can just make out their features—three wire-haired wolfhounds, gray heads weaving and drooling in perfect synch.

The middle dog lunges forward, baring his teeth. It leaps at me with a speed that's unexpected given the dog's massive size. Blake braces himself against me, ready to take the bulk of the blow, his sword raised. I jump to the side, though there's no way to avoid the massive creature. As I do, my hand and shoulder fall into a hollow gap. I throw my arms around Blake and pull him with me through the crevice. We land hard in the sand.

I scramble to my feet, facing the cliff, waiting for the hounds to plunge through. Blake is already up, his jeweled sword in his hands. We stand like that for several minutes, our bodies frozen, our breath coming in shallow pants. The heavy, salty air blows around me and I breathe it in and out, letting it fill me with power. My arsenal is stocked and I itch to unleash it.

The animals never cross over. Blake stalks forward, his sword raised. As he walks in front of me to investigate the cliff, my outstretched hand follows him, keeping him in my sights.

Blake senses the shift in me. Tied as we are, it isn't like we can sneak up on each other. He stops his examination of the cliff and turns to face me, his eyes flashing silver. "What are you waiting for?" It's both a warning and a dare.

It's so much easier to see Blake for the killer he is as he stands bathed in light, the sharp sword raised. Every beautiful inch of him glows with dark power. His eyes are the eyes of a killer, one who'll stop at nothing until the enemy is vanquished. His muscled body is designed for one purpose: to chase down and overpower the weak.

But I am in no way weak. My survival instinct implores me to eliminate the danger, to take out the enemy. My eyes travel to the sharp blade in his hands, and I can't help but recall the blood that flowed from Dart's neck and throat. It should be enough. I should be able to let loose with a wall of fire.

But there's something else, something harder to grasp. Whether it's the product of the bonding of our souls or something else, it stops me from pulling the trigger.

Blake disappears in a burst of light. One second he's there, poised to fight, and the next he's gone.

I blink, adjusting to the darkness now that the silver light is gone.

There's a flash behind me. Before I can turn around, Blake's arms close around my chest, pinning my arms to my side, the blade pointed at my heart.

"I told you," he says. "No hesitation."

I stare at the knife, the tip pressed close enough to my chest that a thin line of blood trickles down my skin. I let my veins fill with water, drawing on the ocean waves and freezing from the inside, until Blake is forced to step away from the icy cold along my skin.

He laughs as he watches me shiver. "Nice." Then he disappears again, but it's only a second before he reappears in the same spot. Not Blake the warrior god, Blake the boy whose face I've memorized.

I collapse into the sand, still shivering even though the power I just used is no longer anywhere near the surface.

Blake looks back at the cliff wall. "I don't think they can cross over to our world." He ignores the fact that I posed at least as much threat to him as the giant dogs. "We can't go back there."

"No kidding." I'm more than happy to limit our conversation to the monsters on the other side of the cliff. It's far easier to deal with that than with the monster lurking in my heart. "What were those things?"

"I'm not one hundred percent certain. I'm pretty sure they're Arawn's hounds."

"In English?"

"The guardians of the gates to the underworld."

"Tell me you mean that metaphorically."

Blake sits next to me in the sand. His arms come around me, bringing a welcome warmth. "According to ancient mythology, Avernus is a gateway. Legend is that the dead passed through Avernus by crossing a river, and there's definitely one of those there. The dogs are meant to keep the dead from crossing back to the living."

"So that place is the gateway to hell?"

"Not just hell. All the mystical worlds."

"If it is what you say."

"It is."

"Then what does that make Austin?"

Blake laughs. Not the reaction I expect. He stops when he sees my face. "You're not joking? I thought you realized this before."

"Realized what?"

"Where did you think the gods came from?" Blake sets his hands on my shoulders and waits. Even with the heat that flows through his hands, the temperature seems to drop ten degrees.

It shouldn't be a surprise. I'm the descendant of a crazy goddess, after all. I'm a mercenary in a vengeful army. Beautiful poison.

"You've been there before," I say. "To the Underworld."

"I've never been down to the water, just along the rocks. I've never seen anything there before tonight. Just rocks and water and that icy wind. Not a living thing."

"But we're not dead."

"Not yet, anyway."

I can't look him in the eye. We both know how close I came to losing it. What he doesn't know is that it's happened before. Eventually, I won't be able to stop it. My emotions will win. Fire will beat out cold logic every time.

"Don't worry about it, okay?" he says.

"I could have killed you."

"You didn't. And you broke the most important rule—you have to strike before we realize an attack is coming."

"Show off." I push his shoulder.

"I liked that thing with the cold. Can you make it happen faster?"

"I don't know."

He moves his hand up and down my side, from my waist to my hip, chasing the last lingering chills from my body. "We should go," he says, but he's already pulling me to him as we lie back on the sand. I turn to face him, letting my hands run across his chest as I lean down to kiss him.

"Now, where were we?" I ask.

He laughs a little as I kiss his throat. When I lick the lobe of his ear, he shivers. My fingers twist through his hair and I kiss him, deep and slow. His hand brushes along my neck to my collarbone, sending little shocks of lightning along the path of his fingers. His fingers swoop to the hollow of my throat and along my shoulder, sliding down my arm. Then he freezes.

The fire inside him is gone in a heartbeat, replaced with a chill I can feel in my bones. My eyes blink open. His eyes hold only fear, icy and sharp.

"What? The dogs?"

He moves his hand along my wrist. "Brianna." His voice is barely a whisper. "Where's your bracelet?"

TWENTY-NINE

I pace in a circle. "We have to go back in!"

Blake's hands are both in his hair now. "We're no match for those hellhounds. They won't let us out a second time."

"What difference does it make? I'm not going to make it to my birthday without that bracelet." My frustration and Blake's combine, which only makes me pace faster, as if that will somehow help.

Blake grabs my arm, pulling me to an abrupt halt. "You can't risk going back there."

I pull away and keep walking. "I can't risk not going back."

"It's only a few more days, right? We can keep you hidden somehow."

Where have I heard that before? "How? Jonah will be looking for any opportunity to expose me. And he won't let it go. He came to the ranch today on crutches, for

God's sake. You think he's going to wait around until I turn seventeen and get all my powers?"

"Jonah we can handle. Those things in there are purebred creatures of the underworld."

"I'm going back."

"You can't." Blake grabs my shoulder. "It's too dangerous."

"For some, maybe. Not me. After all, I'm a creature of the underworld, right?"

Blake's face is serious. "There's more than just hell down there, Brianna. And you're also half human. That's the more important half."

"Says the guy committed to ridding the world of all magic except, of course, his own."

Blake smiles. "I never said I was perfect."

"Why didn't you just kill me and get it over with?" His sword had been close enough to draw blood. I start to move around him. "Or if the wolfhounds get me, it'll be that much easier for you, right?"

He grabs my hand. "Here's the thing. You can't help what you are any more than I can. My whole life has been dictated by my place in the Circle. Every important decision in my life has always been made for me."

Including this one. So I'm just another choice that's been forced on him. The ache in my gut shouldn't be there now that he's touching me. I know he feels it too, because his eyes narrow.

"Let's just forget it," I say.

He reaches for my chin, looking into my eyes. "Oh hell, I've screwed this up, haven't I?"

I try to shake my head, but he holds me still.

His thumb traces a circle on my cheek. "I'm sorry if I suck at this. I've never had a girlfriend before."

"I've been watching you for a year, and I don't think I've ever seen you without some girl hanging all over you."

"*Some* girl, not the same girl." I feel his frustration building, but then it stops. "Wait. You've been watching me?"

Whoops. I feel the blood rush to my cheeks. "It's not what you think. You were kind of a science project."

He grins. "For a year?"

"What about Portia?" I blurt.

"Portia? What about her?"

"Didn't you go out with her?"

"It was nothing."

"So tell me."

"She's Rush's daughter. Her mom is seventh generation too. You'd think that would give her some standing in the Circle, but she's only a first generation breeder. A one. The Circle can be cruel. I thought maybe I could help her improve her standing. We went out a few times. Before I saw you."

"You were with her after the poker game." I can't stop the black emotion that swirls inside. I don't want to feel it. Still, it comes, an inky sea teeming with bloodsucking parasites, latching on and not letting go.

Blake's anger is there too, melding with mine. "What

did you see, Brianna? I thought I could forget you if I just focused on someone else. I tried. I couldn't even give her a ride home. Since the night you walked into the kitchen at the party, there hasn't been anyone else."

My stomach churns with a dizzy cocktail of jealousy and indignation. "What about the Boobsie Twins? Sierra? Kendra?"

"Now you're mad about girls that I talked to before we ever went out? Because if we're going to go there, I seem to recall having to chase you out of a dark bedroom or two."

"Once." My voice is quiet.

"You still want him. I've felt it."

I want to tell him that Austin means nothing. He might be a god, but everything he made me feel was fake. Smoke and mirrors. Yet my pride won't let me tell Blake the truth.

"Maybe it has something to do with the fact that it didn't take Austin over a year to notice me while he dated virtually every available girl in Rancho Domingo," I say. "Or that he didn't turn away when I smiled. Maybe it's because he didn't forget that he was actually introduced to me at least six times."

Blake's hand is in his hair. "You know that's not fair."

"It's still the truth."

"So now you blame me for the power you wielded with that damn bracelet? In case you haven't noticed, Austin can make you feel things that aren't even true."

"Like this damn bond?" I want to take the words back as soon as I say them, but I can't.

Blake's anger and my sadness converge into a numb depression that settles in my chest like it's going to stay awhile. I know I should stop. But I want to hurt Blake, to pay for the fifty-seven little hurts he's inflicted on me.

"At least when Austin kissed me, it wasn't with the knowledge that we would end up in a twisted soul bond that could only end in death."

"Is that what you think?" Blake's voice is so low, I feel it more than I hear it.

"You knew what I was. Maybe you didn't believe it at first, but at some point, you knew exactly what you were doing."

My arrow hits the mark. Trouble is, it's hard to tell whether the pain that rolls me in nauseating waves is his pain or my own. It hardly matters. We're a match made in hell.

Blake doesn't say anything more. He turns and walks back to the parking lot. I'm free to go back to Avernus and look for my bracelet, to be mauled by a trio of hellhounds if that's what I want. But I won't give Blake the satisfaction. If I'm going to die, he's going to have to be the one to pull the trigger. I'm not letting him out of this that easy.

Blake doesn't say anything when I slide into the passenger seat. He just stares straight ahead and drives me home. I sit not six inches from him. Without my bracelet.

And I've never felt more invisible.

THIRTY

I get ready for school, even though I feel naked without my bracelet. I'm not afraid. Blake's already introduced me to Micah and Jeremy, and I doubt I'll run into Jonah at R.D. High. But it doesn't really matter—I want Jonah to come after me. It will save me having to hunt him down myself.

Still, it's awkward when I walk into the kitchen and Dad tells me how nice I look today. I'm not sure how to react, so I just grab a muffin from the box on the counter and pretend I don't hear him.

The walk from the parking lot into school is more bizarre. I'm used to guys never looking at my face, never looking at me. It's a shock when Mark Briggs grins at me and waggles his eyebrows as I get out of my car. "Looking good, Paxton!"

"Dude, you're smoking." Rob Schrader sidles up next

to Mark. The two have bonded over their mutual love of PlayStation and porn.

Not being noticed by guys like Rob and Mark has never been a problem for me. I walk by without acknowledging them. Welcome to the invisible zone, guys.

A low whistle assaults my ears with an ominous ring. I stop, the hair rising on the back of my neck. I'm torn between turning to look and forcing myself to keep walking. It's probably just a couple of dorks like Rob and Mark, feeling the need to publicly comment on my transformation.

I'm lying to myself. The fire that flows through my veins tells me everything I need know.

I turn my head to the right, craning my neck toward a cherry-red truck with custom black stripes. It takes up nearly two parking spaces with its oversized tires and huge wheel base. Jonah Timken leans against the bumper, sipping from a cardboard coffee cup. A pair of crutches rests against the tailgate. So much for Christy's banishment spell.

I turn all the way around and march toward him. The fire inside me is already tickling my fingers, and I want retribution.

Jonah looks up from the coffee. His Adam's apple slides up and down as he swallows. For a second I have the upper hand. I shouldn't hesitate. I should burn him up now, before he realizes what's coming. I only have to picture Dart lying in a pool of his own blood.

But I don't attack him. Maybe it's because Dart is alive. Maybe it's because Jonah's relaxed body language tells me he's not here to fight. A small part of me hopes it's because I'm not the same kind of monster he is.

Jonah's eyes are thirsty, despite the drink in his hand.

I stop a few feet in front of him. "What are you doing here? Slumming? Shouldn't you be out getting your rich girlfriend wasted or something?"

Jonah can't hide the surprise in his voice. "Where's your disguise, bandia?"

"Who am I hiding from? You and I don't have secrets."

His smile is sickening. "What game are you playing?"

My eyes go to his right hand, remembering how it closed around my neck at Joe's party. I have to fight not to back away from him. "I don't need to hide from you. I'm not as weak as you think."

He laughs at that. "I never thought you were weak. The magic that surrounds you is crazy strong. It's what makes you such a hot mess."

Bile rises in my throat as his gaze rakes up and down my body. I've never wanted to disappear more. I paste on a smile of my own.

"I think I get why Blake wants to keep you around for a while. I may decide to do the same once he's out of the picture."

"What, you don't want to kill me now?" He's the worst sort of coward. "Of course not. Why would you go after someone who could burn you to a crisp? Defenseless animals are more your thing, is that it?"

Jonah sets down his coffee and reaches for the crutches. "Animals? I don't know what you're talking about. Sounds a little kinky, but I'm open-minded." He licks his lips. "You and I have some unfinished business."

"You won't touch me again." I summon as much strength as I can.

Jonah laughs like I've said something funny. "You're not mine to kill. It's only dumb luck Blake found you first. You think that means something, but it's just your DNA seeking out a mate. Soon it'll be my touch that makes you burn. My soul that mates with yours. My hand that spills your blood."

My stomach heaves at his words, the muffin threatening to come back up. "How do you know about the bond?"

His smile gets wider. "You were born with the same curse we all were, this sick connection that forces us together and tears us apart. I didn't realize Blake got to you first until he jumped me. Blake was smart to seal the deal before you caught on. I only wish I'd found you first. I bet you're pretty hot in the sack."

I know Blake didn't bond with me on purpose, even though it's what I accused him of myself. But Jonah makes it sound so much more twisted. And if Blake wanted me dead, I would be dead by now.

Jonah hobbles forward on his crutches, closing the gap between us. "We didn't think there were any bandia left. And then there was that blue fire. I'm surprised Blake didn't kill you first thing, after what you did to his house. But here you are, dripping with magic and sexy as hell. My money's on you—I can hardly wait until the bond is broken and you're up for grabs again." He makes an obscene gesture with his hand.

I'm filled with a mixture of hope and dread. "You know how to break the bond?"

Jonah raises an eyebrow. "I understand it's quite painful."

"How?"

"It's simple. One of you dies."

Not the answer I'm hoping for, but about what I expect. "If I die, you'll never get near me." Not a great option, but an option.

"Who said anything about killing *you*?"

He can't be implying what I think. "Blake is one of your Circle."

Jonah shakes his head. "You think *he* cares about alliances? If he did, he would have told the Circle about you. He kept you to himself, assuming you'd be dead before any of us even knew you existed."

I don't want to hear this. I want to cover my ears and sing at the top of my lungs like a five-year-old. I can't let him see how much he's affecting me, but I'm shaking with rage and something darker.

"Even if you somehow killed Blake. I would never let you near me," I tell him. "I would sooner die than bond with you."

He shrugs. "It's your call." He winks at me, then turns back toward his monster truck, leaning on his crutches.

My blood is hot. A fireball appears in my hand before I can even think to conjure it. It's just there, as natural as a sneeze or a tear. The part of me that wants to take him out is right there with it, as much a part of who I am as breathing. But there are people here, bystanders who've done nothing to me.

I take a breath and start counting. 5. 25. 125. 625. Better.

Before Jonah can take a step, I send the blue flames sailing over his head into the bed of his truck. Instant car-b-que.

"What the hell?" He scrambles to get away from the truck.

"That's for Dart."

"Who the hell is Dart?"

I close the distance and slap him. Hard. "If you so much as go near my horse again, it won't be your truck that's burn-ing."

A group of students gathers, staring at the fire as it grows bigger. A siren wails in the distance. The first bell rings. I step around Jonah and walk the rest of the way toward school. Mark Briggs starts to say something to me, but wisely shuts up when he sees the look in my eyes.

I'm smiling by the time I get to class. I didn't kill Jonah. I should be disappointed, but instead I'm hopeful. If Jonah can live, maybe Blake can too.

My first four classes go by without incident. I catch a few curious glances from some of the guys, but no one tries to approach me. Which is fine with me, because my life is complicated enough at the moment. I meet Haley at her locker just as Braden Finley comes by for his daily ritual of asking Haley out to lunch.

"Hey, gorgeous." Braden opens his locker without looking at her. When he shuts it and leans against it, he grins at Haley appreciatively. Then his eyes move past her. To me. "Who's your friend?"

Haley has to turn around to see who he's looking at. When she turns back to him, her cheeks are red. "You mean Brianna? Haven't you guys met?"

"I think I would remember meeting Brianna." He's talking to Haley but staring at me.

I can't stop the smile that grows until I'm sure I'm grinning at Braden Finley like an absolute fool. He raises his eyebrows speculatively. "A few of us are heading off campus for lunch. You should come."

Whoa. Braden just asked me to lunch. I'm not seriously considering saying yes—I know the game. I've seen it played out enough. I also know that Braden is currently dating Gia Davidson. And I have a boyfriend, even though it's kind of twisted and messed up at the moment. Still, it's nice to be asked. Really nice. I wonder if this is how Haley feels all the time. "Sorry," I say. "I have plans."

"Next time." Braden starts to walk off. As he walks past me, he leans in so close that his shoulder touches mine. Then he stops and whispers in my ear, "Don't make me wait too long." As he walks away, a laugh escapes my lips before I can stop it.

"What was that?" Haley stares at me like I'm an alien, complete with a third eye and slithery tentacles. Her expression slowly changes from disbelief to contemplation. "Do you think he's trying to make me jealous?"

I force myself to stop smiling. "Obviously."

Haley doesn't catch the hint of sarcasm in my response. "Is it bad that it's working?"

"I think that's the point."

"Yeah, you're probably right." She puts her hand on my shoulder. "Sorry about that."

"Sorry? Why?"

"It was kind of rude of him. Flirting with you to get to me. I mean it's not very nice for him to play with your feelings like that."

It's not enough that the only possible reason Braden Finley would flirt with me is to make Haley jealous. No, now she has to assume that my poor feelings are hurt because of course, I must have thought he was really flirting with me.

"What a jerk." I don't even try to conceal the sarcastic tone this time. "He must've gotten the idea from Austin."

Haley's lips twitch for a second before she can mask it. "What are you talking about?"

I shrug. "Well, it explains why Austin showed up at the ranch yesterday and tried to get me to go home with him. He must've assumed I'd tell you and then you'd be jealous."

Haley's eyes narrow to points. "You're lying. Austin doesn't need to make me jealous. Besides, he asked me to meet him at McMillan after school today."

"Austin is not who you think he is."

"I think I know who my own boyfriend is. It's you I'm starting to wonder about."

I close my eyes, instantly regretting calling Haley out. By the time I open them again, she's gone.

THIRTY-ONE

I fall back against a row of lockers, exhausted. I didn't mean for the stuff about Austin to come out like that.

"Jesus, Paxton." Sherri Milliken grabs my arm and pulls me down the hallway. "Are you trying to get yourself killed?"

"Let go of me."

"Where's your bracelet?"

"Why do you even care?" I'm not in the mood for a lecture.

"Because you're putting us all in danger. You think the Sons won't find you here? Hell, there might even be a few on campus."

"There's not."

"What do you mean, there's not?" She searches my face. Crap. I've said too much.

"Wait. You know who they are, don't you? I *knew* it. It's the only reason you survived the weekend."

I shake my head. "You're not wearing your talisman."

"That's different. I'm seventeen. I can control my powers. They can't tell what I am just by looking at me. You, on the other hand, are a flashing beacon of magic. You might as well be wearing a neon sign that says 'kill me now.'"

"Fine. I'll leave. As soon as you tell me what happens when I turn seventeen."

Sherri spins around in a circle, her arms wide. "You get to be beautiful." A group of guys stops a few feet away to watch her. "Well, you always got to be beautiful. But now people will notice. And it's fricking awesome! All those guys that wouldn't even look at you before will be drooling at your feet."

I'm not so sure it matters now. "Tell me about the power."

"Believe me, Brianna, beauty *is* power."

Was she always so shallow? "That's not what I meant."

Sherri rolls her eyes. "Okay, okay. I told Sasha we should tell you from the beginning. I knew what you were from the first day of ninth grade, when you walked into class with that fricking bracelet on. I couldn't believe it at first, because you looked amazing, like you weren't hiding at all. But the guys didn't notice. They didn't even look at you. It was like they didn't see you at all. Meanwhile, I looked like Supergeek."

"Tell me what happens."

"It's like you can feel it inside of you. Fire, water, air, even the earth. And then you want to use it. Almost like you have to."

I've felt it. In my veins. In my blood. How it wants to be unleashed. Has to be. "How do you control it?"

Sherri looks at me like I'm crazy. "It's part of who you are. Just embrace it, Paxton. It totally rocks. And you'll need it when the Sons find you again."

"You sound so certain they will."

"Oh, they will. Sasha says they date a lot of girls, always looking for potential breeders. And let's face it—we have the traits they're looking for."

"Traits?"

"Beauty, strength, power." Sherri glances over her shoulder at the group of guys hanging back to watch her. Watch *us*. "Our kind was almost exterminated. As far as the Sons were concerned, we were all dead. So they won't be expecting more of us." She eyes me skeptically. "Will they?"

"I wouldn't know." I clasp my hands in front of me, worrying my thumbs. She wants to blame me for outing us, but I'm not the one who started a magic blaze that took out two hundred homes. "How would I even know if I've found one?"

"You'll know. Supposedly, it's really hot when they touch you. It sounds amazing. I can't wait." She looks back over her shoulder at the group of guys and waves her fingers. "Not that I'm not enjoying the trial and error."

"Then what?"

Sherri shrugs. "Then you do what you were born to do and reel them in. Once you confirm their identity, you take them out."

"You make it sound easy. Like you could just kill some-one?"

"And you make it sound like it's going to be hard. Like you're not what you are. We were made to do this, Brianna. This isn't some grand moral dilemma. It's simple. Kill or be killed."

"Not if I have anything to say about it."

"You don't. You never did."

I finally get to the question I've wanted to ask since we started talking. "What do you think would happen if you didn't ... take them out?"

Sherri's eyes flash. "What do you mean?"

"You said, yourself, that they're supposed to be hot?"

"You can't mess with them, Paxton. If you wait, you run the risk of getting killed, or worse, bonding with the murderer. Which is not only sick and twisted, but will hurt like hell when you finally do kill it. Or worse, when it kills you. You can't afford to let your soul get bound up with a Son of Killian."

Sherri glances back at the group behind her. A couple of the boys have given up and presumably gone in search of easier prey. Sherri flashes me a look of annoyance. She's waited years for this, after all.

"Why is the bonding thing so bad?"

Sherri blows a perfectly straight bang away from her face and looks longingly over at the last boy, who's linger-ing a few feet away. "Sleeping with the enemy is always dangerous, but in this case it's suicidal. Don't kid yourself about them. They might be hot, but they're murderers who will cut you to pieces at the first opportunity."

"And we're different, how?"

"Easy, Paxton," she says, then turns her back and moves toward the remaining boy, her hips swaying. "We're the good guys."

I try to imagine a world where Sherri Milliken is one of the good guys. I swear. I try.

THIRTY-TWO

I go directly to my car after school. Sherri's right about one thing—I need my bracelet. I might be able to make it to Friday on my own, but what about the Seventh Daughters who come after me? The bracelet was never mine. It was on loan from the daughters who came before.

Instead of turning on the road that will take me west to the beach, I keep driving toward McMillan Prep. It's a calculated risk, but I'm betting that Austin is the key to getting my bracelet back.

The campus is smaller than R.D. High's, but everything else about it feels bigger. Grander anyway. The football stadium is state-of-the-art, with actual restaurant vendors and a bar for the alumni and parents. The buildings are painted in fresh white, accentuating the red tile roofs. Stone pathways wind through shady trees and floral gardens.

The parking lot is full, but there are no students outside.

I look at my watch. I don't know what room Austin might be in, so there's nothing to do but wait for class to let out. I find a spot on a low wall near the entranceway and wait. At the sound of a bell, students pour into the walkways.

I spot Austin right away. He walks with a backpack slung over his shoulder, flanked by other students. He keeps his head low and his hands in his pockets, as if he's purposefully trying to blend in. Now that I know he's not human it's easy to see that everything about him, from the too-long hair to his casual walk, is calculated. Of course, he can't hide his high cheekbones and handsome face, but even his crooked smile is a mask, a premeditated imperfection to make him seem more approachable. Nothing about Austin feels real to me now.

His eyes shine gold for just an instant when he sees me.

He picks up his pace, weaving through the crowd of students with undisguised grace. He stops in front of me, blocking me from their view. "And to what do I owe this pleasure?"

I stand to face him. "This isn't a social call."

"A shame. I think we both would enjoy it more if it was." His eyes darken, and I feel the fog forming around my brain. Some kind of mind manipulation. I let ice fill my veins until the fog fades away.

I meet his gaze, clear-eyed and focused. "What's the matter? Don't you trust your own charm anymore?"

He laughs, unfazed by the fact that I've stopped his power. "You're right. I didn't have to work very hard to convince you to come to my room that first night, did I?"

He goes right for the jugular. I'm shaking, embarrassed, and angry. But my pride can take more than a few hits; it's had lots of practice. "I think you might have something that belongs to me," I say.

"Your heart?"

God. It's all I can do to keep from hitting him. "My bracelet."

"Oh, right. You left it behind, didn't you?"

He knows exactly where it is. "Give it back."

"For someone who claims not to be interested, you ask for a lot of favors. And now you show up at my school out of the blue. If I didn't know better, I'd say I have a bit of a stalker." He looks behind him. "What if one of the Sons sees you?"

"It's a little late for you to pretend to be worried about me fighting the Sons." He's the one who said Jonah should pay.

He shrugs and sits down on the wall, patting the spot next to him. "Sit." When I don't move, he adds, "I promise to behave. Unless you don't want me to." He shakes his head. "I'm kidding. We need to talk. You need to understand about me. And Blake."

"Said the spider to the fly." I sit down next to Austin, careful to keep a few extra inches of space between us. "So, spill."

Austin looks into my eyes and smiles. For a second, I'm back at the quarters table that first night, laughing, flirting, reveling in the attention of a beautiful boy. I shake my head, and he laughs. Like he knows how easily I've slipped.

"I knew that if I stuck with the Sons long enough,

eventually Danu's daughters would show up." He takes a breath. "I've been waiting for you for a very long time."

I try to process this. "You were waiting for me? For how long?"

"Not counting the thousand years that I was banished to the underworld? Three years."

"What?" None of this is making sense.

"There was a time, Brianna, when the gods lived on earth and ruled humans. The humans turned on us, abandoning us in favor of the God of All Things. As if he would bother with them."

"They went over your head?"

"Something like that." He sighs. "A powerful group of warriors in a crusade for God succeeded in vanquishing our leader. We were tricked into splitting the earth. The Milesians selected the upper earth and gave us the under-world, knowing we'd be trapped there for eternity."

Again, I've got to hand it to Sasha. She knows her stuff. "But you're here?"

"A loophole. The gods were trapped over fifteen hundred years ago, but I've always ruled the underworld, and with it the gateway to earth."

"You can travel back and forth."

He nods. "As long as I haven't been personally banished."

"So what does this have to do with Blake?"

"The Sons are the Milesians. They want nothing more than to rid the earth of magic and gods, even as they covet their power."

I know this part of the story. I just don't know if I believe it. At least not when it comes to Blake.

Austin's fingers trail the length of my hair. "They won't stop, Brianna. Not until you're dead." His eyes meet mine. "We're on the same side here."

"If you're some kind of god, why don't you just kill the Sons yourself?"

He shakes his head. "It's not permitted. The last time I got directly involved, I was personally banished. I couldn't cross over for a thousand years. I could do little more than wait, watching the world carry on without me. Now that I've returned, it's almost too late. The Sons are winning. If you don't stop them, they *will* win. We're running out of options. I need your help."

Somehow, I'm not convinced that the gods ruling the humans would be a good thing. Not if they're anything like Sherri Milliken. "What about the humans?" I say. It feels weird to call them that.

"You only ask that because you were raised by them. You don't know what you are yet—not fully. You're not one of them. You can control them. True, the gods are angry, but you needn't worry—the humans will be put in their place, but most will survive to serve the gods. To serve you. If you live."

I scoot further away on the wall. *Most* will survive. That can't be good. "Blake won't kill me."

"Don't kid yourself about him. You have a piece of his soul inside you—it clouds your judgment. He may not want to kill you today, but eventually, he'll have to. He claimed the right to do it. His path is set."

"What do you mean?"

Austin laughs again. "It's what tipped me off about you. That flash of magic at my party. It was all very dramatic, Blake claiming the right to kill you in my kitchen."

Isn't that what Jonah said too? I'd thought that frozen moment just meant my craziness was back. And it was. But if it meant something else...

Mine.

My lower lip trembles. I don't want to believe it. But hasn't Blake admitted as much to me? That he didn't want to do what he was going to have to do?

Austin reaches over and takes my hand. "He's going to kill you. Unless you end it first."

How? By killing Blake? By killing them all? *No.* The word pounds in my heart, resonates in my head. *No.* Blake is not a killer. *I* am not a killer. I didn't kill Blake when I had the chance. I didn't kill Jonah. I didn't even kill Derek and Cassidy when I set the chem lab on fire.

"I want to help you." Austin waits for a reaction, like he expects me to throw myself in his arms and beg him to help me kill my boyfriend.

I pull my hand away. "I'll figure this out on my own."

"Then you're a fool." His eyes turn dark. The fogginess is back, but I'm ready for it this time, letting my veins flow with ice. I want to tell Blake that I can do it fast now, but of course, he's not here.

"I should go." I stand up from the wall. Most of the

students have left. Only a few mill around the parking lot, hanging by their shiny BMWs.

I'm a few steps away before Austin stands up. "Forgetting something?" He dangles my bracelet from his fingers.

I almost forgot. I practically run to him. He raises his hand over his head, keeping the bracelet just out of reach. "What do I get if I give this to you?"

"Some self-respect?"

He shakes his head. "You owe me."

I'm instantly back in the stall with Dart. What had Austin said after he healed him? "For Dart?"

"That, too. For now, I'll settle for a small recompense for recovering your bracelet."

"What?" I step back. It can't be good to owe Austin anything.

His lips curve up. "One kiss."

"No."

He twists the bracelet around his fingers. "What are you afraid of Brianna? Afraid you won't be able to stop at just one?" He doesn't advance further, a fact for which I'm grateful. "Face it. You weren't meant for him. You were meant to kill him."

It's not like that. Not now. It can't be. "I wasn't meant for you either, was I, Romeo? This is a tragedy, remember?"

He laughs. "That doesn't mean we can't have a little fun in the meantime." He leans against the wall and folds his arms against his chest.

I move a step closer. "You don't think it's sad that the

only way you can get a girl to kiss you is to resort to extortion?"

His smile grows. He knows I've just caved.

I stand frozen as he closes the last few inches between us. His hand comes to my cheek. My skin is still cold from the trick I used to fend off his power. The heat of his hand sends prickles of pain across my skin. I flinch away from his touch.

His voice is a low growl. "Don't play with me."

"Last time I checked, I wasn't the one blackmailing you into kissing me." I turn my head away from his hand.

He holds my chin, forcing me to meet his gaze. "Am I so horrible?"

He looks radiant, his brown eyes flecked with gold. And he saved Dart. But he's not real. I can't forget it. He leans toward me, and this time, I stay put.

His lips touch mine slowly. So slowly. He pulls away, and I exhale. Okay, that wasn't so bad. I open my eyes. Austin's face is too close.

"It doesn't count if you don't kiss me back." He lowers his face to mine. I hold my breath.

"What the *hell*?" Haley's voice is a high screech.

Austin jumps away, bumping into the wall behind him.

Haley's perfect silhouette is outlined in the sunlight. Christy drops her car keys onto the concrete beside her.

Haley advances on me. "Oh. My. God."

I want to back up, but there's nowhere to go unless I

want to end up in Austin's lap. Probably not a good idea under the circumstances.

"I knew it. I knew you couldn't leave him alone." Haley's face is twisted into a venomous scrunch that she obviously hasn't practiced in the mirror.

"It's not what you think."

"Don't look at me." Austin holds up his hands in mock surrender. My bracelet still hangs from his fingers.

I spin toward him. "Give it back."

He closes his fingers, flashing me a crooked grin. It's all a game to him.

"Now," I say.

Fire fills me so fast that I have to grab the wall to keep from falling over from the pain. The heat chases away the last remnants of ice in my blood. I face Austin, sending fire to the bracelet still trapped in his fingers. He opens his hand with a start, dropping the glowing blue bracelet on the grass.

Wind whips around us, wildly at first. I focus on the silver chain until the wind catches it and sends it flying toward me. I snatch it out of the air, closing my fingers around it. My internal temperature drops as the bracelet cools in my hand.

Austin blinks. It's my turn to smile.

"What was that?" Haley looks from Austin to me and back again.

I step around her on my way to the parking lot. "Just getting something that belongs to me."

I don't look back.

THIRTY-THREE

I just drive, without conscious thought of a final destination. The pain is worse now. The dull ache is still there, but it's accented by sharp pangs, like shards of glass swirling inside me.

On some level Blake knew what would happen between us that night on the beach. He knew what it would mean. How it must end.

It's not so much like a GPS as something more intuitive that sends me to the parking lot near Magic Beans. I only know I need to see Blake, and I move accordingly. When I get out of the car, I head toward the sidewalk that leads to the park. I follow the path as it winds to the fake lake at the center. The park is quiet as the last rays of sunlight reflect off the water.

I don't see Blake, and for a second I worry that I've got it wrong. Then I feel him, a soothing balm that coats and covers the jagged cuts inside. Warmth spreads from my chest, lower and lower, until my whole body is wrapped in it. His footsteps barely register in the soft dirt path, but I'm attuned to every single one. When he steps into the open, it's all I can do to keep from launching myself at him.

He watches me, his eyes wary, unsure. We just stand staring at each other, and I realize he's waiting for me to attack him. I can't stifle a giggle, because I do want to attack him. Badly. Just not in the way he thinks.

"Fancy meeting you here." I step closer, savoring the electricity that charges the air between us. I feel the change in him, the trepidation replaced by curiosity, then the growing heat that mirrors my own. He starts to reach for me, but puts his hands in his pockets instead.

He lifts his chin. A current of energy flows around us. He shifts from one foot to the other, but doesn't move closer.

"Are we okay?" I blurt.

He rubs the back of his neck and looks past me to the lake. "Define okay."

"I'm sorry for what I said last night." I take a tentative step closer. He doesn't back away. "It's just all happening so fast. And it's hard to remember that I'm not that girl you would never look at. Because, well, I am."

His eyes travel to my wrist. "You got your bracelet back."

"Austin had it."

The flash of silver in his eyes is all the warning I need. I can feel his anger too, and the double impact makes me back up again. "You saw him again?"

"What to do you mean, again? I went to get my bracelet." And there's the part where I let Austin kiss me. It's not like I kissed him back.

"He's dangerous, Brianna, don't you get it? You can't trust him."

"Like I can trust you?"

"It won't be me that ends this."

"Why not? Because you'll let Jonah do your dirty work for you? Or is it the older Sons who will be the ones to take me out? You know there's only one way for this to end, and something tells me that you're not going to make some noble sacrifice so I can live."

He finally moves toward me, breaking the tension. He puts a hand on each shoulder and his eyes find mine, searching. "Is that what you want? For me to fall on my sword for you? Prove my love like some crazy martyr?" His eyes sparkle with silver. And then he's gone. Vanished.

"Blake?" I spin around, but he's nowhere. "Blake!" I shout at the air. I run up the path, frantic to find him before he does something supremely stupid. I stop halfway to the parking lot, aware that I'm not running toward anything. He's not here. He's not anywhere that I can follow.

I wait to feel something, any inkling of where he's gone. My built-in GPS is on the fritz, which means he hasn't come back. Only the pain in my gut tells me he's still alive and breathing. I turn back down the path. My steps are slow, in no hurry now. When I get to the lake, I sit on the grass and wait.

It's not until the sun disappears completely and the big

dipper is fully visible in the sky that I feel him again, just before he materializes in the grass next to me. He sits down beside me and stares out at the lake.

"I can't do it," he says quietly, like he's almost sad.

"Thank God." I lace my words with a touch of sarcasm, doing my best to mask the desperation I'd felt waiting for him. It's not like he can't feel it now that he's here, but that doesn't mean I have to acknowledge it. "I would never ask you to do something like that. Never."

"You'd sooner kill me yourself?"

"I'm not a killer." I hope it's true.

He barks out a laugh. "You shouldn't bother lying to me. I can tell what you're feeling."

Fine. If he wants the truth, I'll give it to him. "I don't know what I am. What I'm becoming. But I do know I want to live. And I'll fight if I have to."

"I don't doubt that for a second. And though I've never given it much thought before tonight, it turns out I want to live too."

"So where does that leave us?"

"We're both alive at the moment." He takes my hand in his, sending shivers along my skin.

"There's that."

He waits for me to look at him. "I'm sorry," he says.

"You're sorry ... "

"That I didn't see you sooner. I wish I could take back all those times I didn't. I feel like I've wasted the last year. All those times when you were right there in front of me. If I'd just bothered to look."

My heart skips and races at an unhealthy pace. "You weren't exactly lonely."

He laughs at that. "You have no idea."

"All those girls?"

"All those prospects. For the breeding program. It's my role in the Circle. I'm a prospector."

"Prospector?"

"There aren't many breeders, but they're out there, and it's my job to find them."

"How?"

"We look for certain traits. Those girls you saw me with were potential breeders. I only had to get close enough to get a few strands of hair for DNA testing. Then I moved on."

"So it wasn't that you liked all those girls?"

"I didn't say that. Some more than others. But it wasn't like I could stick around to see where it went. Less than one percent of them have anything we can use, and I have to keep moving. It's too risky to bring pure humans into our Circle. I'm not even supposed to have a girlfriend until I settle on one of the breeders."

"What does that make me?"

"You do have a hell of a gene pool."

"So you're just using me for my DNA?"

He laughs. "I wish it were that simple. Brianna, I haven't worked for the Circle since I saw you at the party. You're all I think about. Even before the bond."

"You knew the bond could happen." Finally, I say what I've come here to say. "You knew what it would mean."

"I didn't believe it. Even if I did, it probably wouldn't

have mattered. I just knew I wanted you. More than anything I've ever wanted in my life. And when we kissed ... I don't think I could have stopped it."

I'm desperate to believe him. Every part of me wants to believe that he wants me. That there's nothing else. I press forward anyway. "When you saw me, at Austin's party, you planned to kill me. You claimed the right."

His face pales. "Who told you that?"

"It's true?" My heart plummets to the fiery pits of hell. I shouldn't have said anything. I don't want his admission after all.

"It wasn't something I could control," he says quickly. "When you walked into the room, I didn't even see you at first. Then there was this weird flash of light and everything went black. When the room came back into focus—"

"Everything was frozen."

He stares at me. "You saw that?"

"Nobody moved, and then you turned your head and looked at me."

He shakes his head. "You looked at me, and that's when I knew. I knew that you were the bandia, the one we were looking for."

"And you claimed the right to kill me?"

"I claimed you, but I didn't kill you. I already told you, I won't. Not unless you come after me first."

"But you set us on this path, knowing how it had to end. What are we supposed to do? What if I end up killing you?"

"You won't."

"You can't know that."

Sparks of silver illuminate the green in his eyes. "I know you, Brianna. Not just what you are. *Who* you are. If you come after me, you'll have a damn good reason for it."

"I hope you're right." My birthday is now just four days away and I have no idea what to expect. "I torched Jonah's truck today."

"Thank you. I hated that truck." He laughs. "You don't have to convince me that you're dangerous. I get it. And it's not like I'm going to go down without a fight. I just won't be the one to start it."

I lean into him, letting my shoulder touch his. His arm comes around me, pulling me closer. I close my eyes. "I hate this."

"Really?" His hand rubs light circles along my back. "Because I kind of love this part."

I smile into his shirt.

His lips press light kisses along my neck. Lower. He watches me as he unbuttons the top button of my shirt. "I can't imagine my life without you in it." His smile is almost sad, like he knows that our time is short, that we have to make the most of the moments we still have.

His finger trails down the opening in my shirt, between my breasts, underneath them, then back up to my neck. Everywhere but where I want them. I twist my fingers in the hair at the back of his head as his lips follow the path of his finger. My skin is on fire, only briefly cooled where his tongue licks.

I lie back in the grass and he rolls on top of me. He kisses his way to my ear, his labored breaths fueling me. Then his lips cover mine the same way his body does. And when I kiss him, it is with everything that I am, good and bad, human and goddess, friend and enemy. It's somehow perfect.

THIRTY-FOUR

I sit in the back room at Hunter's, waiting for Blake to finish up a poker game. Fishnet, who is apparently Sierra, sits with Jonah two tables away. They make no effort to include me. Every now and then Sierra makes a point of looking in my direction just before she whispers something in Jonah's ear and laughs. It's all very mature.

Portia serves drinks to the poker players, but I have to get mine directly from the bartender, an old guy who makes a face every time I ask for refill on my Diet Coke. I try to ignore the way Portia touches Blake when she gets near him. A hand on his back, his shoulder, his arm, so casual I can almost believe she's just being friendly or supportive.

If Blake notices, he doesn't react. At the card table he has a singular focus. His attention never wavers. It's easy to see the predator in him as he watches his three remaining opponents.

Mr. Stevenson pushes a large stack of chips toward Blake. Colonel Lydon and Mr. Basker fold.

My role here is simple. I'm a living mood regulator, close enough to ease the ever-present ache when we're apart, far enough away to avoid the distracting hum of pleasure while Blake works. It's Thursday night, but Blake promised to have me home well before midnight. I don't plan to be anywhere near this place when my birthday rolls around. Like Cinderella in reverse, at midnight I'll go from humble servant girl to belle of the ball, no faerie godmother required. Of course, there's always the risk I'll turn the handsome prince into a pumpkin. And that would be letting him off easy.

Joe ambles into the room in a black leather bomber jacket. He nods at Jonah but keeps walking, sliding into the seat across from me.

"How's he doing?" Joe nods in the general direction of the game.

"He has the second highest chip count, and Mr. Stevenson is on tilt, so he'll probably be out soon."

"You follow poker?"

"My dad watches it when there's no golf on." I don't tell him how I used to make a game of calculating the odds of each player winning the hand before they showed the numbers on the screen. True geek confessions will have to wait another day.

Joe still watches the poker table, but his words are only for me. "You know it's not too late to get away from here."

It's not like I haven't given it some serious thought. "Are you trying to get rid of me?" I ask.

"Nah. It's been a long time since things were even halfway interesting." Joe pulls out a pack of cigarettes and sets it on the table.

Something about the distant look in his eyes triggers a thought. "How long have you been with the Sons?"

"A generation or two." We both know he's lying. "You lose count after a while."

So I'm guessing the giolla aren't historians because of their scholarly pursuits—they live the history they report. No wonder Joe is behind the times. I feel a little sorry for him. It can't be easy staying the same while the rest of the world grows up around you.

"Have you known others?" I ask. "Bandia, I mean."

"Goes with the territory. Last time was nearly eighty years ago. She wasn't around long, mind you, but she killed three Sons before they got her. Regular bitch on wheels, that one."

"What happened to her?"

"Same as always." Joe pulls a cigarette from the pack and rolls the filtered tip between his thumb and forefinger. "Knife to the heart."

I know he means it literally, but part of me can't help but wonder if it's figurative as well—if she was betrayed by someone she loved. "Why didn't you turn me in the first time you saw me?"

"It's not my war. Besides, it looked like you were gonna

take up with Austin. I didn't think it was in the best interest of the Circle for them to get into it with him."

He knows about Austin. "Why not?"

"He's more powerful than the rest of you. You'd do well to remember that. He doesn't see the world the same way. He won't back away from a fight."

"He backed down from Blake." I think about how Austin left us alone in Avernus. He didn't fight Jonah either. Not even when Jonah had a knife to his throat. What had he said the other day? That he couldn't get directly involved?

"Austin doesn't back down from anyone unless he's got a reason." Joe's eyes travel to the bar. "Speak of the devil."

We both turn as Austin walks into the room, his arm thrown casually around Haley's shoulders. His brown hair falls across his forehead so that he has to tilt his head to look out from beneath it. He pulls Haley closer. To the casual observer, he appears harmless. Human. But if I look closer, I can see how he almost floats across the room.

It's a second before Haley sees me. She immediately looks away and beams up at Austin, staking her claim.

"What's he doing here?" I feel the moment when Blake sees him, his focus dissolving into a thick knot of animosity.

Austin removes his arm from around Haley and travels the rest of the way to the poker table. He pulls a wad of cash from his pocket and sets it on the table. "Room for one more?"

Blake glares up at him. "This is a private game."

The other three players eye the stack of bills like a pack

of stray dogs around a steak. "His money looks good to me," Colonel Lydon says.

Austin nods at the Colonel, ignoring Blake's hard gaze. The dealer counts out the cash and slides a stack of chips across the table. Haley comes up behind Austin and hangs over his chair, letting her arms fall across his shoulders.

He takes Haley's hand and brings it to his lips, but he stares at me. "Lady Luck." His voice is a seductive purr. "Just what I needed."

I don't know if it's Blake or me, but I have to force myself to stay in my seat. The urge to drag Austin from the room is strong. I hate the way Haley drapes herself all over him. For a second I worry that I really am jealous. But it's not jealousy at all. I'm terrified of what Austin has planned for her. Because the way he's holding her hand while smiling at me is not some sick game to make me jealous. It's a warning.

The dealer shuffles the cards and passes them around the table. Blake looks at his two cards and I feel him try to reign in the seething anger, to concentrate on the game. It's a pointless attempt.

The betting starts. Mr. Stevenson opens with a bet of five hundred. The Colonel folds. Blake throws in some chips. So does Mr. Basker. Austin slides his entire stack into the center of the table. "I'm all in."

Blake scoffs. "It's a little early for you to throw it all away."

Austin's grin exudes confidence. "Why wait if you don't have to?"

Mr. Basker and Mr. Stevenson fold. Blake hesitates, and I can practically feel the gears turning in his head. He doesn't trust Austin, but he doesn't know anything about his game yet. It's too early in the hand to even guess what cards Austin might be holding. He should do what the others did, fold quickly. Instead, he slides the bulk of his stack of chips to the center of the table. "Call," he says, not so much taking the bait as throwing down a challenge of his own.

The entire room falls silent. Everyone watches, holding their breath, as Austin turns over his cards. A seven and a three.

A stone-cold bluff.

Blake grins as he flips over an ace and a jack. The odds are in his favor. I let out a breath. Austin doesn't react. He brings Haley's fingers to his lips for one more kiss, winking at me from across the table.

I realize then what I should've known all along: Austin has already won. The odds may be small, but there's still a chance that he'll draw the better hand. That's the thing with odds—no matter how small the probability, so long as it exists, the outcome is possible. Not just possible; it has to happen at least some of the time. And Austin already knows the ending.

The dealer lays three cards face-up on the table. A six, a ten, and a jack. Blake's made a pair. Austin has nothing. Austin's odds of winning just dropped into the single digits.

Austin puts his elbows on the table and leans forward. "Shall we raise the stakes?"

Blake laughs. "I don't take candy from babies."

"It's not over yet." Austin stares at me again. A chill runs down my spine, like someone dropped an ice cube down my back. I hope Blake feels the warning in my fear. Whatever Austin is up to, it's not good. Austin squeezes Haley's hand. She smiles down at him. It's the same smile I've seen her bestow a thousand times, but there's something off about it. The spark that is Haley Marvell isn't there. She's phoning it in. Weird. Haley is more into Austin than any of her previous guys. The least she could manage is one of the stock performances she's perfected over the last few years.

The dealer deals a fourth card face-up on the table. A three. Austin has a pair of threes. Blake is still winning with a pair of jacks. There's only one more card left for the dealer to turn over.

"Now it's getting interesting," Austin picks up a red chip and flips it back and forth through his fingers, weaving it over and under in smooth fluid strokes. It's the kind of thing that takes years of practice to perfect, a way of communicating experience at the poker table without saying a word.

Blake's mood shifts again, his blood pressure rising even as he leans back in his chair casually. "How much?"

No, no, no, no. I want to scream it across the room. There's easily twenty thousand dollars in the pot as it is. It has to be a set-up.

Austin falls back in his chair, mirroring Blake's relaxed

pose. "You have something I want." His gaze moves over Blake's shoulder until he finds me again.

To his credit, Blake doesn't take the bait. He smiles. "I don't see how that matters, seeing as how you don't have anything that I want."

Haley doesn't take offense at the comment, even though it's exactly the kind of thing that should set her off. In Haley's world, everyone wants her. She keeps her head down, her eyes following her hands as they weave patterns along Austin's chest.

Austin drops the poker chip. It lands with a clatter that echoes across the otherwise silent room. Everyone is watching them now. "Naïve of you to think that I don't have what you want," he says. "I know things your half-breed brain can't begin to process. And I can help you keep what you have." His eyes get darker. He lowers his voice. "No one has to die."

"Die?" Mr. Stevenson scoops up his chips. "What's going on here?"

Blake's heart races, sending waves of nervous energy pulsing through me. I can't sit still. I stand up and cross the room to the table.

Blake doesn't look at me as I stand next to him. He's still focused on Austin. "You can stop it?" His voice is low, almost a whisper. But I feel Blake's hope as it rises in my own chest. "How?"

Austin's eyes are black as they bore into Blake's. "There is a way."

I feel Blake falling into the abyss, his energy focused

only on Austin, on what Austin promises. A way for us to be together. A way for us to both live. An end to the war between our kind. I feel how impossible it all sounds, and I know that Austin doesn't intend for any of the Sons to live.

I can't reach Blake, even with my hand on his shoulder. Blake is already circling in Austin's orbit; he's right there with Austin, not fighting him off at all, just wanting.

Mr. Stevenson stands up and stuffs his pockets with the cash in front of him. No one stops him as he hurries from the room. Everyone watches Austin.

Austin knows he has Blake now. His lips curve up into a crooked grin that now looks almost twisted to me. "Are you in?"

I squeeze Blake's shoulder. Hard. "He's lying."

Blake doesn't look up, his eyes still fixed on Austin. He wants to believe the lie so badly. The lie that we can be together. The lie that one of us doesn't have to die.

I try another tack. "Haley," I say. I have to call her name again before she finally looks up. "Don't you see what your boyfriend is doing? He wants Blake to give up his claim on me." The Haley I know would do something, say something. She wouldn't sit by and let a boy insult her this way.

Haley's turquoise eyes are tinged with black. "You," she says. "When are you going to understand that Austin is not interested? It's getting to be a little pathetic the way you pant after him."

I want to shake her out of it. "Pay attention to what he's doing. I'm the prize he wants."

Her eyes narrow to black slits, and for a second she looks exactly like her mother. I back up a step. "You've always been a loser when it comes to guys, Brianna. So you've had one boyfriend for a whole week. Don't let it go to your head."

I know that Haley is trapped in Austin's spell, with limited control of her own mind. That doesn't stop the words from ripping fresh wounds over scars that should be healed. I'm still standing tall, but on the inside I'm laid open, bleeding profusely.

Haley lets her hand trail down Austin's chest, kissing his ear as she whispers something to him. He smiles again, then looks at me and laughs. He's got my best friend, and now Blake. Pulling my strings in the most painful way possible.

Then there's a roaring in my head, a cacophony of waves and wind. It's coming from Blake, and I realize he's finally trying to push back against Austin's pull. I have to grab the back of his chair to keep from collapsing on the ground. I summon what strength I can. But I can't reach him, not with Austin there. I feel the shadow of false promises as they grow. And then there's silence.

Blake leans forward in his chair, fingering his two cards. "I'm in," he says.

THIRTY-FIVE

The truth has never seemed clearer to me than it does right now. We cannot change the past. We cannot change our future. The ending was written the moment Blake kissed me on the beach. Sooner. We might fight against it, but Austin's twisted smile tells me everything I need to know. I can't stick my head under my pillow and wait for this to go away. The war is coming. It's coming for me.

Austin looks at the dealer. No one moves as the dealer removes the top card from the deck and starts to turn it over.

Before he can lay it on the table, there's a sharp wind that starts at the center of the room, whipping the cards into the air and sending them flying in every direction. The card in the dealer's hand flies into the melee as the entire deck is blown around the room, along with cocktail napkins, straws, and assorted scraps of paper. But not before I see the card.

A three.

Austin stands, glaring at me. I shake my head at him—it wasn't me.

There's a movement by the doorway, and everyone turns to look. Sherri and Sasha walk in with the grace of supermodels, wearing crimson red gowns that cling in all the right places and heels that are impossibly high. They're dressed for sipping champagne, not fighting demigods.

Sherri Milliken laughs as Rush and Jonah surge toward them, outing themselves as Sons.

Sasha smiles her gorgeous smile. "Hi, boys."

Austin is still watching me, but his face changes as he laughs. "Juliet, you've been holding out on me."

Haley looks confused. She watches Sherri and Sasha circle Rush and Jonah.

Sherri looks over at me and winks. "Nice work, Paxton."

Blake rises from his chair and grabs my arm. His eyes are dark, green with a hint of silver. I wish to God I could blame the look in Blake's eyes on Austin, but Austin's not influencing him anymore. The raw emotion in Blake's eyes is nothing compared to the lancing pain that slashes through me as I feel Blake's anger. More than anger—betrayal. My heart sinks, plunging with the weight of all that Sherri just implied in her statement to me.

I should have told Blake about Sherri and her death squad. But I couldn't tell Blake about her any more than I could tell Sherri about Blake. I walked away from Sherri and her bloodlust. But in the process, I led her straight to the Sons.

I need to say something now. The window on Blake's willingness to listen to me is closing even as all hell is about to break loose. "I can explain," is all I manage to blurt.

There's a flash of silver light, and Rush and Jonah vanish. Sherri and Sasha are in trouble. They've lost the element of surprise; their advantage is already gone and they're about to find themselves on the business end of a very sharp knife.

If I don't do something, Sasha and Sherri will die. I can't sit back and wait for it to happen.

Blake lets go of my arm abruptly. The flash of silver light is the only warning I have before he disappears into thin air.

"Holy crap!" Haley is finally coming out of her Austin-induced coma, her eyes bugging out of her head.

"Stay here," I say, as I race toward Sherri and Sasha. Austin's laugh is the only sound I'm aware of as I launch myself at Sherri, knocking her to the ground.

"What the hell, Paxton?" Sherri pushes at me but stops when Rush appears right where she'd been standing, his dagger drawn to slice at just the level of her neck.

Jonah stands with his arms around Sasha, his bright silver light only serving to illuminate the dark crimson that spills from Sasha's chest where his knife plunged. Sasha falls to the floor soundlessly, blood pooling around her in a dark circle.

"You can't stay in one place," I tell Sherri. "Get up and get moving."

I hear screaming from the back of the room. Crap—Haley's still in here.

I send a gust of wind at Rush, throwing him off his feet before he can disappear again. His back hits a stuffed moose head hard enough to make a cracking sound. He lands on a table, unmoving. Sherri is back on her feet but Jonah has already disappeared. Then there's a flash of silver near Sherri's back.

"Move!" I scream.

She's not fast enough. Blake appears behind her, his sword poised at her heart.

"Don't," I plead. "Blake."

He stares at me like I'm a stranger. Like he doesn't understand a thing about me. "Please," I whisper. There's a flash of silver behind me and I concentrate on water, bringing the icy cold to the surface as quickly as I can.

I feel the blade of Jonah's knife at the base of my throat, but it's gone just as quickly, as Jonah recoils from the freezing cold of my skin.

Blake's face changes. He lets go of Sherri and lunges at Jonah. There's a clattering of sword and knife and then a blur of movement. They move so quickly, the only way to follow the path of their fight is by the crashing tables and smashing glasses.

I seize Sherri's arm and drag her from the room. We run to the parking lot. We go as fast as Sherri can manage in her five-inch heels, anyway.

"Get out of here," I say. "You saw what they did to Sasha. You can't win this fight. There's too many of them."

"No duh, Einstein." She pulls off her heels and runs toward a car parked near the front entrance. She has the door open before she realizes I haven't followed.

"We don't have much time, Paxton. We need to disappear for a while."

I'm tempted. I've never wanted to run away more. But I can't leave Haley in there. I can't leave Blake. "I can't."

They're the words of a coward, but they might be the bravest words I've ever said.

"It's been nice knowing you." Sherri slams the door. She starts the car and peels out of the parking lot, disappearing in a cloud of smoke, leaving only the smell of burned rubber in her wake.

I'm running back toward the restaurant when I feel the first blast of pain, so strong I fall to the ground. The pain isn't mine, but it might as well be. My head snaps back like it's been hit. Blake is hurt. I have to get to him. I force myself to my knees, crawling along the sidewalk into the front door of the restaurant. I try to block the pain from my mind. I don't have much time.

Joe meets me halfway to the back room and helps me to my feet wordlessly. I lean on him for support as we work our way inside.

Jonah is standing over Blake, his shirt bloodied. I pray that it's Jonah's blood. Blake lies on the ground, his sword a few feet away. I feel how weak he is, nearly unconscious. Before Jonah can raise his knife, I send a ball of ice at his wounded leg, hitting him square in the shin. Jonah collapses to the ground. I turn on Rush.

Rush seems to have recovered from his run-in with the moose head. He looks at me and then looks away, and I realize why he hasn't attacked me yet. I'm still wearing my bracelet. Even when he knows he should look at me, he can't.

Blake stirs beside me, rising to his elbows. When he sees me, a vein in his neck twitches. "What are you still doing here?"

"Saving your ass." I can stand up without Joe now that Blake is out of danger.

Joe laughs and removes the arm he'd draped around my waist. "I knew I liked you."

Jonah scowls at me from the floor but doesn't strike, and I know the immediate danger has passed. Haley is huddled in a corner with her face buried in Austin's shoulder. One look at Austin's face tells me everything I need to know. Austin is not happy.

Sasha's body lies on the floor, her crimson dress stained black. Blood coagulates around her. I cover my hand over my mouth, fighting against waves of nausea.

Rush steps forward and grabs Blake's arm. At first I think he's going to help Blake off the floor, but instead he pushes him back to the ground. "In my office," he growls. "Now." Jonah's satisfied smile disappears when Rush turns his glare on him. "You too. And bring the girl." Rush doesn't even look at Joe when he addresses him. "Take care of this mess." He turns on the high heel of a gray cowboy boot and walks away.

My eyes dart from Joe to Haley. "Take care of … he didn't mean … ? Is Haley going to be okay?"

Joe nods. "Have you heard of hypnosis?"

"Yes."

"It's like that. A little stronger. The humans will remember a bar fight, but it will all be fuzzy, like they had too much to drink. The players will wake up tomorrow with limited memory, and more chips than they came with, so they won't complain."

"What about Haley?" Between Austin's mind games and Joe's hypnosis, poor Haley's brain is going to be a scrambled mess.

"She'll be fine. She'll just think she drank too much, and what little she remembers will be pleasant."

I want him to make her forget everything. Especially what she said to me. I want him to make me forget it.

Blake is on his feet. He walks out of the room without looking at me.

Joe's hand squeezes my shoulder. "He'll come around."

Easy for him to say. He doesn't feel Blake's rage as it burns inside me, so strong that I barely feel the throbbing ache in my head anymore.

Jonah glares at me and tilts his head toward a door in the back. He doesn't touch me, and I'm not complaining. I don't want to be anywhere near Jonah Timken.

Rush's office is a large room in the far corner of the restaurant that looks more like a lounge than a traditional workspace. There's a table with two chairs, and a huge wrap-around couch. Rush is pacing by a blackened window. Jonah takes a seat in the center of the couch; Blake sits on the end farthest from the doorway. I don't sit. I can't afford to let myself get too comfortable. Not that the couch appears comfortable. It's a shiny patent leather that looks like it would stick to your skin.

"Who is she?" Rush points at me even though he can't meet my eyes.

"Isn't it obvious?" Jonah leans back and stretches his arm out. "She's the bandia."

Rush laughs at that. "We just saw the bandia, fool. One's dead on the floor of the game room. The other one got away. You saw what they were. More beautiful than any human girl. Capable of great power." Rush crosses the room. He stands in front of me but doesn't look at my face. "This *girl*"—he says it like it's a bad word—"is the least like a bandia I've ever seen."

Blake sits on the couch in silence. He's staring straight ahead, not rushing to my defense, not even watching as Rush picks up a lock of my hair and *smells* it. I only know he's aware of Rush's invasion of my personal space by the surge of adrenaline that isn't mine.

Jonah barks out a laugh. "She's the one that sent you flying into Colonel Potter's head. If she's not a bandia, I don't know how you begin to explain it."

"It was the other one." Rush turns on Blake. "Why did you protect this human from Jonah? What's she to you?"

Blake still stares straight ahead. He doesn't even stop to consider his response. "Nothing."

No, no, no! *Please*, I silently plead with him. *Let me explain.* But he's closed me off. I can't feel anything now but a wall of dark emotion.

Rush forces himself to look at me. I can see the effort it takes for him. "She knew how we fight. She pushed the dark-haired one out of the way."

I nod at him. "I'm a breeder, sir."

Jonah snorts from the couch. I'm glad at least one person is enjoying himself.

"Is this true?" Rush stares at Blake.

I half expect Blake to deny it, to throw me to the wolves and be done with it. Instead, he nods his head. "Ask Dr. McKay. Her DNA is off the fucking charts."

It's my turn to feel the pain of betrayal. He actually tested me? When did he get my hair? Wait, who am I kidding? When *wasn't* he close enough to grab a few strands of hair?

"Why didn't you tell me about her sooner?" Rush eyes me with more interest now, his eyes actually traveling from my head to my feet despite the effort it takes.

Jonah laughs openly now. Bad idea. If there's one rule that seems to apply in Rush's office, it's that anything remotely fun is checked at the door.

Rush walks over to Jonah and kicks him hard in the leg, sending Jonah down to the floor with such force that even I gasp. "Don't think you're out of this. What the hell did you pull back there? Attacking Blake until he was unconscious? For a minute there I thought you were going to do the unthinkable."

It's a few seconds before Jonah can stop writhing enough to respond, his voice a rasp. "He started it."

Blake stands up, smoothing his thighs with his palm as he does. "Are we done here? I'll see if Joe needs help."

Rush nods, as much a dismissal as a response. "Tell Joe to set up an initiation for the new breeder on Saturday."

I want to say something, to remind them that I'm still in the room, but I can't. I'm too busy trying to gather the thousand tiny pieces of my heart as Blake walks past me.

THIRTY-SIX

I'm nearly home before I realize it's been my birthday for five minutes. I don't feel any different. There's no swell of magic, no flood of power. For a second, I dare to hope that they've all got it wrong. I'm just a girl, a girl missing a crucial pheromone who has a perfectly normal, if romantically challenged, life. A girl who can fit virtually any aspect of her world into a perfectly logical, science-based box. It's a second of peace that I don't deserve, but I give it to myself anyway.

In school on Friday, I don't take off my bracelet. It's probably safe to let guys see me now; the magic won't slip out and give me away anymore. But I don't want to be seen. Not now. Maybe never. And, birthday or no birthday, the bracelet still seems to shield me with some level of anonymity.

I find Haley at her locker. She turns so I'm staring at her shoulder. Christy makes a sad face and mouths "Sorry."

It might not be her call, but she's not going to cross the line that Haley's drawn in the sand, either.

It shouldn't matter. After what Haley said to me, I should just let it go. But unlike Blake, I don't drop people the first time they disappoint me. And it can't be easy watching everything she thought she knew about me get turned on its head. It sure as hell hasn't been easy living it. I let her walk away. I'll be back, though. After lunch, and again on Monday, for as long as it takes.

When I get to the ranch, Marcy waves me over to the center of the ring. "Parker's dad is back in town. We can have the check today."

I flinch. "I'm not selling Dart."

Marcy's smile falls. "I know it's emotional for you. But he recovered from the mountain lion attack just fine, and this is a better price than you imagined. He'll be right here. You'll still see him every day."

She's right. I shouldn't let my personal feelings about Parker Winslow stop me from earning my college tuition. It's not like Dart won't be well taken care of. "I'll think about it."

"That's my girl." Marcy's smile is back.

Jenna rides up on her little bay pony. "Hi Brianna," she says shyly.

"Hi," I say, noticing that the heel of her boot drops below Peppermint's belly. "Hey Jenna, remember when I said you could ride Dart some time?"

She nods without stopping, her chin bobbing up and down and up and down.

"How's now?"

She can't stop the excited squeal that flies out of her mouth. "Really?"

I tack Dart up and bring him to the ring, taking Peppermint while Jenna cinches her saddle into place and climbs on Dart. She looks cute on him. He's not so big that she looks out of place, nor so small that she'll grow out of him.

"She'll be graduating to a horse soon, right?" I ask Marcy as Jenna takes Dart along the rail.

I can practically see the dollar signs floating away from Marcy as she realizes where I'm going with this. To her credit, she smiles. "It might be a good fit. You realize that her parents can't pay half of what Parker will pay."

I nod. The price will still be more than what I'd hoped for when I first found him, enough that I can go right into a four-year program at U.R.D. The thought of going to the same school as Blake gives me a little thrill that I have no right to feel under the circumstances, especially since Blake hasn't tried to contact me once since last night. Not even to text Happy Birthday.

"I'll talk to her mother." Marcy shakes her head.

Jenna reaches down to pat Dart's neck as she eases him into a canter, and I know I've made the right decision.

After Dart is groomed and Jenna has fed him an entire two-pound bag of carrots, I go in search of Parker. Not to gloat. I have some questions. There's something that doesn't make sense now that I know the truth about Austin. Why did Austin date Parker for two years?

When I find her in the tack room used by Sam's students, she doesn't say a word to me. I don't know if she knows that I'm not going to sell Dart to her, or if it ever really mattered to her that much, but she just goes on cleaning a bridle of butter-soft leather like I'm not even there.

"Parker."

She finally looks at me.

I'm not sure how to ask, so I just say it. "What was the deal with you and Austin?"

She rolls her eyes at me. "Really? You came all the way over here to ask me about Austin? Like you have any real chance with him? Please. Or are you just a masochist? I'll tell you exactly what Austin loved about me. Is that what you want to hear?"

"Spill."

"Well, for starters, I'm beautiful. And of course there's rich. I was class president of McMillan. As a sophomore. It was only natural that the two of us would end up together."

"That's it?" I don't disguise the complete disbelief in my tone. There has to be more to it than Parker's popularity. I'm sure Austin is popular in his own right. He wouldn't need Parker on his arm to seal the deal.

Parker's mouth opens and closes, and for a second she resembles a giant fish. "Well, he did always tell me I was descended from a beautiful goddess."

"But you weren't," I say with a certainty I feel in my bones. "And let me guess. He broke up with you shortly after you turned seventeen."

She opens her mouth again without saying anything.

I don't wait around for her to get it together. Parker Winslow has told me everything I need to know.

Austin was prospecting, looking for a Seventh Daughter to help him fight his war against the Sons. Only Austin doesn't have the aid of the latest advancements in genetic science. Austin is flying blind.

Austin is not as all-powerful as he claims.

THIRTY-SEVEN

It's not until my mom hugs me and tells me Happy Birthday that I realize how long I've been waiting for someone to say those words. It's been nineteen hours and twenty-seven minutes.

Mom sits down at the kitchen table and holds up an ad mock-up for *R.D. Magazine.* "Do you like this one?" She waves the glossy picture of herself, complete with perfect smile and anchorwoman helmet hair.

"It's nice."

"I thought you were going out with Haley and Christy?" she asks. It's kind of a tradition for the three of us to go to dinner together—no parents—on our birthdays. Tonight we were supposed to go to Olive Garden, eating too many breadsticks and not enough salad.

"Change of plans."

Mom goes through another stack of photos. "I'm not

sure whether to feature the new listing or the big ranch house from last month." She holds up two more photographs.

"Definitely the ranch." I plop myself down on the leather couch in the family room next to the kitchen. "It's flashier."

Mom scrunches her face at the pictures. "So you'll be home tonight for your birthday? Your dad and I were planning to take you out tomorrow. You could invite a friend."

I don't bother to say that the list of potential invitees, never huge to begin with, has dwindled to zero. I shrug.

"Oh, honey." Mom gets up from the table and sits down next to me. "You're not still worried about Nana's superstitions? It might be kind of cool, having powers."

Mom did *not* just bring up something as uncomfortable as my effed-up legacy. "Trust me. It's not cool. It's the supernatural equivalent of someone putting an Uzi submachine gun in your hands and telling you to shoot," I say.

Her lips pucker. "Has something happened?"

I'm not sure what to say, so I don't say anything. "I think I might have a buyer for Dart."

I know Mom won't be able to resist the chance to change the subject to a more comfortable topic, and she doesn't disappoint. "Is that what this is about? Well, you knew you were going to have to sell him eventually. Will you get a good price?"

I nod.

"That's great! It's what you've been working so hard for."

I get up from the couch.

"Should I make the dinner reservations?"

"Sure." Might as well take a page from Mom and try to

act like nothing's happening. The act might be the only normal thing I have left.

Mom smiles again, satisfied that she's fulfilled her duties as a parent while successfully avoiding the messy stuff. "Will Haley join us?"

"I'm thinking of having it be just us this year."

Mom doesn't hide her surprise. "Really? That sounds great." I can't get a read on whether she's truly happy or not. Now that we're talking again, she might be nervous about trying to sustain a conversation for a couple of hours without a friend as a buffer. She stands up and walks back to the table, already rifling through her photos.

For some reason, I can't not talk about it anymore. "Mom."

She stops, frozen.

"Can you sit back down?"

She walks back slowly, as if afraid that if she moves too fast she'll spook me and I'll bolt. But I don't. I wait for her sit down on the couch.

And then I tell her everything. About the night on the beach with Blake. About Austin and his plan to use me to kill all the Sons. I tell her about Jonah, how he attacked me and attacked Dart. I tell her about Sherri Milliken, about how I blew up Jonah's truck. How Sasha was killed. How Blake doesn't trust me now.

To her credit, my mom doesn't flinch. She doesn't ask a lot of questions. She doesn't even attempt to lecture me about safe sex or responsible magic. She waits until I'm done before she asks, "Is that all?" with a soft smile playing at the corners of her lips.

I nod, then add, "And I'm kind of in a fight with Haley."

She laughs, a kind laugh, and I find myself laughing with her. Finally, when we stop, she sits up straight. "Well, it does sound like a lot at once, but if anyone is smart enough to figure out how to make things right, it's you."

"You're supposed to say that. You're my mom." But the truth is, I've missed hearing it. She used to always tell me how smart I was and how I could do anything I wanted to, until the fire and then Nana getting sick. Then she just stopped talking to me about anything that mattered.

"It's the truth. What research have you done so far?"

"Research?"

"It's the first thing to do, right? No need to reinvent the wheel. All the big breakthroughs are just extensions of the thousands that came before."

The scientific method. Mom was the first person to propose the idea that a chemical reaction in the lab must have been what started the fire. She gave me the gift of logic when I couldn't deal with the reality of what was happening to me. She's handing me the same lifeline now, but this time it's not just an avoidance method.

"The problem is, when it comes to this stuff, I *am* reinventing the wheel. I don't know anything about our past—not the secret one, anyway."

A crease appears on my mother's forehead. "That's not entirely true."

"What do I have? A bunch of rumors about what I might become and a bracelet that I wasn't allowed to take off."

Mom shakes her head. "Maybe our history wasn't spelled out for you, but it was always there. Nana never let you forget the old ways."

Nana told me about witches and faeries and black cats. I fail to see how any of that could prepare me for *this*. But Mom's eyes are teary and I don't have the heart to fight her, so I just nod.

"What?" Mom must see the doubt in my eyes.

"I just don't see what witchcraft and superstitions have to do with anything. I'm not a witch."

Mom smiles. "Nana never said you were. She said if you practiced magic you'd be burned as one. 'Witch' is just a word used by your enemies to demonize your power."

"But I don't think it works that way. There aren't any spells or anything like that. I can just *do* things."

"Have you ever tried to do a spell? Nana was so adamant that you not try."

I have tried. Twice, with Christy's book. But both times nothing happened. Well, not nothing, exactly. I did pass out and have those weird dreams about Danu.

"What did Nana tell you about me, exactly?" I ask.

Mom blinks. She doesn't say anything at first, and for a minute I think I've lost her.

"She said you would conjure blue fire and control the sky and earth. I thought she was speaking metaphorically." Her voice cracks as she speaks. "Then there was the fire at the school."

"You told me it was the chemicals in the lab." I guess Mom and I aren't so different after all. On some level we both wanted to pretend this wasn't happening.

"I just wanted you to have a normal life."

"But I'm not normal. Nana knew exactly what I was. She knew I made the fire."

"She was terrified. She believed in the curse so much that she swore she wouldn't have any children. Then she ended up pregnant with me. She decided to risk having me since I would only be the sixth generation, but she moved to San Francisco shortly after I was born. She thought if she could keep me far from Ireland, then my children might be safe. Even so, she tried to talk me out of marrying your father. She tried to talk me out of having you."

"She thought I would become a killer."

Mom looks away, but not before I see the tears in her eyes. "I didn't believe her. I still don't. But she was convinced. And there was the fire. The blue flame. Those two children were inside the building with you."

"I didn't kill them. Why didn't you tell me everything then? There was no reason to keep secrets at that point. I needed to know."

"Nana was worried about you. She said you shouldn't have been able to conjure fire at that age. She thought it was better if you didn't believe that you'd caused it. It was better if you didn't try to use it again."

Oh God. Nana wasn't protecting me as much as she was protecting everyone else. Nana knew about the monster in me. She just wanted to keep it tucked safely under the bed.

Mom rubs her lips together. "Nothing else happened after that. Even I was convinced the fire was an accident."

"But not Nana."

Mom sighs. "She always believed in magic. She said the men who burned witches would come for you eventually, and we shouldn't interfere."

Shouldn't interfere? "You mean, you should let them kill me?"

"No." She looks back at me, more certain. "No. She said that you would be strong enough to fight them on your own."

"What if I don't want to?"

Mom's eyes widen with worry, and I realize she's taken my statement the wrong way. "I don't have a death wish or anything," I assure her. "I don't want any of this. I just want to be something close to normal, if that's even possible."

Mom finally smiles. "That's what I want for you too."

"But let's just say it's not possible. If I had to fight, did Nana say anything about how I was supposed to defeat them?"

Mom shakes her head. "I wish I could help you more."

"It's okay." For now, it's enough to know that I'm not alone in this. The fact that my mother and I have even had this conversation is a miracle itself.

I hug my mom.

I spend the next three hours researching. There's some information online. I find the story of the Milesians taking the earth from the gods and sending them to the underworld, but nothing about *how* the gods were made to stay there.

Hadn't Austin said he'd been personally banished for a

thousand years? So it must be possible, even now, to banish him. To stop him from trying to spark this war with the Sons. To keep the gods safely in the underworld.

I've found my hypothesis. My theory.

I've even tested it—with Haley and Christy, when we tried to banish Jonah. The spell didn't work, but that doesn't mean my theory's dead. It just means I need to keep testing it under different conditions.

I find the book I took from Christy. My spine tingles as I flip to the banishment spell.

The introduction states the spell should be performed at a gateway. Didn't Blake say that Avernus was a gateway? I could try the spell if I could get Austin back to Avernus. With Austin gone, I could convince the Sons that I won't fight. That I'm on the side of humans.

At least I can try.

My cell phone starts barking. I consider ignoring it, but then the howling sets in. I grab the phone, intent on turning off the sound, when I see the message flash across the screen. It's from Haley. Short as the message is, it has my full attention.

HELP.

THIRTY-EIGHT

There's no other message. I race to Magic Beans first. Matt stands behind the counter, cleaning the espresso machine with a damp washcloth.

"Is Haley here?"

He shakes his head. "She got off an hour ago. Her boyfriend picked her up."

Boyfriend? *Austin.* Shit. This is not good.

Blake storms into the shop, his eyes wild. "Are you okay?" He flips a silk strand from the beanstalk out of the way.

I feel his concern mixing with my own, and it's not helping. "Haley's in trouble." I hold up my phone and show him the message.

"Thank God. I thought it was you."

"I have to find her."

Blake follows me out of the shop. "I'm coming with you. I have a bad feeling."

"She's with Austin."

"It's not like they haven't gone out before. You don't think he's going to hurt her?"

"You're the one with the bad feeling." I spin away from him and head toward the Blue Box. He grabs my arm, stopping me.

"I'll drive."

I don't question it. I'm going to need all the help I can get. "Can you call Joe?"

Blake nods. "Any ideas where they went?"

"Maybe Avernus?" I can't help but hope so. Two birds with one stone. "Haley told me he took her to the beach once."

"I don't know if a pureblood human could get in there. At least not alive."

"The beach, then. He'll want to be close to home." His real home.

Blake calls Joe and tells him to meet us at the beach.

I wait until we're in the car and driving before I ask the question that's been on my tongue since the moment Blake showed up. "Why are you here?"

"I told you. I thought you were in trouble. I can't explain it. Something's not right."

"What do you care?" As I say the words there's a slicing pain in my stomach, only eclipsed by the sinking feeling in my heart. "I'm nothing to you." I know he still thinks I set him up to be killed by the other Seventh Daughters.

I wait for his reaction, practically begging for him to deny it. At the very least I hope for righteous anger, something strong I can use to distract me from the grief that's already ripping at me from the inside.

There's no denial. No anger. His reaction is far more disturbing. He glances at me, his eyes sad. Pitiful. Then I feel what I should've felt from the moment he arrived: the wall between us, solid as the stacked stones in the field in my vision, piled high and packed with clay dried harder than cement.

I have to work hard to sense the resignation I can see in his eyes. He's past being angry with me. Way past. He's walled me off. Doing everything he can to keep me out.

I laugh, a harsh sound that doesn't mask the pain behind it. Anger, I can use. I gather the slings and arrows that have been tearing around my chest and prepare to fire. "I don't know why you're so disappointed in me. You always knew what I was. Why wouldn't I return the favor and let my sisters do my dirty work for me? It would've been poetic justice if they'd killed you."

He doesn't take the bait. He looks straight ahead in silence, the wall in place, no sign that I'm breaking through.

"Of course I sent Sasha and Sherri to kill you. That's what you think, right? Which explains why they had no idea what they were doing. Obviously they came to die as martyrs. I mean, if you know Sherri Milliken, you know what a selfless person she is. And Sasha..." My voice trails off and my anger suddenly seems so pointless.

Sasha is dead. I may not have been the one to send her into that den of Sons, but her blood is on my hands all the same. I could have warned her. I could've told her how the

Sons would use their power to kill, taught her how to fight them. I could've talked her out of going after them in the first place. I did nothing.

In a way, Blake is right about me. I betrayed him. I betrayed Sherri and Sasha. I betrayed myself. I sat passively by and did nothing until it was too late. Too late to help the Seventh Daughters. Too late to help Blake.

So I didn't kill him. I didn't set him up to be killed.

I didn't choose him, either.

Blake's voice is quiet. "Were you close to her?"

I shake my head. "I met her once. The night Jonah attacked me. When you picked me up in Mira Mesa."

He nods. There's another tense silence before he speaks again.

"You don't get it, do you? I'm here because I thought you were in trouble. You still are. And whether I want it to or not, it still matters to me that you're okay." He laughs then. "Who am I kidding? I want it to matter."

He doesn't say anything else. He just reaches across the car and takes my hand. As his fingers lace with mine, the wall comes down with a crash. I feel him all at once, a flood of sensation. Anger, disappointment, and pain are there, but they're not his. My dark emotions are mixing with something else, something that threatens to overtake them. Not quite hope—it's richer than that. It's the most powerful magic I've ever felt, filling me with such force that I almost smile.

"You're as much a part of me as breathing," he says. "I'm tired of pretending you're not."

I let out a breath. "So don't."

The car stops at a light. Blake looks at me then. Really looks. And it's not just that he sees me. Or even that he likes what he sees. There is something else behind his eyes.

He doesn't say anything at first, and for a moment I think maybe he won't. That he doesn't have to. The stoplight flashes green, reflecting off the windshield, but the car doesn't move. Blake closes his eyes and then opens them again. Then he leans forward, bringing his lips so close to mine that they're nearly touching. He exhales; I feel the hot breeze against my mouth. "Do you feel it?" he asks.

The emotion that fills me is so potent, so full, so pure, that putting a name to it would diminish it somehow. My heart expands to soak it all in, until I can't tell where Blake begins and I end.

"Yes," I say.

His lips finally touch mine. And in the moment, I believe.

THIRTY-NINE

I'm only partly relieved to see another car in the small parking lot at the beach. The other half of me is terrified. Blake clasps my hand as we walk down the path and make our way along the sand next to the base of the cliff.

The air is colder than it should be this time of year. And there's something else off about it all ... an unnatural smell that wafts on the wind, a hint of sulfur. I hold my hand out, using my power to form a mini pressure system that forces the air to flow around us. Only then do I let myself take another breath.

"There's something in the air." I say.

Blake nods. "I know. I feel it."

"I mean literally. Something's here that shouldn't be. I'll try to keep it away from us, but hold your breath if you get hit by a gust."

"Do you think Austin would really hurt her?" Blake asks.

"Maybe. I don't know." My gut is telling me he would. "Don't look in his eyes. His promises are empty."

We see the fire first. It's a huge bonfire, with stacks of wood that rise several feet out of the pit. The flames flicker and stretch, higher and higher. Instinctively I reach out to them, test them. The fire recedes on my command, quieting down to a slower burn.

Haley's laugh carries across the beach. She whoops and throws her arms around Austin's neck. He stumbles back, folding her into his arms and spinning her around in a circle. From here they look blissful, romantic.

Blake stops. "She looks okay to me."

Haley's voice is too loud. "Let's go skinny dipping!"

My veins turn to ice. "She's not okay." Haley doesn't know how to do anything she can't learn from watching others or practicing in her room. Haley would never suggest skinny dipping. Okay, maybe in a hot tub, but never in the ocean. Haley can't swim.

I let go of Blake's hand and run the rest of the way to where Austin is still holding Haley in his arms.

"Easy." Austin's voice is soothing, lilting accent and all. "You'll get to swim soon enough." He grins when he sees me. "For a moment I was worried you weren't coming."

"Let her go."

Haley's eyes are so dark I can barely make out a thin ring of turquoise. "Brie! Are you stalking us now?"

Blake steps up behind me. As he does, the wind shifts,

changing directions and blowing toward Blake. I have to react fast to stop it, convinced now that whatever is in the air is dangerous.

"Haley, listen to me. I'm not stalking you. You know me better than that. And Blake is here too. We're here to help."

Haley's laugh is too high. "Last time I checked, Austin and I were doing just fine on our own." She moves her lips to his neck and kisses a trail to his ear. Her smile is too big. It's not the coy smile that took her two years to perfect, the one that shows just a hint of teeth, and the promise of more. "We're going skinny dipping!" She lets go of Austin and stumbles away, pulling her long-sleeved tee over her head. The cold wind whistles around her but she doesn't flinch.

"You can't swim." I keep my voice low. Embarrassing Haley in front of Austin and Blake won't help me convince her to come with me.

"You think you're so great now, don't you? So you got a boy to notice you. La dee dah!" She spins in a circle. When she stops in front of me her face is contorted into a grotesque sneer. "I bet I could get him too, if I wanted. Except I would never do that to you. I have boundaries." She unbuttons her jeans and starts peeling them off.

"Haley!" I grab her arm. "Listen to me. This isn't you talking. He's in your head. Don't let him do this."

She shakes off my hand and continues pulling off her clothes until she's standing on the beach in only a thin pair of black lace panties and matching bra she's managed to keep hidden from her mom since she bought it at the mall three weeks ago. When she looks at me again, her face is almost wistful. "Why can't you understand?" She looks over her shoulder at Austin. He stands in the firelight, smiling at her with his crooked grin, looking for all the world like a smitten boyfriend. "I love him. It's not like before."

The air turns colder, even as I push the wind away. It's too cold.

"Haley." Blake's voice is smooth. He touches her shoulder, fighting fire with fire. She can't look away from him. "Aren't you cold?"

Haley blinks, a lost look in her eyes. "Blake?" Her arms come around her chest and she rubs her arm, finally feeling the chill in the air.

Too late, Austin realizes what's happening. No longer content to sit back by the fire, he's on us in three strides. Haley is already grabbing for her clothes and shivering.

"Good." Blake keeps his voice low. "Get your stuff. We need to go home."

The golden light that flares behind us is so bright we all turn at once.

A ring of gold surrounds a patch of darkness so black that it seems to swallow everything. The light-ring grows and changes shape until it forms the outline of a man. Not a man. A god.

The creature that stands before us is like nothing I've ever seen. It almost hurts to look at him. It's not so much that he's illuminated in sunlight as it is that he's the sun itself. His light and heat shine on everything in his orbit. The cold air turns to a warm tropical breeze; hot waves dance along my skin. He's wearing what looks like a suede cloth, draped across his chest and tied around his waist, barely covering him. His boy-band good looks, so approachable as a human, are now anything but. His face is chiseled—sharp lines cast in granite with the skill of a master, so perfect that it's a shock when he flashes that crooked smile and my insides warm to an uncomfortable degree.

Haley drops her clothes in the sand and moves toward Austin, enchanted. She doesn't even notice the silver flash behind her.

With Blake's appearance, the beach is lit up like it's high noon, silver and gold light attempting to outshine each other. Blake's sword is drawn; his eyes watch Austin warily.

Austin holds out his hand to Haley and pulls her to him. She sinks into him, her eyes still huge. He strokes her hair as he whispers in her ear, and from a distance it almost looks like he cares about her. But I hear the last word he says as he pushes her away. "Swim."

Haley turns her back on him and starts to walk toward the water. I grab her arm but she pulls away easily. "Leave me alone." She starts to run.

A flash of lightning strikes right where Blake is standing. Blake disappears, before I can tell whether he's been hit. I spin around, looking for him.

Austin's laugh heats me through. It's a stark contrast to the icy cold heart that beats inside him. "Who's it going to be, Brianna? You can't save them both."

I call the wind, using it to blow Haley backward, doing what I can to keep her from making it to the water.

Blake appears with a flash to my right. "Go after Haley. I can take care of myself."

"He can't kill you," I say, remembering Austin's comment about not being able to interfere. "If he kills you, he'll be banished to the underworld."

Blake grins. "So it's a win-win." He disappears again as I run to Haley.

She's fighting against the wind. It's strong enough that she falls to the ground. She struggles to get on her hands and knees, crawling with tiny steps.

"Haley!" I call her name three times before I'm close enough for her to hear me in the howling wind. A sandstorm rises around us, beating us with a million tiny bits of pebble. I smell an odor on the wind again, a stagnant damp smell that reminds me of underground. I hold my breath but it's too late—I already feel the air swirling in my lungs, coating my thoughts with a filmy drowsiness. Haley is a blur of movement as the wind stops.

I'm barely cognizant of her moving closer to the water; my mind is cloudy and dark. I just know that I have to stop her. It's like walking in quicksand. My feet feel so heavy, it takes all my concentration to keep them moving forward. I know I can't hold my breath much longer. I'm not even sure why I'm holding it in the first place. Then, just as I'm about to suck in a huge breath of air, my head clears. I push the wind away from me as quickly as I can before taking in big gulps of oxygen.

I hear the splash as Haley dives into the water. I call to the water, manipulating the waves to push her back toward the shore. I wade in until I'm almost waist-deep, reaching for Haley's arm. She dives under just as I make contact. She slips away. Her hand pops out of the water a few feet closer to shore. I surge forward. She's only knee-deep in water, but she's still face-down, panicking. I grab her arm and pull her to her feet. She struggles against me, even as she's coughing and choking, until she finally stops coughing long enough to get some air in her lungs. The air is fresh now, with no sign of the putrid odor that hung in it before.

When Haley looks at me, her eyes are clear and blue. She looks down at her wet, nearly naked form. "Brie?" Her voice is shaky. "What's going on?"

There's a clash of metal hitting rock, and we both look up to see our boyfriends-turned-gods facing off by the cliff wall.

I grab Haley's arm. "Come with me!"

She doesn't move at first, her eyes glued to the spectacle in front of us. "Is that...?" She can't bring herself to finish the sentence. "Oh. My. God."

It is quite a sight. Two men, too beautiful for words, bathed in the light of the stars and the sun. They fight, the clang of their swords ringing out across the beach.

I grab Haley's arm again and pull her away. We run along the beach until we're far enough away that the night becomes dark again. I lead her up the path to the parking lot.

Joe steps out of a white convertible just as we come over

the crest. He takes off his leather jacket and places it around Haley's shoulders, ushering her into his car.

"Stay with Joe," I say. "No matter what." I calculate the odds of my coming back in one piece if I really try to banish Austin. They're not so good. "If I don't come back, don't worry," I tell Haley. "Austin won't have any reason to hurt you."

Haley nods, but her eyes are vacant, lost. "What about you?"

"I have something to take care of. Don't worry. I can handle it."

I have no idea if the words are true. It hardly matters. I can't sit by and do nothing anymore. My days of being a scientific observer are behind me. It's time to take action.

"Are you going to tell me what's going on?"

"Of course." I hug Haley close. "You're my best friend."

She hugs me back. "I'm going to hold you to that."

I don't know if she means my telling her everything, or being her best friend. It doesn't matter. I plan to follow through on both.

There's a flash and a large boom from down on the beach. I leave Haley in the car and run back down the path. I don't stop running until I get to the firepit.

Austin stands behind Blake, his arm tightening around Blake's neck. He holds Blake's sword in his free hand. "You're just in time," he says to me.

Blake's eyes plead with me. "Brianna, go back. He can't kill me, right?"

"Is that so?" Austin runs the sword along Blake's chest, drawing a thin line of blood.

Blake doesn't flinch, but I feel the effort it takes for him to stay strong. The sharp stinging sensation ripples on my own skin. "It's a trap, Brianna. Get out of here."

Austin laughs. "A trap? For who? I have no intention of hurting her. You, however, are a different story." The sword cuts deeper.

I fall to the ground as Blake does, the pain slicing through me, as real as if the sword were breaking through my own skin.

Austin's golden voice carries across the sand, reverberating in my spine like a deep bass. "Do you feel his pain too? So sorry. I'm afraid it's going to hurt quite a bit more before I'm through."

Blake vanishes from Austin's arms, and in a flash Austin is gone too. I push myself onto my hands and knees, still trying to get my bearings as the pain begins to ease. The next flash of light is behind me, farther up the beach. Blake is drawing Austin away. His silver light flickers as he struggles to reappear.

Austin appears in front of him, his back to me, sword raised. He thrusts the sword toward Blake's heart. A killing thrust.

Before I can even think, I'm on my feet, consumed with fire. There's a silver flash and a ball of blue flames dancing in the palm of my hand. I throw it at Austin's back without a second thought. Just as the fire is about to hit its mark, there's another, golden flash. Austin is gone.

The relief I feel, at the realization that his sword never made contact with Blake, lasts only a fraction of a second. Then my fireball takes the sword's place, hitting Blake square in the chest.

My heart explodes in the same instant. It breaks into a million tiny shards, which rip through my body like jagged bits of shrapnel. Even as I scream, I plead with Blake to hang on. But he's pulling away. There's a tearing sensation so strong it's as if my body is being torn from the inside out.

As my soul splits in two, everything goes black.

FORTY

It's cold. Dark and cold. I shiver, my shoulders shaking against the chill. I want to embrace the iciness, to wrap myself up in it until I'm numb.

Austin's warm hand smooths my hair, running from my crown down my back. I'm pulled into a sitting position. My shoulders fall back against the wall of his strong chest as his arms come around me. I keep my eyes closed. Even as the heat of his body starts to warm me through, I fight against it. I'm not ready for the pain that comes with thawing out. I'm not sure I can endure it. I just want to go back to the anesthetic of the cold.

His hands run down my arms, sending prickles of pain along my arms as my nerves come back to life. *No.* Fear and panic twist around in my stomach, competing for dominance in the empty space that once was filled with Blake.

And then the cold disappears all at once and I can't help

but feel it. Not the all-consuming pain and grief I expect, but something far worse. My heart is empty, drained. Utterly alone.

"Blake!" I call, but there's no trace of him. Not a hint of emotion, good or bad. I can't feel him at all. He's really gone. My eyes fly open; I'm no longer able to keep the panic at bay.

Blake lies on the beach a few feet in front of me. I start to move toward him, but the arms around my waist fold tighter, holding me back.

"Shhhh," Austin whispers. His voice is soothing, a comfort I can't afford to indulge.

"Let me go." I pull away, and this time he doesn't stop me. I scramble across the sand, throwing my arms around Blake's lifeless form. I don't bother to check his vital signs; I already know there won't be any. The hollow place inside me tells me everything I need to know.

I don't cry. I don't deserve the luxury of tears. Blake is back in human form, in dark jeans and a vintage concert tee. He looks almost normal, other than the streak of blood and the black burn marks that mar the front of his shirt. His skin is still slightly warm, the last bits of life holding on.

Austin walks up behind me. "Destiny is a funny thing. It always finds a way, doesn't it?"

I want to kill him. I *meant* to kill him. He should be the one lying on the beach, his heart frozen for eternity. "This is your fault."

He holds up his hands, turning them over as he looks

at them. When he speaks his voice is laced with sarcasm. "Out, damned spot."

I launch myself at Austin, my fists connecting with his chest as hard as I can.

He grabs my wrist, stopping another blow before it connects with his rib cage. "You think you know what this means, but you don't. His death means your life. You get to live, Brianna. You win."

I pull my wrist away from him, stepping back. "You can save him."

He almost looks sad. "I can't."

"I saw you do it. With Dart."

He laughs. "You think I'm some kind of healer?"

"I saw you. Dart was dead. You brought him back. You healed him."

"I'm not a healer." The smile that plays at the corner of his mouth tells me he believes what he says. He's mocking me.

"How do you explain what you did with Dart, then?"

"A sacrifice of sorts. A reversal spell."

"A spell? I thought you were a god."

"Magic in a god's hands is a powerful tool, Brianna. Surely you've discovered that."

Not exactly, but it does lend credence to my theory. I might still be able to banish Austin. But first I need him to heal Blake. "How does the spell work?"

"I called back the magic."

Semantics. He healed Dart by reversing the magic. He

healed him. "So, you can reverse the magic that killed Blake. You can save him," I repeat.

"I told you I can't." He shakes his head. "I can only reverse my own magic."

My head fills with white noise. Loud static that hurts my ears. I fall to my knees in the sand. It was never Jonah. It was Austin's magic. Austin killed Dart.

I feel sick. The blue flames arc across my fingers. I throw the fire right at his gorgeous face. He disappears in a golden flash and the flame lands harmlessly on the sand before vanishing from lack of fuel. He appears again a few feet away, shining like the sun.

How could he do something so horrible? Dart had nothing to do with this fight. Nothing.

I hurl another ball of fire at him. He disappears just before it hits him, appearing again directly in front of me.

"Why?" I barely hear myself ask the question.

Austin steps closer, but he's watching the fire that dances in the palm of my hand. "To spur you into action. I thought for certain you would go after the Sons. Revenge is a powerful motivator."

"No shit." I throw another ball of fire at him. He disappears again.

I collapse in the sand, defeated. It's all too much. Austin killed Dart to spark a war. A war he needs me to fight in order to win. I'm just the foot soldier, a weapon to be manipulated and used. And now Blake is dead, and Austin won't rest until the other Sons are dead too. Once the gods return, the humans will be the ones to suffer.

Austin appears next to me, dressed casually in a T-shirt and jeans. He kneels in the sand. "I've made a bit of a mess, haven't I? Brianna, I only ever meant to keep you safe. Don't you see? If you don't go after them first, you can't win. They mean to kill you. They always have. Are you so willing to throw your life away?"

I swallow my pain. Bury it deep. Maybe Austin can't save Blake, but I can keep him from hurting anyone else. I force myself to meet his gaze, suffocating the instinct to fight him. This is the only way I can think of to stop him. To hurt him. "Okay."

"Okay?"

I reach for the clasp of my bracelet, unhooking it and letting it fall to the sand. Although he's said the bracelet doesn't affect him, I need every arrow in my quiver. Austin's answering smile carries me forward.

I hold out my hand and he takes it, pulling me to my feet. "I'll need your help." My voice is strong, surer than I feel.

"Of course." His eyes search my face, and for a second I wonder if he's suspicious.

I step closer to him, deliberately brushing my breast against his arm. I lower my eyelids and look up at him from beneath my lashes, attempting a look I've seen Haley perform countless times. "I'll need you."

The firepit beside us sparks and flares with blue flame, warming my skin from the outside even though my blood runs cold.

Austin's eyes ignite, in unison with the fire. "I'd be lying if I said I wasn't looking forward to that."

I force myself to lean in closer, bringing my hand to the back of his head, running my fingers through his hair. I tilt my head up toward him, licking my lips. A muscle in his neck spasms in response. I feel an unexpected surge of power. Not magic; something baser, human. I turn my head, just enough so my breath warms his throat. My lips brush against his ear. "Do you still want to take me home?"

His breathing is loud. Hard. His arms come around me, pulling me against him. "What do you think?"

I let my forehead fall against his shoulder as I gather strength. When I look up, I manage a smile. "What are you waiting for?"

"Indeed." His smile sends an icy shiver down my spine. I'm playing with a time bomb. I hope I'll know when to cut the wires. I hope I'll cut the right ones.

He slides his arm around me and starts to walk, heading in the direction of the parking lot. I stop, shaking my head. I curl into him, press into his side. "It's too far. Let's go to your real home."

He hesitates. I place my lips against his neck, grazing my teeth on the sensitive skin where his pulse beats. He moans and grabs the back of my head, pulling me closer.

When our eyes meet, I know I'm winning this battle. He shakes his head, but he turns around. He leads me to the crevice in the cliff wall and pulls me inside.

Everything is still. There's no breeze. No life. Just the rocks and the river and the stark waterfalls in the distance.

I hear my own breath coming fast, fear finally catching up with my recklessness. My theory might not be correct. It's not like I have the best track record or anything.

My heart beats faster as he leads me to the flat boulder and pulls me into his lap. I stop him before he kisses me. He tenses, and I know I've made a mistake.

I bring my finger to his lips and then trace the line of his jaw. "Wait," I whisper. "Don't rush this. I want to remember every second." I lean forward and kiss the spot where his collarbone peeks out from his shirt. I feel him relax, melt, beneath my touch.

I'm running out of time. We're here. I have to finish it.

I kiss my way up his neck, whispering against his skin. "*Bane of all that is true.*" A swirl of cold wind blows around us, which I take as a good sign for once. "*Come out of the weeds.*" I scratch my nails along his back, trying to distract him as the wind lifts my hair. "*Make your last strike.*" The wind picks up, biting and stinging with cold.

Austin tenses again. He lifts his head. "What are you doing?"

I bite down on his neck, harder than is necessary.

He pulls me tighter. I nibble my way to his ear. "*Your time on earth is at an end.*"

Too late, he realizes I'm up to something. He pushes me off him, standing up. The wind whips around us wildly now. It's hard to stand. I grab his arm for support.

I fall into him but manage to stay on my feet. It starts to rain, big fat drops that gain in speed and number, slanting sideways in the wind. Austin's arms close around me.

I have to shout to hear myself over the wind. "*A thousand years of otherworldly night!*"

Thunder claps, so loud that the ground shakes beneath us. I nearly lose my balance again, but Austin is holding me to him. "What are you doing?" he screams over the howling wind.

"Ending this badly."

The sky opens up with a pounding rain. It pours so hard I can barely see Austin, even though he's right in front of me.

He screams a string of obscenities that I can barely make out between the hammering sheets of rain. A gust of wind blows me back. I fall onto the rocky ground. I can't see anything in the downpour.

I clamber to my hands and knees and crawl in what I hope is the general direction of the cliff wall. I manage a few steps against the wind and rain. My hand finds empty air in front of me, and I realize I've gone the opposite direction. I'm at the edge of the ravine. I try to back up a step, but my foot hits something hard. I spin around.

He stands above me, a ring of golden light surrounding him, fighting back the rain. "What did you do?" His eyes are full of fury.

There's nowhere for me to go. He's blocking the path to the cliff wall. His face contorts as he repeats, "WHAT DID YOU DO?"

I look into his eyes. The eyes of a god. A very angry god. I rise from my knees, standing to face him. The rain falls more lightly than before, but it hardly matters; I'm soaked through.

"Nothing you haven't seen before." I say. I still have to shout over the wind. "The world will just have to manage another thousand or so years without you."

"How . . . ?" He closes the distance, and I can't help but back up a step. I feel a rock slip beneath my heel and fall into the ravine behind me.

I smile up at him. "Magic."

"Bloody fool." It's unclear if he's referring to himself or me.

There's a rumbling noise. The ground shifts, sending me back to my knees. A huge rock falls from the cliff wall and rolls toward us. I dive to the side to avoid getting swept up in its path.

The river churns below us. It seems to pick up speed on its winding course to the depths of the underworld. More rocks fall from the sides of the walls lining the canyon. The entire place feels like it's about to come down.

Oh hell. It is. I can see the cliff wall now that the rain has let up. More rocks, big and small, are coming loose, collapsing in on themselves. A large boulder lands directly in front of the crevice. Sealing us in.

I rise to my feet again. Austin still stands in my path, a pillar of strength, oblivious to the ruin that's falling around him.

"Are you going to let me through?" I ask.

He still doesn't move.

"If you don't let me go, who's going to fight your war for you?"

His voice is tired. "You're not going to fight them. If you wanted to fight, you wouldn't need to trap me here, would you?"

I look back over my shoulder. The river is rising, devouring the ravine from the inside.

His hand finds my chin, turning my head back toward him. "You still owe me a favor."

"Blake's dead. Isn't that enough for you?" Another loud clap of thunder booms overhead.

The earth shakes.

Austin grabs me by the arms, holding me against his chest. "You owe me this." He leans in close, his mouth at my ear. "Stay alive, Brianna. Whatever it takes." He pushes me with such force that my feet come off the ground.

At first I feel like I'm flying, sailing through the air, floating in the wind. But I'm not flying, I'm falling, down into the ravine. The churning water gets closer and closer. I barely hear the sound of my body smacking against the water before the waves close around me and the river swallows me whole.

FORTY-ONE

I cough and cough and cough. I can't seem to stop. I puke up what feels like a gallon of water. My hair is sticky and knotted with seaweed, scratching my arms as I cough some more. When I finally stop and collapse on the sand, I'm staring up at the stars. They don't seem nearly bright enough.

Then I remember. Blake. I sit up and look around the beach. The fire still burns, smaller than it once was. Blake's body lies in the sand beside it. I struggle to my feet and move as fast as I can, then crumple next to him.

His blond hair looks almost silver in the moonlight. His hand is cold, no trace left of the life that flowed through him. The bloodstains on his shirt look nearly black, but they're not as dark as the charred area around his heart, the place where he was hit.

I double over as the tears finally come. I cry out, screaming to the sea. This gut-wrenching ache is different from the physical sensation of our soul bind. So much worse. There's nothing except a black hole, a light-sucking void that can only collapse in on itself, absorbing everything in its path, including me.

I don't know how long I cry, my teeth chattering and clacking. I glance up at the fissure in the cliff wall, half-expecting Austin to step out and say "I told you so," but of course he can't.

There's no denying the reality of what I am now. A killer. Not in the way that Austin or Sherri wanted me to be, but a killer all the same.

A different path to the same place.

I should go find Joe. We need to move Blake before someone comes by. We need to take Blake to his family. I don't even know Blake's parents, but the thought of telling them that their son is dead sends me into another round of sobbing.

I put my hands on the charred area of his shirt, over the blackened flesh covering his heart. The skin is still warm. I pull my hand away. The rest of Blake's body is cold. His skin should be cool to the touch, but the magic still burns in him.

My magic. It's still there. What did Austin do with Dart? A reversal. I try to remember the foreign words that Austin used when he ran his hands over Dart's cuts. I place my hand over the burn mark on Blake's chest.

"*Draiocht leasaigh,*" I whisper, hoping I'm pronouncing it right.

Nothing happens. Blake is so still, so empty.

"Please."

Blake's hair is wild, sticking out in all directions. It's somehow exactly right, mirroring my crazy desperation as I say the words again.

The skin beneath my palm starts to cool, and for a second I think it will work. Then I realize the opposite is happening. My magic had been the last bit of life force left in Blake, the final holdout. Even it couldn't stay there forever.

As the last of the magic leaves his body, I slam my fist into his chest. As if I can beat the life back into him.

There's a blur of motion. A hand grabs my wrist and I'm thrown back into the sand. "What was that for?" someone yells.

Blake—*Blake!*—pins me to the ground.

I throw my free arm around him and pull him closer, grinning like a maniac. I hold him as tightly as I can. "Thank you," I say into his neck. I can't believe he's here.

Alive.

"Easy," he says. "You're choking me."

I loosen my hold, reluctantly letting him sit up. I keep my hand on his shoulder, unable to let go completely.

Blake looks up and down the beach. "Where's Austin?"

I bite my lower lip. "I might've banished him from the earth for a while."

He crinkles his nose, apparently noticing that I smell like something close to a beached seal. "I have a feeling there's a story here."

The air makes contact with my wet clothes, but it's the icy chill on the inside that makes me shiver. I drop my hand from his shoulder, shaking my hair in a pointless attempt to get the sand out.

We both look out at the ocean, neither one of us in a rush to have this discussion. I just want to sit here and breathe him in. I reach for him, but let my hand fall at the last minute when I realize he's not even looking at me.

He breaks the silence first. "I can't feel you. You're right here next to me and I don't feel anything."

Ironic, that. Because I feel everything. I may not carry a piece of his soul, but every beat of my heart is alive with him. *Blake. Blake. Blake.*

"Did you find a way to break the bond?" The hope in his voice is a shot with a poisoned arrow.

"That's one way of putting it." My jeans are still wet and starting to chafe. I pull my knees to my chest. "I killed you."

He laughs, and I almost let myself laugh with him. It would be so much easier to pretend it's all a joke. It's not like he can feel me anymore. He wouldn't even know if I lied. But I don't lie. I ramble instead.

"Austin was going to kill you. He had your sword. I tried to stop him, but he disappeared and you were too weak to get out of the way. I thought I was saving you." I'm crying now, remembering the look on Blake's face as my fireball hit his chest. "I was right about Austin. He couldn't kill you himself. I had to be the one."

Blake looks at me sideways. "Brianna, chill. You're missing something kind of important." He runs his hand through his hair. "I'm not exactly dead."

"Not now."

He laughs again. "Did I get hit in the head? Did you? Is that what broke the bond?"

He's not getting it. He still thinks Austin is the one who hurt him. I've told him the truth—it's up to him whether he wants to believe it. I should be relieved, so why can't I let this go? For some stupid reason, it's important that Blake understand. Who I am. What I am.

"You're not listening." I wait until he looks at me. "I. Killed. You." There's a question in his eyes. He's alive, so of course none of this makes any sense to him. I try again. "I used a reversal spell."

"A reversal?"

"Let me see your hand." As he puts his hand in mine, I conjure a fireball. He pulls back his hand with a shout.

"Christ!" He holds up his reddened hand. Blisters are popping up along his fingers and there's a large piece of his palm with the skin missing. The smell of burnt flesh rises in the air.

"Watch." I place my fingers over his hand again, feeling the magic as it courses through. I repeat the reversal spell. As I say the words, his palm cools and the magic retreats. Within a few seconds, the blisters are gone. His skin is back, perfectly smooth, no trace of the wound.

"Oh my God." He's looking at me like I'm some kind of freak, like I've broken every law of nature. Which I have. There is no scientific explanation for bringing the dead back to life. His face is white. "I was dead?"

I nod, taking in the pained look in his eyes without

feeling it. I want to feel it with him. For him. I owe him that. But there's nothing but emptiness where his emotions should be.

Before I can say anything else, Blake turns away. I follow his gaze to the dark figure approaching us.

Joe pulls out a cigarette and puts it between his lips. "You've looked better."

I look down at my still-soaked clothes. My hair hangs in a knotted mess of sand and sea water. Blake's shirt is covered with blood and burn marks. There's a fresh stain where the cut along his chest has started bleeding again. His hair sticks straight up.

I try to smile, not quite managing it. "Nice to see you too."

Joe offers his hand and pulls me to my feet.

I make a half-hearted attempt at brushing sand from my jeans. "How's Haley?"

Is it my imagination or do Joe's cheeks redden? "Good. Worried, but good."

Blake doesn't move to get up. He stares back out at the ocean.

"Coming?" Joe asks.

Blake finally looks at Joe. Not at me, even though I'm standing right here. "Not yet. Can you take the girls home?"

The girls. Plural. Haley and me.

Joe nods. "No problem."

Blake looks back to the water, his eyes vacant. I've been dismissed.

"Wait." I walk toward the firepit. Blake doesn't turn to

watch me. My bracelet lies in the sand right where I left it, and I lean down to pick it up. Before I do, I look at Blake one more time. I'm not two feet away from him, with no magic to hide me, but he doesn't turn around. I curl my fingers around the charm. I don't need its protection anymore, but at least I can pretend it's the reason Blake doesn't look at me.

Joe picks up Haley's jeans and shirt from the beach before taking my arm to lead me back toward the parking lot. "You gonna tell me what all that was about?" he says as we walk.

"No. Are you going to tell me what you and Haley were doing while we were out here saving the world?"

Joe's lips turn up into a closed-mouth smile. "Nope." He reaches into the front pocket of his jeans and pulls out a lighter. He stops walking just long enough to scratch the flint and bring the dancing flame to the cigarette that hangs from his lips.

He inhales deeply before turning up the path to the parking lot.

FORTY-TWO

On Saturday morning, Joe calls to give me directions to Rush Bruton's house for my initiation as a new breeder. "It's not too late to back out," he says halfheartedly. He knows I'm not going to change my mind.

I should. I should get as far away from the Sons as I can. But I have to try to make them understand that I don't want to fight.

Dad stops me on the way out the door. "Hot date?"

"You know it." It's even less true than he realizes.

"I got the oil changed in the Blue Box today. I was thinking you might want to trade her in now that Dart is sold. We could go to some dealers tomorrow."

I don't think I can handle losing Dart and the Blue Box in one weekend. "No thanks. She's got at least another fifty thousand miles in her."

"Okay." Dad stares at me, which is weird in itself. "Is that a new dress? It looks nice."

"It is." I spin around so he can see the blue silk dress that Mom got me for my birthday.

"You look great."

"Thanks." I'm in my car before the full implication of what Dad said hits me. I rub the bracelet on my wrist. The charm isn't working anymore. I can't hide behind the little silver blossom. Today, the Sons will meet the real Brianna Paxton. Whoever that is.

Rush lives in the Heights, in a sprawling house that didn't burn in last fall's firestorm. Everything about the house is proud, from the long driveway to the huge round pillars that frame the front entrance. A six-car garage is attached to the side, but a red Ferrari sits in the driveway, uncovered. Large double doors are framed in an intricate pattern of blue and green stained glass.

Micah answers the door at almost the exact moment I press the bell. "Dude, you look amazing! Are you trying to blow your cover?"

I accept his kiss on the cheek. "Can't a girl just look her best?"

He laughs. "Hell yes. If you weren't already with Blake, I might even consider breeding with you."

I raise my eyebrows.

Micah laughs. "What? You have to admit we'd make some damn fine babies." He leads me down an elaborate hallway with archways every few feet, then stops at another set of double doors. "It will just be the Sons for the ceremony.

You'll meet the rest of the breeders for refreshments in the sunroom, afterwards."

"You make it sound so civilized."

"Mrs. Bruton wouldn't dream of anything less. Right down to the crustless cucumber sandwiches. It's completely lame."

I smooth out the skirt of my dress, grateful that I've dressed appropriately for the occasion for once.

Micah smiles. "Relax. You look hot." He knocks on the door and we wait.

After an awkward minute, Jeremy opens the door. He looks at me twice, as if he isn't sure it's really me, then he grins. "Hel-lo, new blood."

As I enter the room, I feel them staring, hear the murmurs that roll on the air. None of it means anything. There's only one person who matters.

Blake is leaning against a wall in the back corner of the room, next to a giant picture window that opens up to what must've been an amazing view at one time. Now, the black, barren canyon looks like a war zone. It's somehow fitting. Blake sips a glass of dark wine, the deep crimson color of blood. His eyes meet mine over his glass.

My heart flutters, skipping in places like a scratched record. But there's no indication of his emotions. Nothing I can feel. Nothing I can read in his dark gaze. For the first time since coming here, I feel the fear I should have felt all along. It's not the fear that my enemies will not accept a truce, although that's certainly a possibility; it's the fear that there's nothing left between Blake and me now except my breaking heart.

The twins flank me as I walk to the center of the room. I nod politely at two large men sitting at either end of one of the two black leather couches. I recognize one of them as Dr. McKay, the geneticist who came to my school. I force myself to look at Jonah, who sits opposite him.

I turn my shoulder, blocking him out as I smile at Jeremy and place a hand on his arm. Jeremy puts his hand on top of mine and squeezes. Blake is no longer leaning against the wall. He stands at attention, easing closer. My pulse picks up speed with every inch of distance that closes.

Rushmore Bruton stands in the center of the room. He's wearing a dark suit. Instead of a tie, his shirt is topped with a deep red neckcloth tied in a fancy knot that flows in an intricate cascade.

"Well, Jonah, it seems you're not completely insane." Rush looks me in the eye. His stare is hard and I immediately look away. "She's quite pretty, isn't she?" He places his hand on my shoulder, his thumb moving along my collarbone. "She might make good breeding stock after all."

It's an effort not to pull away from his touch.

Blake takes another step toward me. I don't have to feel him to know that he's on the verge of violence. His shoulders tense. The vein at the base of his throat expands and throbs. I swallow. If Blake wanted to attack me, he wouldn't do it here. At least that's what I tell myself.

Rush finally speaks to me directly. "On your knees."

I automatically respond to his command, but my eyes

watch Blake, who moves another step closer. The wine in his glass is lapping and churning though his hand is still.

Rush places both of his hands on my shoulders. "You will swear your fealty to me and mine. Repeat after me." From this angle Rush looks even taller. "I will to the Sons be faithful and true."

I repeat the words, going through the motions.

"And love all that we love."

All that they love. I can't help looking at Blake. He lifts his wine glass to his lips, downing half the glass in one swallow. I wait for him to look at me. "And love all that we love."

Rush closes his hands tight on my shoulders, pinching the skin. "And shun all that we shun."

I say the words, though my mouth is dry and sour.

"Putting the good of the Sons above all."

I hesitate.

Blake moves another step closer so that he's standing right next to me. Waiting. For what? For me to swear fealty so he can expose me as a fraud?

Rush repeats the words, louder this time.

I won't let him do it. I won't give him that power.

"Is there a problem young lady?" Rush glares down at me. My shoulders tremble.

Jonah laughs, a sound that barely registers as I pull away, breaking the contact with Rush's hands. Although my legs feel like Jell-O, I find enough strength to stand, forcing myself to meet Rush's hard eyes.

I may be a killer, but I am not going to be anyone's

monster but my own. It's now or never. Every man in the room is standing at full attention now, nerves on alert, waiting for some sign from Rush.

I gather my courage. "I've agreed to be faithful to the Sons. But I will not fall to my knees for you, and you have no right to ask." My voice shakes.

"On your knees!" Rush's eyes turn silver.

It's almost enough to send me back to the floor. I force myself to stand firm.

Blake has moved so close I can smell vanilla and mint. I close my eyes, breathing him in. It's almost too much. I might cry. Some stand against tyranny that would be.

I open my eyes and focus on Rush. "Mr. Bruton, you have my word that I will not harm the Sons. I will protect you if I can. On my terms."

Blake's hand slips into mine and he gives me a light squeeze. A shock of heat flares where he touches me. My heart dances in response. Blake wasn't about to attack me—his anger is directed at Rush.

Rush's eyes drop to our joined hands, then he glares at Blake. "You will pay for this," he whispers. It's far more powerful than if he'd yelled.

Blake doesn't move from his place beside me.

"I offer a truce." My legs wobble, barely holding me upright.

"Why would I want peace with you? You're no threat to us. A lowly human with an attitude not fit for breeding."

I hold on to Blake tighter as I let the earth seep into my bones. The clinking of the glasses above the bar is the first indication, and then the earth shakes in earnest. Blake starts to laugh as the roar fills the room. Rush steps back, off balance. A blast of air pushes him the rest of the way, so that he falls back onto the floor.

The rumbling stops. "Let's try this one more time," I say. "I will protect the Sons from others like me, and you will ensure my safety from the Sons."

Rush scrambles to his feet. "How dare you!"

Blake pulls at my hand, moving me away from Rush. I have no intention of running. Not this time. I hold my ground. "Perhaps you misunderstood. I offer peace, not war."

"This is impossible." Dr. McKay gets up off the couch. "We tested you. You have the Killian gene. You're one of us."

It seems even Dr. McKay needs to be reminded of basic genetics. Danu's heirs are Killian's heirs just as surely as the Sons themselves are. "I am an heir of Killian," I state. "I am descended from his son Brom."

Rush gasps. I turn to look at him just as he disappears, reappearing as a bright, powerful demigod, a large sword in his hands. The power that flows through me is a swirl of wind waiting to be unleashed. I send the wind at Rush, picking him up and throwing him against the window. A large crack forms down the center of the window as he smacks against it and slides to the floor.

Dr. McKay steps back.

"Anyone else want to play?" I look directly at Jonah, practically begging for him to take me on.

"I hate to say I told you so," Jonah says to Rush. He

looks back at me. "It's a shame we have to kill you. We would've been good together." He disappears and reappears, holding his jeweled knife, his silver eyes flashing.

Seconds later, Dr. McKay turns, then the man sitting next to him, who I assume is Levi. I am surrounded by Sons, nearly blinded by the light that surrounds them. So peace is out.

Austin would be thrilled to know he was right. They won't let me live. My only choice is to fight. I raise my hands just as Dr. McKay leaps forward, sword drawn.

"Enough!" Blake yells, throwing himself in front of me. Dr. McKay sees him too late. He twists to the side, glancing Blake's shoulder with the butt of his sword and knocking him down.

"Stop!" Blake shouts from the carpet. "Think about what she offers. Protection against the others. And there *are* others." He glares at Rush, who's only now pulling himself up from the floor. "You've seen them."

They close their circle around us, but Blake's distraction is exactly what I need to gain the upper hand. I can take them all out in one fiery burst. The flames build in my blood until it hurts. I shake from the fire that rages inside me.

Blake turns to face me, his eyes pleading.

Move. I pray for him to understand, even though I know he can't feel me anymore. I can't attack them with Blake in the way, but if I don't strike soon, I'll lose my only chance. My hand itches with heat. But I won't kill Blake. Not again.

Yet another cruel irony in my twisted life. My weakness is not the killer inside me at all. It's the girl.

Weak, weak, weak.

I shake violently now.

Blake sees my struggle. He looks at the gathered Sons. "Last chance before I let her at you."

I grab the couch again. My legs start to give out as the power and heat build with each second. I need to let it out. Now. "Blake. Move." My voice is a rasp.

"Hang on. They'll come around."

I can't take the fire much longer. The flame burns my blood, boiling it from the inside. My ears are ringing, a blaring siren perfectly suited to the fire that consumes me.

I love you. I'm not sure if I say the words or not, but I hope he hears them. Then it's too late for me to do anything but scream as I fall to the floor.

FORTY-THREE

The first thing I'm aware of is the cold. I float in the fog and mists, embracing the stark chill as it eases the raging fire inside, vanquishing the killer. A shadow drifts toward me in the clouds. And then I fall to the muddy, wet ground. A man stands over me. Not a man. A god. His blond hair is almost white, a glowing mane that frames his perfectly chiseled face. His green eyes are infused with starlight.

"Am I dead?" I ask.

I've been here before, in the field with the rocks that appear to grow up out of the earth. It seems unlikely that I survived the last few minutes. If the fire didn't kill me, the Sons surely did.

His smile is wicked, in a totally good way. "Not yet." His lilting accent is smoky, curling around me like a soft blanket. "So you're the lass that everyone speaks of, the last of the Seventh Daughters."

"There are others."

He shakes his head. "Ahh, but their destiny is not yours, is it? You are the last, the one who will end the war."

"Things aren't going too well at the moment."

"No one said it would be easy. Nothing worthwhile ever is."

"You think any of this is worthwhile? Fighting over something that happened a thousand years ago?"

He shrugs. "It is already done."

"What is it, exactly, that I'm supposed to do?" It might help if I had a game plan. Or if I knew what the end was supposed to be.

"Killian!" Danu appears behind me. "Leave her be."

He backs up a step. "I just wanted to meet the girl that everyone speaks of. She is more powerful than you let on, if she can travel here."

Danu's face is white. "We are not to interfere."

Killian laughs. "It hardly matters. The curse was made a thousand years ago. The end is already written."

"What curse?"

They look at each other, silently debating whether to tell me. Finally Danu shakes her head. "Go ahead."

Killian's lips curve into a self-satisfied smile. "I lived above, once. My life was dedicated to ridding the world of dark magic and vanquishing the demigods who lived among the mortals. The Milesians had already banished the Tuatha De Danaan to the underworld centuries before, but the gods were rumored to have left their half mortal spawn behind. I barely believed it until I met one for myself, a gorgeous creature with beauty and power beyond my comprehension."

He glances at Danu. She raises her eyebrows.

"She was everything I was sworn to conquer, and I could not allow myself to fall under her spell. I fought against it, but I was only a mortal man, and no match for her wicked ways."

"Please." Danu shakes her head.

"Her powers were far stronger than I imagined. She could travel between the earth and the underworld. She brought me here, where the very air is magic. It is here that she bonded my soul to her own, binding me and cursing my ancestors to covet the very dark magic I fought against."

Danu laughs. "Such a hardship you've all endured. Blessed with the power of the gods. Using it to destroy my family, one generation at time. It is my family that has suffered, cursed to fall in love with men who will only destroy them. Forced to kill to stay alive."

They glare at each other.

For a second I wonder if they've forgotten I'm here. "So how do I fit into all this?"

They finally look back at me.

"It ends with you," Killian says.

"How?"

Danu steps forward. "That," she says, "is what we'd all like to know."

"I don't want to die," I say. "I don't want to kill anyone either."

Danu's eyes get misty. "There is little choice."

"You'll do what you must." Killian takes Danu's hand, and for a second I see the heartbreak in her eyes.

She blinks, recovering quickly, then pulls her hand away from Killian and runs. As she runs down the hill, the purple flowers that crowned her head blow in the wind, leaving a trail of petals scattered across the grass.

Killian watches her, doing nothing to mask his desire. He still wants her, after all.

And all at once I know the truth. "You didn't kill her." My voice is a whisper.

Killian sighs. "Some warrior against magic I turned out to be."

The entire war with the Sons has been based on a lie. Killian didn't kill Danu. Someone else did. Someone else with an interest in spurring a war against the Sons, someone who was not supposed to interfere.

Austin.

FORTY-FOUR

The carpet of the den is soft and plush. I open my eyes, but
everyone's attention is on Rush as he paces near the cracked
window.

"You're sure? She thinks she loves you enough to offer
her protection to the Circle?"

"Yes, and she can help us find the others." Blake's words
are a wine opener to the gut, the corkscrew turning tighter
and tighter.

"And she won't turn against us?" Dr. McKay asks.

"She won't," Blake says.

"He's kept her a secret from us all," Jonah whines. "We
can't trust him."

Blake moves across the room, grabbing Jonah by the
throat. "This from the traitor who would have killed me if
the witch hadn't intervened."

The *witch*. The poisonous word seeps into my bloodstream, traveling with quiet speed to my heart.

Rush steps between them, pulling them apart. "She must not be allowed to come between us."

Jonah and Blake glare at each other. Rush narrows his eyes, and they both bow their heads in submission. A tacit truce.

"She's awake," Micah says from behind me.

I push up on my elbows. Dr. McKay extends a hand and pulls me to my feet. "Welcome to the Circle, bandia."

Rush moves in front of me. "We have accepted your offer of a truce."

I smile like this is the best news I've heard in months. But everything feels wrong.

"Killian didn't kill Danu," I blurt. Everyone stares at me. It's not the obsequious answer they were expecting, I guess. "The entire war between us has been based on a lie."

Rush laughs. "We are the Sons of Killian, bandia. You think we don't know that Killian is not responsible for Danu's death? We didn't start this war." He steps toward me and grabs a curl of my hair. "But make no mistake about it. We will finish it."

I'm shaking. I can't stop it.

Blake stands beside me. "Back off." He puts his arm around my shoulder. My body warms to his touch, but the rest of me is torn. I can't feel his emotions anymore. I might have trusted him before he told the rest of the Sons that I would lead them to the others.

Before everything.

"Hang on," Blake whispers. "I'll get you out of here soon."

I lean into him. I can't help it. I want to believe him. More than anything.

Micah comes to my other side. "Blake won't let them hurt you."

But who's going to stop Blake?

Rush narrows his eyes at Micah before looking back at me. "You have our word that we will protect you as long as you are loyal to our Circle. You will do what is required of you. Your betrayal will be your death."

I swear the guy speaks only in platitudes. I gather my strength. "Great to know I'm completely expendable."

Rush's smile is more chilling than his usual glower. "Not completely." He walks to the door and opens it. "Let's go eat, shall we?"

The Sons file out in silence. God forbid those cucumber sandwiches go to waste. Jonah winks at me as he walks by. Micah squeezes my shoulder before he turns and follows.

Blake and I are the only ones left in the room.

I'm afraid to look at him now that we're alone. Afraid of what I'll see in his eyes. Of what I won't see.

"Why didn't you do it?" Blake's question is not one I'm expecting. "You had us all in one room. You had the advantage. You could have ended it, Brianna."

"I'm not a killer." It's not true. Still, it's easier than admitting how I feel about him.

"I thought we were past that." He turns to face me.

Forces me to look at him. His green eyes are watching me, searching for some truth behind my lie. "Why can't you just say it?"

Like I need that humiliation. I can't admit my feelings for him now. It's too late. "I should go meet the rest of the breeders."

"Brianna..." His voice trails off.

But I'm already halfway to the door before he can finish his sentence.

His voice is almost a whisper, but I hear him. "I love you too."

FORTY-FIVE

I spend an hour mingling with people I don't know, and avoiding those that I do. Sierra and Portia spend most of the afternoon finding ways to openly shun me. Bring it on. I've had years of training when it comes to being invisible. I'm far more comfortable being ignored. I could almost hug them.

Blake doesn't try to approach me again. It's almost like old times, except I don't look for an opportunity to put myself in his path. And I don't harbor some secret hope that today will be the day Blake sees me.

There's no physical ache when he talks to Portia by the wine bar. There's no hum of pleasure when he walks by on his way to the buffet. I don't feel the anger that I see in his eyes when I catch him looking in my direction. There's nothing left between us but my broken heart.

She'll lead us to the others.

The witch.

I love you too.

I leave as soon as I can get away. When I get home, Christy and Haley are waiting to take me to a belated birthday lunch at Olive Garden. We OD on breadsticks, laughing and talking about nothing more important than whether Jennifer Aniston will ever find the right guy. It's exactly what I need.

Christy entertains us with a poem Matt wrote for her, a bizarre combination of iambic pentameter and Suessian rhyme that manages to walk the line between light romance and serial murder. Say what you will about Matt, the guy knows how to take direction.

Haley hasn't mentioned last night, but I'm still planning to tell her the truth. About everything.

Haley twists her hair around her finger as she looks out the window. "So, did you hear about Sherri Milliken?"

Christy nods. "I heard she transferred to McHenry High because they have a better math team."

Haley shakes her head. "I heard she ran away with the father of the kid she babysits for. He's, like, thirty."

I haven't heard a word from Sherri. "The second one sounds more likely."

"Really? That's so gross." Christy grabs the last breadstick. "So Matt and I are going mini-golfing tonight. You guys want to come? Maybe bring Austin and Blake?"

"No," Haley and I both say in unison. We look at each other and laugh.

"What?"

"Austin and I kind of broke up." Haley bites into a breadstick. "He turned out to be kind of a jerk."

Christy shrugs. "Cute, though." She turns to me.

"I've got dinner with my parents." Thankfully, Christy doesn't press further.

A waiter comes by with another basket of breadsticks. He's not much older than us, and he makes a point of smiling at Haley. Haley smiles back, one of her trademark "I know you want me but you'll have to wait" grins.

The waiter blushes and walks away. Christy elbows Haley. "Total hottie! You should invite him to come golfing with us."

Haley shakes her head. "I don't think I'm going to go out with anyone for a while."

"What?" Christy's mouth falls open.

"I think I need to figure some stuff out." Haley's eyes find mine, and I know she's talking about more than just some internal soul-searching.

I nod. "Be careful what you wish for."

"I can handle it." Haley pops the last bit of bread into her mouth. "I'm tougher than I look."

She doesn't have to convince me. "So," I say, "it's like this … " I start with Austin's party, and keep going right through to the initiation into the Circle of Sons.

When I'm done, Haley speaks first. "I tried to break up with Austin that day I saw you at McMillan. He convinced me to stay. It was almost like I couldn't say no. And then at the beach. It was crazy. Brianna saved my life."

"And banished your boyfriend to the underworld."

365

Christy laughs. "I can't believe the spell actually worked! I can't wait to tell Delia."

Oh no. I should've known Christy would think this was a good thing. "You can't tell Delia. Or anyone. Christy, trust me, you don't want to mess with magic. It's scary stuff."

But Christy is already going through the possibilities in her head. "And the love spell! Omigod, Brie! It worked, didn't it? You and Blake, and me and Matt, and Haley and ... " She stops. Haley and Austin were not exactly a success.

I shake my head. "You and Jonah?"

Christy shakes her head. "False start. All our guys were there. I know it."

Haley's cheeks redden. "You really think so?"

Christy and I both stare at her. I have a sinking feeling in the pit of my stomach. Haley's self-imposed celibacy is going to be short-lived.

"Who?" Christy looks thoughtful as she mentally goes through the list of potential candidates. Austin. Jonah. Matt. Blake. Please not Blake.

Haley's smile holds a secret that would make the Mona Lisa proud. She looks at me. "So, what can you tell me about Joe?"

FORTY-SIX

Dinner with my parents is nice. We talk about schools I might apply for in the fall and whether I might be able to put some money toward another rescue horse now that Dart is sold. It feels so normal.

Back home, we sit on the couch watching a DVD of the *Lion King*. Dad orders a pizza even though we just ate. When the doorbell rings, he goes to the door, cash in hand. When he walks back into the family room, there's no pizza on him.

"Brie, it's for you."

"Me?" I get up, wondering why Haley or Christy wouldn't just come in.

When I walk past my dad, he whispers, "It's a boy."

My hands go to my hair, smoothing the curls with my fingers. My heart is already beating out the equivalent of a glam-rock drum solo.

Blake stands in the doorway, leaning against the frame. He's holding a small box in his hands, flipping it around and around and around. His smile when he sees me is tentative, unsure.

I can't resist smiling back. "Hey," I say.

"Hey." He stops flipping the box and stands perfectly still. We both just stand there. Waiting.

"Are you busy?" he asks.

I shake my head.

He looks back down. "I didn't expect this to be so hard."

Uh-oh. Warning sirens blare in my head. I think he's given me this speech before.

"Okay, here goes." He looks back up at me. "Do you want to go for a drive?"

Yes. No. Who am I kidding? "Yes," I say. I run back into the house to tell my parents I'm going out for bit.

"Hot date?" Dad says.

"Maybe." I grab a hoodie from the hall closet and practically run back to the front door. He's still there. I haven't hallucinated him.

I follow him out to his SUV. He stops by the passenger door. "I have something for you. I hope that's okay?" He still fingers the small box, turning it over.

I hold out my hand. "I'm not an expert or anything, but I think you're supposed to actually give me the gift."

He laughs and hands me the small white box. There's a tiny shock of electricity when his fingers brush mine. "Happy birthday."

My hand shakes as I untie the tiny green ribbon. I lift

the lid and pull out a delicate silver necklace. At the end of the chain is a round pendant, not much larger than a quarter. The carving is crude, and gorgeous—a flower carved by hand. Wolfsbane.

"Where'd you get this?"

"Joe's been holding on to it for a while. It belonged to a bandia he knew a long time ago. I thought you should have it."

"Thank you. And Joe, too. It's beautiful."

I hold the necklace up, watching it sparkle under the streetlight. Blake takes it from my fingers and places it around my neck. The pendant sits at the base of my throat, the cold metal warming quickly against my skin.

"So beautiful," Blake says, his hands dropping from my neck. He doesn't back away. He's so close, close enough to feel the warmth coming off his skin. Close enough to kiss. He raises his hand, and for a second I think he might touch me again, but he lowers it just as quickly, then turns and walks around to the other side of the car.

We drive to the vacant lot in the Heights, the barren site of his former home. I follow him to the wall at the back.

He sits down and motions for me to sit down next to him. My thigh touches his as I settle in. An ember ignites where our legs meet. I don't pull away, and neither does he.

"What now?" I finally ask.

He laughs. "I have no idea. I wasn't even sure you'd come out with me."

His hand finds mine and our fingers lace together. We

sit like this for a while, watching the world go by from our perch on the wall.

And then I have to spoil it. "Did you mean what you said to Rush today? Are you using me to find the others?"

"You heard that?"

Not a no. Why do I have to ask questions I don't want to know the answer to?

"They wanted to kill you," Blake says into the silence. "I had to come up with a reason for them to keep you alive."

It's what my heart wants to hear. And it's so easy to believe. I wish I could feel him now. To know.

"Do you miss it?" I ask. "The bond?"

"Sometimes." His thumb runs across my palm. "Today, when I couldn't feel you. I kept reaching for you, and there was nothing."

"I know what you mean. It's like a piece of myself is gone."

"Not gone." He holds my hand to his heart. "Right here." My breath catches as he lifts my hand to his lips. "Brianna, you may not have a piece of my soul anymore, but make no mistake about it—you still carry around a part of me." His lips brush my fingertips, feather-light.

His eyes find mine, asking.

I know the danger that lies in wanting. All I've ever wanted was for Blake to see me, as if his wanting me would be enough.

But it's not nearly enough. I can't simply accept the fact that he has chosen me. As much as I'm tempted to revel in being wanted, it will never be enough. I have to want him too, enough to take a risk with my own heart. Enough to trust him with my secrets.

When I don't say anything, he smiles, the arrogant smile that's meant to charm me and every other girl on the planet. "You're scared."

I'm terrified. "I thought you couldn't feel me anymore."

"I'm pretty good at reading body language."

"You're not helping."

"It's okay." His eyes lose their signature sparkle, and I realize that he might give up on me, that he probably should have a long time ago.

"Can we start this conversation over?"

He looks confused. "What?"

"Not just the conversation. Everything. Can we start from the beginning?"

"You want a do-over?"

That's exactly what I want, but hearing it put that way makes me realize how foolish it is to think it can be that simple. It's not like we can go back to that first time Blake walked into Magic Beans and have him notice me. It's not like we can pretend he didn't claim the right to kill me. That I didn't kill him.

"Forget it," I say. "It was stupid."

"I doubt anyone has ever called you stupid. Brianna, I know what you are. Who you are. And you know me. More than anyone. I'm not saying it will be easy. I'm pretty sure it won't be. All I know is that now that you're here, I can't imagine my life without you in it."

"Here's the thing." I say it before I can stop myself. "I can."

He doesn't hide the disappointment in his eyes. For a second, I think I even feel it, but then I realize it's my own disappointment.

"Brianna."

"Let me finish." I let go of his hand. "I *can* imagine a life without you. I've been there, Blake. I thought I'd lost you."

His drops his chin and looks back out over the view, blinking.

I bring my hand up to his jaw, pulling him back toward me. "I don't want to go through that again."

His eyes are wary.

I swallow, choking on my fear. I have to fight to push away every self-protective instinct. This must be what a sky diver feels just before making the jump. I close my eyes and let myself fall. "The thing is, I love you. I think I always have."

His smile is back, dimples and all. "Always?"

"Don't let it go to your head. The last thing I need is you thinking you're some kind of god." It feels good to admit how I feel, how I've always felt. I lean forward, stretching up until my lips meet his, our smiles converging.

There's a flash of silver light behind us.

I pull away with a start. "What was that?"

We scan the yard, seeing nothing. There's a clap of thunder off in the distance.

"Lightning," Blake says. "The discharge of electricity during a thunderstorm." There's laughter in his voice. "For someone who claims to know a lot about science, you don't know much about weather."

"I'm a little superstitious these days."

He leans in to kiss me again. When our lips meet there's no charge of electricity, no flash of light; just the warmth of two people finding each other on a hillside.

It's not a claiming kiss—it's a gift, a promise. I bring my hand to the back of his neck, pulling him closer. His lips travel along the line of my jaw to my throat.

There's another flash of light. This time when I open my eyes, I see it, the silver thread whipping around us.

"Blake." I pull his head from my neck. "Look."

The silver light is dancing, weaving around us in a perfect spiral.

"Is it happening again?" Blake asks.

"Maybe."

His face turns serious. "We should stop."

"We should stop," I repeat, hoping that if I say it out loud I can find the strength to follow through. We both know what could happen if we don't.

Blake leans back, putting distance between us. He's still breathing hard. We watch as the thread of silver light fades into the darkness.

I turn to face him. "You know, it wasn't so bad."

"What?"

"Carrying your soul around."

"Better you than me." He smiles at me and takes my hand.

"I might not mind … " I let my voice trail off.

Blake pulls me into his lap in one smooth motion, laughing. "Yeah, well, you're not the one who has to take on the black soul of a killer, are you?" His smile is the only thing that keeps him from getting blown right off this wall. "I know, I know. I need to work on my moves."

I laugh with him. I'm still laughing when his mouth covers mine; then I'm lost in the scent of vanilla mint and the feel of his tongue as it twists with mine. And for once, I'm okay with the fact that I don't know the answers, that my choices might all lead to the same inescapable place. I still have choices.

And I choose Blake.

Watch for *Gold*,
the next chapter in Brianna's story.

About the Author

Talia Vance has worked as a horse trainer, a freelance writer, and an attorney. She is analytical, practical, and a hopeless romantic. She lives in Northern California with her husband, children, and a needy Saint Bernard named Huckleberry. Talia always thought she'd grow up to write "the Great American Novel," but her tastes ran more along the lines of torrid romances and fast-paced thrillers. So did her life. But that's another story.

Visit Talia online at www.TaliaVance.com.